Titles by Jessica Clare

THE GIRL'S GUIDE TO (MAN)HUNTING
THE CARE AND FEEDING OF AN ALPHA MALE
THE EXPERT'S GUIDE TO DRIVING A MAN WILD
THE VIRGIN'S GUIDE TO MISBEHAVING

Billionaire Boys Club

STRANDED WITH A BILLIONAIRE
BEAUTY AND THE BILLIONAIRE
THE WRONG BILLIONAIRE'S BED
ONCE UPON A BILLIONAIRE

More Praise for the Billionaire Boys Club novels

BEAUTY AND THE BILLIONAIRE

"Clare really knocked it out of the park again . . . This series has been a pure and utter delight."　　　—*Book Pushers*

"I am in love with this series."　　　—*Love to Read for Fun*

STRANDED WITH A BILLIONAIRE

"A cute, sweet romance . . . A fast, sexy read that transports you to the land of the rich and famous."　　　—*Fiction Vixen*

"[Clare's] writing is fun and sexy and flirty . . . *Stranded with a Billionaire* has reignited my love of the billionaire hero."
　　　—*Book Pushers*

"Clare's latest contemporary is gratifying for its likable but flawed hero and heroine, sexy love scenes, and philosophical quotes Brontë perfectly articulates at the right moments."
　　　—*Library Journal*

Praise for the Bluebonnet Novels

THE CARE AND FEEDING OF AN ALPHA MALE

"Sizzling! Jessica Clare gets everything right in this erotic and sexy romance . . . You need to read this book!"
　　　—*Romance Junkies*

"What a treat to find a book that does it all and does it so well. Clare has crafted a fiery, heartfelt love story that keeps on surprising . . . matching wit and warmth with plenty of spice . . . This is a book, and a series, not to be missed."
　　　—*RT Book Reviews* (4 ½ stars)

continued . . .

"Very cute and oh so sexy."   —*Smexy Books*

"[Clare] did a fabulous job of creating a very erotic story while still letting the relationship unfold very believably."
                                               —*Fiction Vixen*

"A wonderful good-girl/bad-boy erotic romance . . . If you enjoy super-spicy small-town romances, *The Care and Feeding of an Alpha Male* is one that I definitely recommend!"
                                               —*The Romance Dish*

THE GIRL'S GUIDE
TO (MAN)HUNTING

"Sexy and funny."   —*USA Today*

"A novel that will appeal to both erotic romance fans and outdoor enthusiasts. Set in the small town of Bluebonnet, Texas, this rollicking story of a wilderness survival school and a couple of high-school sweethearts is full of fun and hot, steamy romance."   —*Debbie's Book Bag*

"Clare's sizzling encounters in the great outdoors have definite forest-fire potential from the heat generated."
                                               —*RT Book Reviews*

"A fun, cute, and sexy read . . . Miranda's character is genuine and easy to relate to, and Dane was oh so sexy! Great chemistry between these two that makes for a hot and steamy read, but also it is filled with humor and a great supporting cast."
                                               —*Nocturne Romance Reads*

"If you like small-town settings with characters that are easy to fall in love with, this is the book for you."
                                               —*Under the Covers Book Blog*

BEAUTY
and the
BILLIONAIRE

JESSICA CLARE

BERKLEY SENSATION, NEW YORK

THE BERKLEY PUBLISHING GROUP
Published by the Penguin Group
Penguin Group (USA) LLC
375 Hudson Street, New York, New York 10014

USA • Canada • UK • Ireland • Australia • New Zealand • India • South Africa • China

penguin.com

A Penguin Random House Company

BEAUTY AND THE BILLIONAIRE

A Berkley Sensation Book / published by arrangement with the author

Berkley Sensation Books are published by The Berkley Publishing Group.
BERKLEY SENSATION® is a registered trademark of Penguin Group (USA) LLC.
The "B" design is a trademark of Penguin Group (USA) LLC.

For information, address: The Berkley Publishing Group,
a division of Penguin Group (USA) LLC,
375 Hudson Street, New York, New York 10014.

ISBN: 978-0-425-26914-5

PUBLISHING HISTORY
Berkley InterMix edition / July 2013
Berkley Sensation mass-market edition / October 2014

PRINTED IN THE UNITED STATES OF AMERICA

10 9 8 7 6 5 4 3 2 1

Cover photos: Crystal strass lamp © Crestock/Masterfile;
Crystal texture © TaraPatta/Shutterstock.
Cover design by Sarah Oberrender.
Interior text design by Laura K. Corless.

PREVIOUSLY

～

Someone had entered the town house.

At the sound of voices, he paused in the foyer of the enormous home. Out of habit, he moved into a shadowy alcove, lest they catch him unawares and stop to stare at him. Even after years of being a scarred, ugly bastard, he was still bothered by the expressions people made at the sight of his face. It was easier to just blend in with the shadows until they were gone. He waited, his ears straining to determine who was there. The only people he'd expected to stop by were Logan's assistant, who'd insisted on picking up some of his books for a donation, and the movers who'd come to clean out the rest of what was left in the house.

He'd thought the place would be empty, so it would be a perfect time for him to inspect it. He hadn't realized someone else would be coming in, much less two women.

There was a shuffle of footsteps, and then the sound of a box thumping onto the ground.

"What is this place?" a soft, pleasant female voice asked. "It's lovely."

"Some dead celebrity's home or something. I don't care." The other woman's voice seemed full of laughter and amusement, but her tone was cutting. "All I care about is how we're supposed to get these damned boxes back to SoHo. What the heck was Audrey thinking?"

"Could we call a cab?"

The women approached Hunter's shadowed hiding place, and he stilled, waiting for them to pass without noticing him.

The redhead was standing not ten feet away from him, her head bent. He couldn't see her face, but she was curvy and tall, her ass a perfect heart from where he was standing, and her hair was a brilliant shade of red. The other girl—a pretty brunette with wide eyes—balanced two boxes and was waiting for instructions from the other woman.

"I don't know about a cab," the redhead said. "That'll clean us out, and I still want to order that pizza."

"So?" the dark-haired one asked.

"Brontë," the redhead said in a crisp voice, and Hunter came to attention. That was a familiar name.

But the redhead was still talking. "You have to understand something about my sister. She's not the most practical creature."

"She's not? She seems practical to me."

"Not when it comes to work. She thinks we're mules or something, as evidenced by all this. And if I need to call and gripe at her to get her in line, then, by golly, I'm going to do it." She put the phone to her ear. A few seconds later, she made a frustrated sound. "Voice mail. I can't believe her. She said there were two boxes. Not five boxes of hardbacks. Does she think we're bodybuilders?"

"It's not that bad," the brunette placated her, adjusting the boxes in her arms. "I'm sure we can manage."

"I blame Logan Hawkings," the redhead exclaimed, catching Hunter's attention. "He thinks the world just belongs to him, doesn't he?"

The look on the other woman's face was sad. "I suppose."

"Ugh. Look at that hangdog expression. You're still in love with him, aren't you?"

The brunette turned sad eyes on her friend. " 'I hate and I love. Perhaps you ask why I do so. I do not know, but I feel it, and am in agony.' "

"Oh, quit quoting that crap at me. You're being dramatic. He's a jerk. You'll get over him."

The redhead turned, and Hunter got a good look at her face for the first time. She was unusual-looking, with round cheeks smattered in freckles. Her expressive eyes dominated her face despite being hidden behind square, scholarly glasses. Her chin ended in a small point, and she looked fascinating. Smart. Annoyed. "Save me from rich, attractive alpha males. They think they're the heroes from a fairy tale. Little do they know, they're more like the villains."

"That's not fair, Gretchen," the one called Brontë protested.

"Life's not fair," Gretchen said in a cheerfully acerbic voice. "I'd rather have a man who isn't in love with his own reflection than one who needs hair product or designer labels." She bent over, and that heart-shaped ass was thrust into his vision again, and his cock stirred with need.

"So you'd rather have a pizza guy with a weak chin and a knight-in-shining-armor complex?"

"Yes," Gretchen said emphatically, and a dimple flashed in her pointed little face. "His looks aren't half as important as his brain."

So she said. Hunter knew from experience that what women said they wanted in a man was soon forgotten if his physical appearance was unappealing. Still, he was fascinated with her. She was brash and clever, and a little sardonic, as if she were as weary of the world as he was. He watched as the two women, arguing and laughing, stepped out of the foyer of the empty home with the boxes of donations that he'd left for Logan's assistant.

Her name was Gretchen. Gretchen. He racked his brain, trying to think of anyone who knew a Gretchen. A lovely redhead with a charmingly unusual face and a cutting tongue. He wanted to know more about her . . .

Hunter touched the jagged scars running down the left side of his face and frowned. Would she find him as hideous as the rest of the world did? Probably. But she'd also said she could look past that. That she wasn't interested in a face as much as the brain behind it.

He was curious whether she'd been telling the truth.

Not that it mattered, since she'd just walked out the door and he'd likely never see her again.

A half-buried memory stirred in the back of his mind as he stared at the now-shut door. The other woman had an unusual name. Brontë. He knew that name, and where he'd heard it before.

He dialed Logan's number, still thinking about the unusual redhead.

"What is it?" Logan said. "I'm about to head into a meeting."

"There can't be more than one 'Brontë' running around New York, can there?" Hunter asked.

The voice on the other end of the line got very still. "Brontë?" Logan asked after a moment. "You saw her? Where is she?"

Hunter stared at the door, half wishing the women would come back through it again, and half relieved they wouldn't. "She just left with a redhead named Gretchen. I want to know more about her."

"About *my* Brontë?" Logan's voice was a growl.

"No. Gretchen. The one with red hair. I want her."

"Oh." A long sigh. "Sorry, man. Haven't been myself lately. She left me, and I've been going crazy trying to find her." Logan's voice sounded strained, tense. "I can't believe she's still in New York. Where are you?"

"At the town house on the Upper East Side." Hunter had been overseeing it to ensure that nothing was out of place. Plus, he'd been bored and restless. And more than a little lonely.

He wasn't lonely any more, though. He couldn't stop thinking about that redhead. Gretchen, with her big glasses and pert comebacks and red hair.

"Your assistant didn't come by to pick up the boxes," Hunter said after a moment. "This Gretchen did, and your Brontë was with her."

"I have to go," Logan said. "I'll call Audrey and see who she sent over."

"Send me information about this Gretchen woman," Hunter reminded him. *I want her.*

"I will. And thanks." Logan's tone had changed from dejected to triumphant. "I owe you one."

"You do," Hunter agreed. "Just get me information on her friend, and we'll call it even."

Things had suddenly gotten a bit more . . . interesting. Hunter glanced at the empty town house and smiled to himself, his mind full of the unusual woman who had been there minutes before.

ONE

Hunter Buchanan didn't believe in love at first sight.
Hell, he didn't much believe in love at all.

But the moment he'd seen the tall redhead standing in
the foyer of one of his empty houses, a box of books in her
arms and a skeptical look on her face, he'd felt . . . something. She'd been bold and fearless with her words, something that attracted him as a man who clung to the shadows.

And when she'd admitted to her quiet friend that most
men bored her and she wanted something different in a
relationship than just a pretty face?

Hunter knew she was meant for him.

She was pretty, young, and single. She had a smart mind
and a sharp tongue. He liked that about her. She was
unafraid and laughed easily. Days had passed since he'd
glimpsed her and he still couldn't get her out of his mind.
She haunted his dreams.

Hunter was smart and rich and only a few years older
than her. It shouldn't have been unattainable.

Unconsciously, he touched the deeply gouged scars on

his face, his fingers tracing the thick line at the corner of his mouth where damaged tissue had been reconstructed.

There was one thing preventing Hunter from pursuing a woman like that. His face. His hideous, scarred face. He could hide the scars on his chest and arm with clothing. He could clench his hand and no one would notice that he was missing a finger. But he couldn't hide his face. When he chose to leave his house, people crossed the street to avoid him. Men frowned as if there were something unnerving about him. Women flinched away from the sight of him.

Just like the woman next to him currently was doing.

Brontë, Logan's big-eyed girlfriend, sat next to him at the Brotherhood's poker table. The dark basement was filled with a haze of cigar smoke and the scent of liquor. Normally the room was filled with his five best friends, but they'd gone upstairs to talk to Logan about the fact that he'd brought his new girlfriend with him to a secret society meeting. Brontë had stayed behind with him. It was clearly not by her choice, either. She sat at the table quietly, nursing her wine and trying not to look as if she'd wanted to bolt from the table once she'd gotten a good look at his face. Her gaze slid to his damaged hand, and then back to his face again.

He was used to that sort of thing. And he wondered if the redhead who was her friend would react the same way to his face.

Experience told him that she would. But he remembered the redhead's sarcastic little smile and that shake of her head. The words she'd said.

"Save me from rich, attractive alpha males. They think they're the heroes from a fairy tale. Little do they know, they're more like the villains."

And he found he had to know more.

"Your friend," he said to Brontë. "The redhead. Tell me about her."

She looked over at him again, those dark eyes wide and

surprised, pupils dilated from alcohol. "You mean Gretchen?"

"Yes." He knew her first name, but he wanted to know more about her. "What is her last name?"

"Why? How do you know about Gretchen?"

"I saw her with you the other day. Tell me more about her."

She frowned at him. "Why should I tell you about Gretchen? So you can stalk her?"

Hunter glanced down at his cards and tried not to suppress the annoyance he felt at her caginess. Couldn't a man ask a simple question? "I am an admirer of hers . . . from afar."

"Like a stalker."

"Not a stalker. I simply wish to know more about her."

"That's what a stalker would say."

Hunter gritted his teeth, glancing over at her. She automatically shied back, her expression a little alarmed as she studied his scars. He ignored that. "Your friend is quite safe from my romantic interests. I simply wish to learn more about her."

After all, what woman would want to date a man with a grotesque face? Only ones who wanted his money, and he wasn't interested in those. He wanted a companion, not a whore.

"Oh," Brontë said, studying her wineglass as if it were fascinating. "Petty. Her last name is Petty. She writes books."

Now they were getting somewhere. He mentally filed the information away. Gretchen Petty, author. He could see that. "What kinds of books?"

"Books with other people's names on them."

He gave her an impatient stare, hating the way she shrank back in her chair just a bit. "A ghost writer?"

Brontë nodded. "That's right. And Cooper's in love with her."

"Cooper? Who is Cooper?" Whoever it was, Hunter

fucking hated him. Probably good looking, smug, and not nearly good enough for her. Damn it.

"Cooper's her friend. It's okay, though. He won't make a move. He knows Gretchen isn't interested in him that way. Gretchen likes guys who are different. She likes to be challenged."

He snorted. Well, she'd definitely get a challenge with Hunter Buchanan.

They chatted for a bit longer, the conversation awkward. Brontë kept turning her face to the door, no doubt anxiously awaiting Logan's return. Logan was a good-looking man, tall, strong, and unscarred. Brontë was a soft, sweet creature, but he doubted she'd ever look at someone like him with anything more than revulsion or pity.

He'd had his share of pity already, thanks.

"Gretchen Petty," he repeated to himself. A ghostwriter. Someone who wrote books for others and hid behind their names. Why, he wondered. She didn't seem like the type to hide behind a moniker. She didn't seem like the type to hide behind anything. And that fascinated him. What would draw a woman like her to him? Did he even want to try? Did he want to see if she looked at him with a horror that she was trying desperately to hide for the sake of politeness, just like Logan's woman? Or would she see the person behind the scars and determine that he was just as interesting as any other man?

He remembered the first time he saw her, standing next to Brontë in the foyer of an empty mansion. She'd declared, *"I'd rather have a man not in love with his own reflection than one that needs hair product or designer labels."*

A plan began to form in his mind.

It wasn't a nice plan, or a very honest one. But he didn't have to be nice, or honest, if he was rich. The good thing about money was that it allowed you to take control of almost any situation, and Hunter definitely planned on using what he had to his advantage.

The Brotherhood played poker into the night while Hunter's bodyguard stood at the door, keeping out anyone that would disturb them. They drank, they smoked cigars, and they played cards. It was one of their usual meetings, if one could ignore the quietly sleeping woman curled up on the couch in the corner of the room, Logan's jacket acting as a blanket over her shoulders. Business was discussed, alcohol drank in quantity, and notes taken for analyzing in the morning. Tips were shared back and forth, investment opportunities and the like.

The Brotherhood had met like this once a week since their college days, vowing to help one another. At the time, it had seemed like an idealistic pledge—that those born with money would help the others succeed and, as a result, they would all rise to the top of the ladder of success.

It had been an easy vow to make for Hunter. When Logan had befriended him in an economics class, he'd been oddly relieved to have a friend. After being home schooled for the majority of his education, Dartmouth seemed like a nightmare landscape to him. People were everywhere, and they stared at his hideous face and scarred arm like he was a freak. He had no roommate or companions to introduce him to others on campus, and so he'd lurked in the background of the bustling campus society, avoiding eye contact and being silent.

Logan had been popular, wealthy, handsome, and outgoing, and he knew what he wanted and pursued it. Women flocked to him and other guys liked him. It had surprised Hunter when Logan had struck up a conversation with him one day. No one talked to the scarred outcast. But Logan had stared at Hunter's scars for a long moment, and then gone right back to their economics homework, discussing the syllabus and how he felt the class was missing some of the vital concepts they would need to succeed. Hunter had privately agreed, having learned quite a bit of his father's business on his own, and they'd shared ideas. After a week or two of casual conversation, Logan had taken him aside and suggested that Hunter attend a meeting he was putting together.

It was a secret meeting, the kind legendary on Ivy League campuses and spoke about in hushed whispers. Hunter was immediately suspicious. As a Buchanan, his father was one of the wealthiest men in the nation, a legend among business owners for the sheer amount of property he owned. Their family name was instantly recognizable, and several of their houses were landmarks. His father's real estate investments had made him a billionaire, and Hunter was his only heir. He'd learned long ago to suspect others of ulterior motives.

But Logan was incredibly wealthy in his own right. He had no need for Hunter's money. And Hunter was lonely, though he would never admit such things to anyone who asked. So he'd gone to the meeting, expecting it to be a scam or a joke—or worse, a shakedown.

Instead, he'd been surprised. The six men attending had come from all walks of life and had a variety of majors. Reese Durham was attending college on a scholarship, and his clothes were ill-fitting hand-me-downs. He'd been ribbed about being a charity case by the other wealthy students, and he had gotten into a few fistfights. Ditto Cade Archer, though he was a favorite on campus with his easy, open demeanor and friendly attitude. His family did not come from money, and were up to their necks in debt to send Cade to college. He did recognize Griffin Verdi, the only foreigner. European and titled, the Verdi family was well connected with the throne of some obscure tiny country and still owned ancestral lands. And there was Jonathan Lyons, whose family had some wealth, but had lost it all in a business scandal.

It was an eclectic group to say the least, and Hunter had

been immediately wary. But once Logan had begun to speak, the reality of their gathering came to light: Logan Hawkings wanted to start a secret society. A brotherhood of business-oriented men who would help one another rise to the top of their selective fields. He believed that the ones that had power could use that leverage to elevate their friends, and in doing so, could expand upon their empire. And he'd selected like-minded individuals that he hoped would have the same goals as him.

Hunter had been reluctant at first, since his family had the most money of all of the attendees. The others had been equally skeptical, of course. But once they began to talk, ideas were shared and concepts and strategies born. And Hunter realized that these men might not be after his family's wealth after all, but to make some of their own.

He'd joined Logan's secret society. The Brotherhood was formed, and over time, he'd gone from no friends to having five men who were closer to him than brothers.

And even though years had passed, they still met weekly (unless business travel prevented it) and still caught up with one another and shared leads.

Until tonight, a woman had never been invited. The others had been unhappy at Logan's invitation to Brontë, but Hunter didn't mind. He was actually inwardly pleased, though he'd shown no outward reaction.

Brontë's inclusion into their secret meant that she would be around a lot more. And Brontë was good friends with his mysterious redhead—Gretchen.

This was information that Hunter could use. And so he didn't protest when Logan had brought her in. She'd given him plenty of information, too. His Gretchen was a writer. A ghostwriter. There had to be a way to get in contact with her. Spend time with her without arousing her suspicions. He simply wanted to be around her. To have a conversation with her. To enjoy her presence.

Of course he wanted more, but a man like him knew

his limits. He knew his face was unpleasant. He'd seen women clutch their mouths at the sight of him. He'd never have someone like Gretchen—smart, beautiful, funny—unless she was interested in his money. And the thought of that repulsed him.

He'd take friendship with a beautiful woman, if friendship was all he could have.

TWO

⌒

Gretchen Petty picked the lemon off her water glass. "Do you suppose if I take enough of these home, it'll make me a decent dinner?"

Across from her, Kat Garvey reached over the table and snatched the lemon wedge from Gretchen's hands. "Stop it. You're not that broke."

"I'm almost there," Gretchen said glumly, shoving a straw into her glass and sipping her water. "The cupboard's bare, and I'm weeks away from an acceptance payment."

"So I take it lunch is on me this time?" Kat asked dryly.

Gretchen set down her glass and fluttered her eyelashes. "Why, Kat. It is so generous of you to offer."

"Don't thank me. I'm taking it directly off the top of your next royalty check."

"In that case, I'm ordering dessert."

Kat just shook her head, grinning, and Gretchen blew a kiss at her. They'd started out as agent and client and over the last five years, had ended up as something more like friends and less like coworkers. It suited Gretchen just fine.

Considering that she spent most of her days in front of the computer trying to keep ahead of deadlines, the only friends she got out to see were usually due to business lunches.

"So how's the book coming, Gretchen? As your agent, I'm obligated to ask you." Kat took a bite of her pasta. "I know it's not your favorite project."

"Favorite would be a grand overstatement," Gretchen said, morosely jabbing her fork into her salad. "Something more like 'greatest torture known to mankind' would probably be closer to the mark."

Kat grimaced. "That well?"

Gretchen shook her head, internally debating how much to share with her agent. She and Kat were good friends, but once she knew how much Gretchen had struggled with this project, it could be tricky. Kat would take the publisher's side, not Gretchen's. Kat was fun and a good friend, but when it came to work, Kat would follow the money.

"Are we on track to turn in at the end of the month, at least?"

"Mmmmmsure." Gretchen gave a tiny shrug of her shoulders and didn't make eye contact. "Or a week or so after. Maybe two."

"Gretchen," Kat said, exasperated. "Are you serious? This is the fourth project you've been late on this year."

She grimaced, expecting this reaction. She didn't have excuses to give, either. She stayed home and worked all day, but the projects she was getting were less than . . . exciting. And it made it damn hard to sit down and work on them every day. "I had to do a lot of science research," Gretchen mumbled.

"For *Astronaut Bill and the Space Vixens of Dark Planet*? Are you kidding me? It's pulp, Gretchen! Granted, it's pulp with a huge following, but it's still freaking pulp. Just write."

"Yeah, but have you read those books?"

Kat snorted. "Not my type."

"Yeah, well that makes two of us. I had to read a few of

them, too. And you know what happens in *Astronaut Bill Conquers the Moon Maidens*? He razes the planet of all greenery. All greenery, Kat! How the hell are they supposed to breathe if there's nothing to produce oxygen?"

"It's space fantasy." Kat waved a hand in the air. "Write in some robot oxygen makers or something."

"But it has to make sense," Gretchen insisted. "I can't just phone it in. I can't write loopholes like that in the story."

She didn't know why it mattered so darn much, but the thought of those stupid, big-breasted moon maidens asphyxiating under her watch made her annoyed as hell. Details mattered. And if she got the details wrong, she'd be blasted by legions of fans for doing a bad job. If she did a bad job, the sales would suffer. And if sales suffered? Astronaut Bill would be assigned to a different ghostwriter.

"I don't know why you get so hung up on that misogynistic crap, Gretchen. Just finish the book and have the copyeditor fill in the holes. That's what they're there for."

Gretchen chewed, saying nothing.

"You know if you turn in late again, they won't re-up your contract. You need this contract."

"I know. I'm just . . . struggling." Every page of Astronaut Bill was painful. They were only fifty thousand words long and the plots were simplistic. Bill gets a mission from headquarters. Bill goes to explore a new planet. Buxom babes are encountered and they need rescuing. Bill ends up saving the day after some spectacular laser gun battles and sexual tension. Piece of cake.

Except she kept getting hung up on the details. And she didn't much like Bill, which made it really hard to spend time with him every day. But Bill was a paycheck, and a good one, so she struggled on.

"Just tell them I'm sick. Maybe someone died and I had to leave town for the funeral."

Kat glared at Gretchen. "I'm not going to lie about your family. I'll just tell them you need another week, max."

"Two?"

"One week," Kat said firmly. "But you know they run on tight deadlines and they won't be happy."

"I know," Gretchen said glumly. The rent was due and now was not exactly the time to have a crisis of faith. "I'll get it finished, I promise."

"Gretchen, you know I adore you, girl. You're my favorite client. But I say this with love—you need to get your act together."

"Consider it together. I promise."

Kat gave her a wary nod. "Well, did you want to hear about another ghostwriting contract? They asked for you specifically."

"Me?" Gretchen sat up straighter, surprised. "You serious?"

"Yeah, I don't know. Do you have connections at any publishers I don't know about?" Her mouth quirked in amusement. "Especially brand-new ones?"

"Brand-new ones?"

"Yeah, someone's launching a small publishing line. I don't know anything about it other than they headhunted one of the best editors I know to head it up, and for their launch title they want you on board."

This sounded . . . odd. Appealing but odd. "I don't understand."

"Me either, kiddo. But they were very clear that they wanted you on this project. Said you had a reputation for ghostwriting and they wanted you on board."

Gretchen stabbed another forkful of salad into her mouth, thinking. She had a reputation all right, but she wasn't so sure it was a good one. She took on a lot of projects to pay the bills, but she was also late a lot. She hadn't been feeling very inspired, and writing could be a damn hard job when you didn't want to do it.

And lately she hadn't wanted to do it. But money was money, and rent didn't pay itself. Her sister Audrey would shake her head and suggest that Gretchen see if she could borrow money from their famous sister, Daphne, but Gretchen hated the thought of it. Being indebted to Daphne ended up being more trouble than it was worth. Gretchen speared another piece of lettuce idly. "So what kind of job is it and what does it pay?"

"It pays three hundred grand."

Gretchen stopped, fork poised in midair. "Three . . . hundred grand? Seriously?"

"So I'm told. Lead title, you know."

"And this is a legit publisher? Really? They're putting out that kind of money?"

"Yeah. Weird terms, though. Ten percent up front, ninety percent upon turn in of an acceptable manuscript. And that's not the weirdest."

Most publishers paid half upon signing. Still, thirty grand up front was more than she'd gotten for her last book, so even if the contract went south early, it was still a good investment of her time, all things considering. "What else is weird?"

Kat suddenly looked uncomfortable. She reached for her wineglass. "Well, there are unusual working terms."

"Uh-oh. Am I going to like the sound of this?"

"Probably not, which is why I didn't mention it when we first sat down. It's strange, Gretch. Really strange. Apparently the project they want you to do is an epistolary novel of sorts. There's some old letters someone found in an attic of a very old, very famous mansion. The publisher said the letters were really romantic, so they're seeing this as some sort of quasi Anne Frank meets *The Notebook* sort of project. They think it'll be huge. But there's a catch. You can't take the letters off the property."

"Okay, that's a little picky, but do-able." She was starting to get excited about this project. Anne Frank meets *The Notebook*? Launch title of a new publisher? With that kind of money for an advance, it sounded promising. "Whose name am I writing under?"

"Don't know yet. They didn't want to release it until the project was agreed upon."

"So where's this house?"

"Mansion," Kat corrected. "And it's in Hyde Park."

Her mouth went dry. "Like . . . the Vanderbilt one?"

"Close. You know the one with the white columns and the crazy rose gardens?"

"Holy shit. Yes, I know that one. Buchanan Manor."

"That's the one. And that's the location of our letters."

"That's so cool," Gretchen said, fascinated. "I'm totally in on this project."

"I think you need to think about it."

"Why? The money's awesome, the house is fascinating, and it's a lead title. What is it you're not telling me?"

"It's the house. You heard the part about the letters not being able to leave the premises?"

"Yeah, but what's the big deal? I'll just drop in on some weekdays and take photos. I don't mind going on location if the pay is right—which it is."

"You're going to be very on location. As in, if you take the job, they want you to live on site for the duration of the project. They don't want you coming back and forth. The owner's a bit of a recluse and doesn't seem to like traffic much, so he's insisting that the ghostwriter live on the premises with him."

"Do *what*?"

"Live. On site. With the owner. He's the one who doesn't want them leaving the premises."

"That's a little . . ."

"Creepy? I know. That's what I said and that's why I think you should turn it down."

She thought for a long minute. The money was nice and the house was intriguing, but the thought of living there with a stranger? That tipped things over from eccentric to downright bizarre. "Exactly how many letters are there, again?"

"Several hundred." Kat gave her a curious look. "You're not considering it, are you?"

"Not seriously," she admitted. "Though it would be cool to visit the house and see what it's like on the inside. And the money would be nice. But . . ."

"Yeah, it's that 'but' that makes me keep pausing. You want me to turn them down?"

Gretchen toyed with her fork, thinking of the expensive salad on her plate that she couldn't pay for, at least not until a payment came in. "Not yet."

Kat shrugged. "Suit yourself."

She shoved a crouton around her plate. Three hundred grand could be several years of financial security, even in pricey New York City. "And they asked for me, huh?"

"Who knows. Maybe the recluse is a big fan of Astronaut Bill."

Yeah, right. Or maybe she was the only idiot available who would actually consider the job. Gretchen sighed to herself and then nudged Kat's fluffy wheat roll. "You going to eat that?"

———

"Never worry, Uranea. I'll stop them with my trusty laser sword." Astronaut Bill put his hand on the sheath at his waist.

Uranea gasped, her small hands flying to her mouth. Her bosoms quivered with distress. "Oh, please be safe, Astronaut Bill!"

"They won't know what hit them," Bill said grimly, dragging his immense blade from its sheath. Uranea gasped again, clearly impressed by the size of it. "Now I'll send them on a one-way ticket back to the stars . . ."

Gretchen rolled her eyes at her own page and took a sip from a water bottle. Garbage. Pure and utter garbage. If Uranea walked into Cooper's Cuppa and ordered a drink,

Gretchen probably would have hauled across the counter to punch her in the face.

Hmm. She made a note to herself: *have Uranea punched in face in next chapter.*

Stupid Astronaut Bill. Stupid Uranea. She kept hoping for a black hole to suck them into another dimension and then she'd never have to write about them again, but nope. No such luck.

Gretchen checked the timer on the oven again. Ten minutes until the next batch of her cookies were done. She could get in a bit more writing. Bracing herself for a few more paragraphs of the hated duo, she began to type once more. The bell at the counter chimed, and she looked up from her tablet, where she'd been drafting the next scene between handling the store's customers.

Cooper moved past her before she could get up, a bustle of white shirt and bright red apron. "I'll get it, Gretch. You're busy."

She was . . . busy? She raised an eyebrow at his back. Here she was, slacking on the job at his business, and he was going to let her? He was either the nicest boss in the world, or . . . hell. Brontë had been right when she'd pointed it out to Gretchen the other day: Cooper was totally in love with her.

Well didn't that just make things uncomfortable.

Cooper was an old friend, a college buddy. They'd both moved to New York at about the same time—him to start his coffee business, and her to pursue a career in journalism. It had seemed natural for them to stick together and remain friends, and when she was lean on money and between checks, Cooper let her work shifts at his cafe for some extra pay.

Except right now? He was being a little *too* understanding.

Brontë had tried telling her a few weeks ago that Cooper was in love with her. Gretchen had denied it. Cooper was just a friend. They were buddies. They hung out together and had each other's backs. There was nothing more to it than that. But as time went on, she began to have doubts that maybe she wasn't quite as aware of Cooper's feelings as she thought. She gave him a wary look as he made lattes and handed them to the waiting customers. When the bar was deserted again, he turned and glanced back at her, his smile too broad for her liking.

"How's the book coming?" he asked. "Still giving you trouble?"

There was one way to find out, she supposed, if Cooper was going to make things uncomfortable for her or not. "Oh, just struggling with a love scene," she said idly. "You know how it goes."

Cooper flushed bright red and his goofy smile got a little bigger and a little, well, goofier.

Hell.

She saved her file and exited out of the app. Maybe it was time to be spending a little less time at Cooper's Cuppa. Usually she only showed up for a shift about once a week, just to pick up some extra money. But ever since her last roomie had moved out, she'd been coming in more or less every day. She needed the cash, and it was a good excuse to avoid writing more of Astronaut Bill and Uranea.

Clearly her coming in so often had backfired.

"Actually, I need to get this scene knocked out," she told Cooper, forcing an apologetic note into her voice as she tucked her tablet under her arm. "If it's okay with you, I'm going to head out early."

"Of course," Cooper said. "Oh, and I wanted to talk to you about something."

The hairs on the back of her neck stood on end. *Oh, God.* Cooper was a friend, but that was all he was. He was more like a little brother to her. A little brother with a cowlick in the back of his hair, barely an inch in height on her, and pit stains on light-colored shirts. Cooper was sweet, but definitely not her type. If he was going to ask her out, it was going to absolutely ruin any sort of easy friendship they had.

It already felt ruined, and that was depressing enough.

She tugged at the strings of her apron, turning her back to him he wouldn't see her wince. "Can it wait, Coop? I really do need to get going. The cookies will be ready in a few minutes, if you can pull them out."

"Oh, sure. I was just going to let you know that I think you'll like your next check."

She turned to face him. "Why?"

He beamed at her. "I gave you a raise."

"A raise? Why? I'm your worst employee."

"Don't say that. You're my favorite employee." The smile on his face grew a little softer.

The discomfort Gretchen was feeling grew. When had Cooper turned the corner from being a friend? Why hadn't she paid attention before now? This made things so incredibly uncomfortable. "You shouldn't give me a raise, Coop. Anyone else would have fired me at this point. I'm late, I'm lazy, and I work on other stuff when I'm tending the counter."

"Yes, but you make an incredible cookie. All the customers love your recipes."

She snorted. "Did you not hear me say the part about being late and lazy?"

"Yes, but you work hard."

"On my books, yes. Not on slinging coffee."

He chuckled. "You shouldn't tell me that. I'm your boss."

"You're my friend," she emphasized, feeling like an ass when his smile faded a little. *Floor, swallow me up right now.* "Actually, I wanted to tell you that I might be scarce for a few weeks," she found herself telling him. That crazy assignment Kat had mentioned was looking better and better. A month away from Cooper might be just the thing to cool his jets and refuel her pocketbook. "I just got handed another contract and it's an on-location one."

"Oh?" He looked crestfallen. "I'll miss seeing you around."

"Yeah, well." She shrugged a little, feeling like she wanted to flee. "I'm sorry. Debbie always wants more shifts. Can you give her mine?"

"Hey," he said, reaching out and squeezing her upper arm as if to comfort her. "Don't stress. You do what needs to be done. You know I'll always be here for you."

Gretchen nodded. "Thanks, Cooper. You're a good friend. I really do mean that."

"I know you do." *Was that a hint of sadness in his voice?*

Now she felt even worse. The last thing she wanted to do was hurt Cooper. Okay, actually, that wasn't true. The last thing she wanted to do was *date* Cooper. The second to last thing she wanted to do was hurt his feelings. "I appreciate it, Cooper. Sorry to run out on you."

"Not a problem," he said cheerfully.

They stared at each other for a long, uncomfortable moment, and then the bell on the counter dinged, saving them from further awkwardness.

"I'm going to head out," Gretchen said, pulling off her apron. "See you around, Coop."

He nodded, taking a client's order, as if nothing was wrong and they hadn't just gotten all weird with each other.

But she felt his eyes on her back as she left the coffee shop.

As soon as she was out the door, Gretchen pulled out her phone and dialed her agent.

"Kat Geary."

"It's me. Is that weird-ass job at the Buchanan place still available?"

"You're not seriously thinking about taking it, are you?"

"I sure am." The more she thought about it, the more this

seemed like a good idea. It was a little unorthodox, sure. But the thought of spending time away from Astronaut Bill and his ladylove was more appealing by the moment. And speaking of uncomfortable love interests . . . getting away from Cooper for a few weeks would do a lot to ease the discomfort she was currently feeling. The money was just a very nice, very pleasant bonus on top of things. "I could use a distraction and this project sounds like the perfect one. When do I get to start?"

"As soon as we get a handshake on it. Gretchen, are you sure? It means living on the premises."

"Yeah, but I've seen the outside of the house. It's huge."

"What if it's filled with coffins and decapitated doll heads inside?"

"Jeez, Kat. You been trolling through the horror fiction section lately? It's a mansion. I'm sure it'll be fine. It's probably so big that I won't see anyone ever. It'll just be me and some dusty library. No big."

Kat sighed gustily into the phone. "Well, as your friend, I think you're crazy. As your agent, I just want to say thanks for the commission."

"You're welcome. I think. Now, can you call my Astronaut Bill editor and tell her I need an extension?"

THREE

⚬

Gretchen stared up at the Buchanan Mansion from the window of the cab as it pulled up the driveway. "Holy doughnuts. This place is insane. I can't believe I'm going to be living here for the next month."

"I can't believe it, either." At her side, her sister Audrey's voice sounded prim and disapproving. "The money is good, but I still think you're crazy for taking this job."

Gretchen was pretty sure that made two of them. "It's a pretty lucrative job, Audrey. And you didn't have to come."

Her sister gave a derisive snort. "Oh, yes I did. You haven't met Buchanan. I have. He's surly and unpleasant and that house is a mausoleum. It's bad enough that you're taking a job that forces you to live in someone else's home. I don't care if he's Mr. Hawkings's best friend—I'm not letting you shack up without checking out the place first. That's so they know you have someone looking out for you. I don't want to have you disappear for a month and then we're calling the news and insisting that someone digs up the gardens looking for you."

Gretchen rolled her eyes. "I'll probably never see the man."

Audrey just gave her a prim look. "Don't argue with me. You know I'm the responsible one in this family."

And because she couldn't really refute that, Gretchen just grinned.

The car moved slowly down the winding drive and, as it did, they passed intricately clipped flowering bushes in fantastical shapes. Spirals, moons, and stars adorned the colorful fall gardens. "I don't think they'd bury me in the backyard, Audrey. Did you see the landscaping? It probably costs more than we both make in a month."

"If you need money," Audrey began for the millionth time that day.

"It's not just the money," Gretchen said. "It's an adventure. Haven't you ever wanted to have an adventure?"

"Not if it involves living with a stranger, no."

Spoilsport. It wasn't as if she and the owner were going to get in their jammies and have pillow fights and cuddle up in the same bed or something. "Look at the size of this place. Odds are that I never see him."

Buchanan Manor was as big as a shopping mall. Seriously. She tried counting windows at the front of the building, but there were too many. Pointed gabled roofs in a dark green decorated the roof, and the building itself was a pale shade. There were windows everywhere, looking out on the spectacular lawns. If she counted up, it looked like the building was four floors. Good God, how many rooms did one billionaire need? He could fit an entire school into this building.

The taxi pulled up to the cobblestone driveway and Audrey paid the cab driver as Gretchen got out of the car, Igor's cat-carrier tucked under her arm. The cat meowed angrily, and she made a shushing noise even as she continued to stare up at the mansion.

She was wearing jeans and a sweater and felt hideously, conspicuously underdressed. And here this was one of her better outfits. Since she didn't leave the house much, she normally spent her time in yoga pants. But this house made her think anything less than starchy collars and tweed jackets were underdressed. Gretchen swallowed hard as her suitcases were set down on the driveway. "This is uncomfortable." ·

Audrey shouldered her small weekend bag and gave Gretchen an odd look. "Where's all your bravery?"

"I didn't realize I was going to be living at frickin' Hogwarts! I—"

The massive wooden front door opened, and a tall, thin man with a bald head and long neck stepped out of the house. Both women fell silent and watched him descend. Gretchen looked at him with keen interest. He wore a small plaid bow tie and a tweed jacket with patches in the elbows. *Fascinating.* Was he the owner, then? Come to greet her? He didn't look very friendly.

"Good afternoon," the man said in a sonorous voice. "Which one of you is Ms. Gretchen Petty?"

She raised a hand. "Here." She immediately lowered it, feeling like a tool. This wasn't class. "I brought my sister for the weekend so she can see me settled. I hope that's okay?"

He gave her a piercing stare, as if she'd displeased him greatly.

At her side, Audrey cleared her throat and stepped forward, iPad in hand. "My employer is Logan Hawkings, a friend of Mr. Buchanan's. When I told Mr. Hawkings that we would be coming here for the weekend, he told me that he had cleared it with Mr. Buchanan and that it would not be a problem for me to tag along." Audrey's tone was direct, crisp, and absolutely business-like in the face of this man's disapproval.

Gretchen wanted to kiss her sister for putting the man in his place. He must not be Mr. Buchanan, then. Thank God. He looked like he had a massive stick up his ass. Not exactly Gretchen's kind of person.

After a long moment, the man nodded. "I am aware of Mr. Hawkings's involvement. If you would please follow me, I can show you to your rooms."

He turned and began to walk back up the stairs, not offering to help them with their luggage. Lovely. "No, no," Gretchen began loudly. "Don't bother. I can carry all the bags. There are Amazons in my ancestry, after all. Me strong like bull." She flexed mockingly.

The man gave her an ugly stare over his shoulder.

Audrey stifled a giggle and thwacked Gretchen lightly on the arm. "Shut up, already."

Gretchen simply grinned and tossed her bag over her shoulder. "Come on. The world's friendliest butler there doesn't look like he's going to wait on us."

They followed behind him, jogging to catch up, as he led them through the house.

When they entered the foyer of the grandiose hall, Gretchen stopped and set down her luggage, her mouth gaping at the sight. A dual staircase curved up the massive marble foyer, and in the center of the ceiling dripped a crystal chandelier. A red runner carpet lined the stairs and Gretchen felt as if she'd been dropped into a TV show. "This place is gorgeous."

The gentleman escorting them turned and gave her a slight sniff of disapproval. "Of course it is."

"I wasn't insulting the place, I was just—"

"Talking. Yes, I noticed." He turned his back on her and began to go up the stairs.

Wow. She made a face at him and turned to Audrey, who was trying to stifle a giggle behind one hand and failing miserably. "Gee, I hope he's in charge of the tour," Gretchen mock-whispered. "He's got some incredible people skills."

Audrey batted her arm, laughing.

They followed the butler—at least, Gretchen assumed he was the butler—up to the second floor and down a long, narrow hall. The house was clearly old but everything was in remarkable condition and of the finest make. At the end of the hallway, the butler turned to them. "I have prepared only one room for guests." And he gave another baleful look at Audrey.

"Oh, it's not a problem," Gretchen said sweetly. "It must be terribly difficult to find space around here. You must only have thirty or forty guest bedrooms. I totally understand."

He stared at Gretchen and then opened the door, choosing to ignore her.

The door opened up into a gorgeous room, and despite the butler's unpleasant demeanor, Gretchen was delighted at the sight. A large canopied bed that looked like something straight out of the Tudor dynasty jutted out from the far wall, and the vaulting ceiling was painted with dancing cherubs and glittered with more chandeliers.

She stepped over the threshold, a bit surprised at the opulence of the room. She'd been expecting something a bit more like a hotel room, with a simple bed, dresser, and table. She would have been glad for that. This . . . was incredible.

"I trust that this suits your needs?" the butler asked dryly.

Gretchen forced herself to close her mouth and gave him an equally grave look. "It's a little small," she lied, "but it'll suit."

"I'll give you a few hours to get settled. Dinner is in two hours and will be brought to your room."

Audrey stopped staring at the gorgeous room and looked over at the butler. "Do we get a tour of the place?"

"And the letters," Gretchen said. "When do I get to look at those?"

"The letters are in the south wing, and the south wing is off limits today." He moved toward the door, readying to leave. "If you need anything else, ring the bell pull. My name is Mr. Eldon. You can ask for me."

"Why is the south wing off limits?" Gretchen asked as he began to shut the door.

"Because today is Friday," he said as the door closed with a click.

Gretchen stared at Audrey, a bit surprised by what had just happened.

"Well. The rich do surround themselves with eccentrics," Audrey said. "Maybe he's very good at being a butler. Or something."

"I'm hoping it's more along the lines of 'old family friend'," Gretchen said wryly. "Because that'll excuse his behavior a little more. Do you think the owner doesn't want me here to do this project?"

"I don't know," Audrey said, moving to the bed and touching one of the thick, luxurious tassels hanging from the bed draperies. "They invited you here, didn't they? So the Buchanan family must be aware that you're here to work."

"Huh." Gretchen wasn't so sure. The butler was kind of a jerk. Still, she could put up with a jerk for a nice fat paycheck and the opportunity to live in an American-style castle for an entire month. It wasn't as if Mr. Eldon was going to be hovering over her shoulder for the entire time.

An angry meow came from Gretchen's bag, and she set it down on the edge of the bed, unzipping. Igor bounded out a moment later, and then hissed at her to let Gretchen know his displeasure.

That was par for the course today, really. It seemed like everyone was in a pissy mood.

Eldon entered Hunter's office after a quick knock. "She is here, and she is settled, sir."

Hunter bolted to his feet behind his desk, then forced himself to remain put. Calm. Relaxed. At ease. "Did she seem pleased?"

The butler's mouth turned down in a sour frown.

"Pleased? I suppose. She asked to see the letters and I told her the wing was off limits."

"You can show her tomorrow."

"Shall I leave the honor to you?"

"I . . . no. Not yet." The surroundings would be strange to Gretchen. Best not to unsettle her more than she was already. Perhaps she was nervous and seeing a man with scars lurking in the shadows would only increase the nervousness. "I shall introduce myself in time."

"Very well, sir." Eldon said nothing else, but didn't leave the room, either.

"What is it?"

"She has brought her sister with her."

"I have no objections."

"Yes." Again, a long pause, and then Eldon's face seemed disapproving once more. "And a cat."

Hunter felt his mouth stretch tight against his scars, smiling. "A cat is permissible. I did not state in the contract if she had to leave any pets behind."

"I see."

"And have you set up the letters for Ms. Petty's project?"

Eldon gave a sharp nod. "They have been placed in an authentic Buchanan trunk dating from the Victorian era and left in the Blue Library."

"And you reviewed them to verify their accuracy? This has to seem like a legitimate project, Eldon. I don't want her leaving early because she realizes it's a scam."

"I have been assured of the age and accuracy of the letters by the gentleman who sold them to me. He insisted that they have been in his family for generations and was only willing to part with them for a large sum."

"I don't care about how much they cost. I just want it to be enough to keep her here for a few weeks so I can get to know her."

"You may trust that it is under control, Mr. Buchanan." Eldon clasped his hands behind his back and shifted on his feet. "This does, however, bring me to the question of the publisher."

"The publisher?"

"The one you formed to push Ms. Petty's project? You hired Mr. Stewart from his publishing house and told him to acquire employees and projects as long as Ms. Petty's book was given premium attention."

He vaguely remembered something about that. It had seemed easier to him that he'd set his own publisher up than to approach one of the others. After all, he didn't care if the business made money. "Is there a problem with Stewart?"

"I believe he wanted to discuss Bellefleur Publishing with you and get your opinion on some of the acquisitions."

Hunter waved a hand, dismissing the thought. He didn't give a shit about what Stewart acquired. "Have him talk with my accounting people."

"They are not fans of this project, just so you know, sir."

"Why does it matter to them?"

Eldon's mouth pursed as if considering something unpleasant. "I believe one does not go into publishing with the expectation of making large amounts of money."

"Then it's a good thing that I didn't go into this expecting to make money, isn't it?" Hunter smiled tightly. "Tell him to contact my accountants. And tell my accountants to give the man whatever he needs to run his business— within reason."

Hunter moved to the window, gazing out at his rose gardens. They were bare and brown this time of year, the beds carefully covered to protect the roots in anticipation of springtime. They'd be gorgeous then, but for now they were barren. He wondered if she'd like them when they were in full bloom. *Did she like gardening? Did she like the outdoors?* "You met Gretchen, Eldon. Tell me your thoughts."

"It is not for me to say, sir." He didn't look pleased at being asked. When Hunter continued to wait, he added, "She seemed . . . strong."

Strong. Hunter rubbed his mouth, thinking of kind Gretchen. She was so beautiful and lively. He'd have no idea how to talk to her. Hell, he still had a hard time figuring out what to say to Logan, Jonathan, and the others and he'd known them for years. Next to someone as lovely and personable as her, he'd be . . . a tongue-tied, scarred lump.

Fucking pathetic.

Eldon cleared his throat. "Will our house guests affect the cleaning schedule, Mr. Buchanan?"

"No, they will not."

"Then I shall be off to resume my duties, sir."

"Thank you, Eldon."

His butler left, and Hunter was once again alone in his study. He forced himself to sit back down, calmly, though his heart was beating rapidly in his chest. Anxiety? Excitement? Or something else?

Buchanan Manor never had visitors. *Hunter* never had visitors. Even the Brotherhood never came to visit. He usually went to visit them, and with a bodyguard in tow.

He felt an incredible urge to head toward the guest hall in the east wing, where she was housed. He wanted to pass down the hall and perhaps spot her exploring. Did she like his house? Or did she find it old and stodgy and overbearing?

His hand touched the scars on his cheek, feeling the deep, ugly grooves still carved into his flesh after all this time.

And clenched his hands on his desk, quelling his excitement.

————

Dawn broke bright and early, shining through the massive windows along the far wall. Gretchen bounded out of bed, already feeling restless and ready to begin the project. On the other side of the bed, Audrey mumbled and rolled over, going back to sleep.

That was fine with Gretchen. It'd give her a chance to get her bearings.

She dressed quickly, considering the bell pull, and decided to head out on her own. Dinner had been brought to them last night but it had been . . . strange. A few meager sandwiches and a can of tuna for her cat. She'd considered that Igor might not be the most welcome here and had brought cans of food and a portable litter pan, but it was downright odd that the cat seemed to be welcome and her sister was not. And since the welcome had been so incredibly warm she decided that perhaps this morning she'd explore a bit on her own before alerting their host that she was awake.

The halls of the house were eerily silent, to the point that she stopped and turned her phone to vibrate. A phone call would alert someone to her presence, and . . . she paused. Why was she feeling the need to sneak around? There was no one in this mansion. And after all, she'd been invited. So why the vague sense of guilt?

Probably because the butler had been such a jerk. If he was the welcoming party, she could see why no one else was here. She wondered if the owner was quite as big an asshole as his employee. Perhaps the unfriendly Mr. Buchanan had given his butler instructions to make their welcome an unpleasant one because he wasn't a fan of the project. Maybe he didn't want her here and was permitting it only for the sake of the project.

Though if he didn't want her here, then why would he allow it? Why wouldn't he make other provisions to take the letters off-site in a controlled manner and have her work somewhere else where he wouldn't be disturbed?

None of it made any sense.

Gretchen wandered the halls, admiring the costly furnishings and the architecture of the place, but the more that she wandered, the more bizarre it seemed to her. Though the place was spotless, she had seen no one at all. Didn't a place this huge need a massive staff on hand? She'd seen enough documentaries about British aristocracy and the huge staff that the manor houses carried. This was practically American aristocracy, right? So where were the employees? She found it hard to believe that Buchanan would be doing his own dishes and dusting his library.

She eventually made it back to the main foyer of the house. Then she headed across the hall to the next wing. For some reason, it was oddly pleasing to hear the distant whirr of vacuums. That meant someone else existed in this enormous mansion.

Following the sounds, she pushed open doors until she found the source—an army of maids thoroughly cleaning one room. There had to be twenty women in there busy with vacuums and dusters.

"Hi there," Gretchen called.

They stopped what they were doing. One woman froze mid-feather-dust, and the one wielding the enormous vacuum shut it off. They were all middle-aged to elderly, and they stared at her as if she were a ghost.

Gretchen gave them a friendly little wave, though she was feeling a bit odd about such things. This place was crazy. "You guys work here?"

As soon as the question left her mouth, she felt like an idiot. They were wearing traditional black-and-white maid costumes that Gretchen thought only existed for costume parties, though a more modest kind than she'd seen for Halloween. Of course they worked here. "I'm staying in the east wing," she said lamely. "Working. Nice to see you all."

"No one's supposed to be in this wing," one woman said after a moment. "Today's Saturday."

"Umm, okay." She glanced around, but everyone seemed to be waiting for her to go. "Why can't we be in the west wing today again?"

"Because it's Saturday," another woman said. "Off limits except to the cleaning crew."

"Yeah, okay, but why?"

The woman shrugged. "That's how it is. We don't make the rules. We just work here."

And now she was making them nervous. *Well, wasn't this awkward.* Gretchen pointed at the door behind her. "I'm . . . um . . . just going to leave, I think. Have you guys seen Mr. Buchanan?"

"No one sees Mr. Buchanan except Mr. Eldon," the eldest maid offered helpfully. "Do you want me to call Mr. Eldon?"

"No, that's okay. I already had my fill of Mr. Eldon." Gretchen glanced at the door, then back at the maids. One wing was closed yesterday because it was Friday. This wing was closed because today was Saturday. "So tomorrow's Sunday. What happens on Sunday?"

"Boathouse and Greenhouse," one of the women offered. "And any outlying buildings or special projects."

"And Monday?"

"No one works on Monday or Tuesday. Wednesday is the north wing, Thursday is the east wing, Friday is the south wing, and Sunday is the west wing."

"You do a different area each day of the week? Huh. Which day of the week is Mr. Buchanan's room?"

"Wednesday."

So he lived in the north wing. Not the same wing as her. "And the rest of the family?"

"No one else lives here except Mr. Eldon and Mr. Buchanan."

In this big house? Only two men? How positively . . . creepy. And lonely. And an enormous waste of all this incredible space. "I see. Well, I think I'm going to finish taking a look around, if that's okay with you guys."

"Are you sure you don't want me to ring Mr. Eldon?" One woman pulled out a phone that looked remarkably like a walkie-talkie. "I'm sure he'd—"

"No, I'm good. I was just heading down to the kitchens. Can you tell me where they are?"

"There's three kitchens," one maid volunteered. "But the only one that's kept stocked is in the north wing."

Spiffy. "Thank you. Is there a kitchen staff?"

"Just Mr. Eldon. He prepares all of Mr. Buchanan's meals. He's probably there right now."

"I see." *Jeez. This was sounding weirder by the moment.* Gretchen knew the rich were eccentric, but this was a little ridiculous. "Well, skip that, then. I'm not that hungry after all. I'll check the kitchens out some other time. Thanks for your help, ladies."

She left, quickly shutting the door before they could protest—or worse, call the oh-so-pleasant Mr. Eldon.

Gretchen headed back to the main hall, heading toward the familiar part of the house before she got lost and someone had to call Eldon on her. It was still early enough that she could get a good day's work in on Astronaut Bill before Eldon returned to show her where they were keeping the letters. She could return, wake up Audrey, spend some time with Igor, and relax. And work on her book like she was supposed to. Even better, she could ring the bell and force that awful Mr. Eldon to make them breakfast. The thought of him slaving over a stove for her and Audrey had a certain appeal.

And yet . . . Gretchen turned. Then, after a moment's thought, she headed up the stairs to the north wing.

She was being nosy, she told herself. She just wanted a glimpse of what the mysterious Mr. Buchanan looked like. Maybe he'd be just as weird and unpleasant as Mr. Eldon. But her imagination was fired up.

Plus, she'd use any excuse to avoid spending manuscript time with Astronaut Bill. Maybe it was time Astronaut Bill met up with a fearsome race of skinny, bald giant butlers that needed to be slaughtered.

It would be satisfying, if not a bit bloodthirsty. At least it was just fiction.

When Gretchen had thought she'd want to see the master of the fabulous house, she hadn't thought that she'd see . . . well, all of him.

After exploring the north hall for a time, she turned down another section of the wing, the faint sound of piped-in rock music drawing her forward. She'd headed toward the sound . . . and stopped.

At the end of the hallway, not a hundred feet from where she was standing, a door was opening. Steam rushed out in a billowing puff, along with the source of the loud music. A man emerged, rubbing his head with a fluffy white towel to dry his hair, humming to himself. His face was hidden from her but . . . nothing else was.

And oh, mercy, he was gorgeous.

He was utterly naked, his skin gleaming with wet drops from his shower. His legs were tanned and shadowed from the wet hair clinging to them, and his legs were thick with cords of muscle. Nice, wet cords of glorious muscle. A tattoo traced across one bicep.

He was hung, too, Gretchen didn't mind noticing. His cock lay semi-erect against his thigh, as if he'd recently pleasured himself.

Her gaze traveled upward, feeling almost lascivious at spying. But his chest was just as perfectly sculpted as the rest of him, deep grooves worn into the muscle and displaying a delicious lack of body fat. This was a man who worked out regularly and with great enthusiasm.

Much like the enthusiasm she was feeling staring at his broad shoulders and washboard abs, Gretchen thought to herself. There was something not quite right about the way one side of his body looked, as if the skin had too much shadow on it, but she was too far away to see what it was. A trick of the light, perhaps? A light dusting of chest hair covered his pectorals.

The towel fell, and she caught a glimpse of dark hair atop his head and strong, handsome features . . . and then the towel revealed his entire face.

Scarred. Broken. His mouth was pulled down on one side.

She gasped, unable to help herself. He'd been so perfectly sculpted that the sight of the ruin on his face had completely thrown her for a loop.

The man froze and turned toward her, as if seeing her for the first time. Recognition flitted across his face, and then he was wrapping the towel around his waist. "Get the fuck out of here," he roared. One hand went in front of his face, shielding it from her gaze.

"Sorry," Gretchen said in a high-pitched voice, taking a few cautious steps backward. "I didn't mean to spy. I just—"

"Get out of here! Go! You're not allowed down this hall!"

"I'm so sorry! I—"

"GO!"

Gretchen turned and ran. She didn't stop running until she made it back to the east wing and slammed her bedroom door shut behind her. She leaned against it, breathing hard.

Holy shit.

She'd just seen the owner naked. Really naked. Hell, she'd practically ogled his nakedness and taken his measurements. And it had been some damn fine nakedness. The only thing that wasn't perfect was his face. It was terribly scarred, but the more she thought about it, the more she was intrigued by it.

Not that she'd get a chance to find out the story behind it. Mr. Buchanan was seriously pissed that she'd seen him. She'd never seen anyone so mad. Gretchen winced, biting a fingernail.

Was she going to be fired from this job before she'd even started it? Just because she'd been bored and curious? *Shit.*

———

Damn it all. That had not been how he'd wanted to meet Gretchen.

Hunter had planned it all carefully in his mind. He'd leave her some friendly notes, letting her know that he had an interest in the project he'd cultivated for her. He'd meet her in a well-shadowed room and let her have the impression that his face was not that bad. After a few chance meetings, he'd reveal to her his face and give her a chance to consider it in stronger light. Not daylight. Daylight was too harsh and unforgiving. Then, maybe when she was comfortable with his . . . disfigurements, they could move past it and be friends.

He'd not intended for her to see him. Naked. Fully exposed in more ways than one. His hands twitched, needing his pruning shears. Time in the greenhouse working on his roses always calmed him. Perhaps a few hours of tending to them would give him a chance to calm down and digest how things had already gone horribly wrong.

Hunter stared at the empty walls of his bedroom. No mirrors adorned the walls. He didn't want to see his reflection staring back at him. Not in this personal space. His hand touched his newly shaved chin, and he thought for a moment, trying to see his face through her eyes. All he could see was one normal side of his face, and the other hideously distorted and scarred. The finger he was missing. The lacerated white lines that remained on his arm and chest.

Hunter dressed quickly and strode out of his room. Try as he might, he couldn't get out of his mind the horrified little gasp she'd given at the sight of him. She'd seen everything. His scars had been laid open.

And she'd been revolted.

FOUR

⌒

Gretchen nervously deleted and undeleted the last para-graph of chapter thirteen, chewing on her lip. Any moment now, that tall jerk was going to show up and ask them to politely leave. Or hey, since it was Eldon, it prob-ably wouldn't be so politely.

And then what would Gretchen tell her agent? Tell Audrey? *I sort of got a look at the owner's junk when I went exploring, and he's not a fan of being ogled.* That would go over well. God, how could she have messed this up so quickly? She hadn't even been here a full day yet. She glanced over at Audrey, but her sister was curled up on the bed, flipping through a magazine and glancing occasionally at her phone.

Next to her computer, Igor flicked his wiry little tail and whacked her on the wrist with it. She idly reached over and rubbed her fingers on his soft head. She had zero inter-est in working on more of sexist Astronaut Bill and his twerpy ladylove. She wanted to go look around. She wanted to take a good look at those letters she'd been sent here to transcribe and somehow turn into a book.

More than that, she wanted to find that naked man she'd spied on and apologize for gawking at him.

Maybe she could introduce herself. He had to be Buchanan. She could have asked Audrey about him, but then Audrey would be giving her suspicious looks and wanting to know just why Gretchen was so curious about the man. Gretchen didn't want to field questions about him. He was a dirty little secret she was intrigued by, and didn't want Audrey to ruin it for her with her disapproval. So she said nothing.

She thought of the curious way his face had been twisted on one side. She wondered what would have caused such—

At the knock on the door, she jumped.

Audrey sat up, swinging her legs off the side of the bed and tossing aside her magazine. "Don't move," she told Gretchen. "I'll get it."

Gretchen remained seated, but her gaze was glued to the door, peeking at it over her computer screen.

Sure enough, the sinister figure of Eldon lurked in the doorway. "Ms. Petty."

"Good afternoon," Audrey said coolly. "Can I help you with something?"

Oh, no, Gretchen thought, unable to look away. Mr. Buchanan had complained about her snooping. He'd told that horrible butler that Gretchen had seen his junk, and now he wanted her gone. This was where her spying would be laid out and confessed, and she'd be embarrassed in front of her cool, competent sister and the unpleasant butler. She was going to be fired before she'd even begun. She just knew it.

"I'm here to show the other Ms. Petty the project she will be working on, if now is a good time." Eldon's lean face turned in her direction, waiting.

Not . . . fired?

Really? She sat for a minute, utterly surprised. Why had Mr. Buchanan not sent her away? She'd seen him in his birthday suit.

"Is now a good time?" Eldon repeated, his voice flat with dislike.

"A good time?" *Was it ever.* Anything to get away from writing. Gretchen snapped her laptop shut with an almost gleeful air. "Now is perfect. Audrey, can you keep an eye on Igor for me?"

"He's a cat," Audrey said with a hint of amusement, walking back to the bed and picking up the magazine. "Exactly how much watching does he need?"

"Just make sure he doesn't eat a tassel or something," Gretchen called out, heading out of the room and shutting the door behind her. She couldn't help but smile at Eldon's disapproving face. She'd thought for sure that he'd come here to send her away.

"Lead on, my friend," Gretchen said cheerfully. "I can't wait to see this project."

The butler began to walk down the hall, glancing over his shoulder at Gretchen as if to reassure himself that she was following him. "Mr. Buchanan wanted me to set proper expectations for you in regards to this project."

"Proper expectations? I think I hear a lecture incoming." She barely resisted trailing her fingers along a lovely mahogany table. Pretty sure that wouldn't meet the proper expectations.

"This will be a quite lengthy project," Eldon droned in his dry voice. "It should take you at least a month to catalog and go through the letters."

"I'm fine with that."

"The letters are very old and should be handled with care."

"Duh. I'll be careful."

He gave her a scathing look. "Further, they are not to

be removed from the premises. They are also not to be photocopied or scanned in. Mr. Buchanan is very concerned about the privacy of the project and the family's wishes."

"Whatever you say," Gretchen told him. "I'm just the hired help. You just point me at the letters and I'll get to work."

"Indeed."

There was a wealth of unpleasantness in that one word, but Gretchen was determined not to let it bother her. "So the letters are from the Buchanan family's archives? Is that correct?"

"I am not at liberty to discuss things," Eldon said, his voice seeming to get even stiffer.

"Well, can I ask Mr. Buchanan about them? I—"

"Mr. Buchanan is busy. He is not going to be involved. Do not disturb him with your questions."

"And that's fine, but I just thought that since—"

"You are not to bother Mr. Buchanan!" He turned a baleful gaze upon her. "He is a very busy man and does not want to be disturbed. Your being on location does not mean he is at your disposal."

Whoa, what had crawled up his ass? Had Buchanan said something to him? Gretchen raised her hands in a defensive posture. "I wasn't suggesting that. I was just going to say—"

"If you are not interested in reviewing the project, Ms. Petty, I can let the publisher know that we are in need of another writer."

"If you'd let me finish a sentence," Gretchen snapped, "you would know that that is not what I'm saying at all. Just show me the damn letters."

She half-expected him to snap back at her, but he only smiled.

"They are right this way," Eldon said, gesturing. His voice was as cool as ice all over again, as if he didn't have to try to be nice now that he'd gotten his way. "Please follow me."

It was apparently time for a new plan. If she wanted to say hello—and apologize—to Mr. Buchanan, she'd have to see him when Eldon wasn't around to glare at her. Maybe a late-night visit?

Nah, that'd probably just be weird. He'd think she was creeping on him.

They moved down a long hall decorated in seemingly old-fashioned gilt and blue furnishings. Gretchen made a mental note of this, because she'd be damned if she was going to ask Eldon to show her where the room was again. Too bad she hadn't brought her phone, since a GPS would be needed for this enormous building. So she noted the surroundings. Blue sofa, old picture with ridiculously ornate frame, case full of Fabergé eggs along the hallway wall, more blue settees, a golden statue, and an old oil painting of the ugliest man she had ever seen (also dressed in blue), wearing a powdered wig.

Then, they turned into a sunlit hallway, and Eldon paused in front of a pair of wooden double doors.

The butler glanced back at Gretchen. "I don't think I need to remind you to keep these doors shut at all times. The library has many old and priceless books, and the hall here is quite sunny and could age them."

"Of course," she murmured, resisting the urge to shove his hands off the doorknobs and sweep the doors open herself. For a moment, she felt like a kid at Christmas. The house had been spectacular so far. What would the library be like?

Eldon pushed the doors open and stepped aside, and Gretchen stepped in, looking around in wonder.

The room was large, though that had been expected. At least as long as a basketball court, the room was two stories, with a flat, painted ceiling of a bright blue mural of dancing Greek characters. The room itself was floor-to-ceiling rosewood, shiny and gleaming. Row upon row of neatly ordered books lined the walls, and there were a pair of curling staircases on the end of each side of the room. Wrought-iron railings lined the second floor, and dotted amongst the endless rows of books were *objets d'art*. A small piano was delicately situated in the far end of the room near a few more dainty settees, a portrait hung off a decorative easel in another corner. A massive Victorian globe held a place of honor near the large fireplace.

It was a room of wonder and imagination. Gretchen was utterly delighted at the sight of it. *Holy crap. I get to work in here for the next month?* But she kept her cool and asked, "So this is where I'll be working?"

"Indeed." Eldon sniffed. "I should like to remind you that nothing is to be removed from the library—"

"Of course."

"And please do not touch anything you do not feel you need for your project. Some of these items are quite valuable—"

"Of course."

"And then I must remind you—"

"Not to open the doors and let the sunlight in because the books will turn to dust. Right." He'd told her that not five minutes ago. She wasn't likely to forget. "Do you want to warn me not to feed Mogwai after midnight?"

He stared at her.

"Never mind. Eighties joke." Gretchen put her hands on her hips, trying not to show her excitement. She couldn't wait to explore this place, but that wouldn't happen with Eldon hovering. She needed to act like this was no big deal, and as soon as his back was turned, then she could do all the leisurely exploring she wanted. Time to seem bored.

Gretchen feigned a yawn. "So where are the letters?"

"Right this way." Eldon made his way to the back of the room and gestured at a matching rosewood secretary desk. She'd seen furniture like this, but only in antique stores or museums. The legs were spindly and painted with delicate designs, and as she watched with growing delight, Eldon opened the desk, revealing a flat writing surface and myriad cubbies used for mail. "This desk has been designated for your work area."

"Mmmhmm." She tried to seem casual and unexcited, even though she wanted nothing more than to sit down and run her hands along the wood.

"The letters are in this trunk."

Gretchen glanced politely at the large steamer trunk set up next to the desk. "The container that holds the letters is in the trunk?"

"No," Eldon said. "The letters are in the trunk." He leaned over and flipped open the lid, revealing the contents.

There were letters, all right. She'd been expecting a lot of letters, of course. Maybe she just hadn't properly visualized exactly how many letters. This trunk was filled top to bottom with envelopes, all neatly left in slit-open envelopes and lined up like playing cards. There had to be more than several hundred letters in that freaking trunk, maybe even a few thousand.

Her mouth fell open and she moved to the trunk, staring at the contents. "All these?"

"All these," Eldon agreed. "They are cataloged by year."

"I see that," she murmured, touching a small tab separating a line of the envelopes. It was labeled 1885. She did a quick glance down the row, looking at the tabs to get an idea of the scope of the project. They started with 1872 and continued all the way up until 1902. "Are there really thirty years of letters in here?"

"So it seems."

Holy crap! Okay, so she hadn't been initially excited about this project, but now she was fascinated. What could these two letter writers have to talk about for thirty years that would have been so interesting that the letters were carefully kept and preserved for all this time? "When can I start?"

"You can start tomorrow."

———

"You're fine with me going back to work and leaving you here?" Audrey awkwardly patted Igor's wrinkly little head, then returned to brushing her hair, readying for work.

The hairless cat meowed and rubbed against her hand in response.

Gretchen, still lolling on the bed in her pajamas, patted the blanket to call the cat. She didn't have a day job like Audrey. She didn't have to get out of her pajamas if she didn't want to. "I'm fine. I start the letters today, and if this weekend is any indication, Eldon's the only one I'll ever see. Mr. Buchanan is either avoiding us or not in residence, and either way suits me fine," she lied.

After all, she knew the truth—not only was Mr. Buchanan in residence, but he was totally, completely avoiding Gretchen.

She knew why, of course. She'd seen the man naked as could be. Strangers tended to frown on that sort of thing, after all.

But Audrey didn't know any of that. If her sister did find out, she'd insist that Gretchen leave at once. Audrey was a bit prudish about that sort of thing. Growing up, the twins had been models of decorum, and Gretchen had been the wild child. Now all the wildness had gone out of Gretchen and seemed to have slid into Audrey's twin, Daphne. As for Audrey, well, she still had that good girl mentality.

"I've met Buchanan a few times, Gretchen." Audrey brushed her pale red hair in rapid strokes, glancing occasionally at Gretchen through the mirror. "He's not what I'd call friendly or pleasant. I just worry about you being here with only that man and that horrible butler."

"I'll be fine, Audrey. Me and Igor will just work on the

book, live off sandwiches, and get this project done as soon as possible. It's no big deal."

Audrey paused from pinning up her hair into her typical workday chignon. "You're sure? It's not that far of a drive from the Hawkings building. I can get into a cab and come get you if—"

"If what? I fall down the stairs and no one notices my crumpled form for weeks? Come on, Audrey. You've seen this place." Gretchen rolled over in the bed and gestured at the room. "This house could fit all of my apartment building in here with room to spare, and there's only two guys living here. The odds of me running into him are slim to none. If I need anything, I just ring for Eldon."

"I know. I still don't like this." She licked a finger and smoothed an errant strand of hair, staring at her reflection in the mirror. "It's a weird setup."

"Yeah, but if Buchanan was a creepster, there are lots of cheaper ways to get women. Hookers don't cost nearly what the publisher's paying me."

"That is so not funny."

"Oh, I don't know. It's kind of funny if you think about it. I'm the literary equivalent of a hooker. Give me a contract and I'll do whatever you want, baby."

"Still not funny."

"Come on. Just a little bit funny."

"Nope."

Igor began to purr, and Gretchen scooped him up in her arms, cuddling him. The cat was surprisingly soft despite his lack of fur. His skin felt like crushed velvet, and she couldn't resist his sweet but ugly face. "Tell Audrey it's funny, Igor."

"Gretch, you've really got to get out of the house more if you're talking to that cat."

She wiggled Igor back and forth, crossing her legs under her. "Tell Audrey that Mommy's out of the house right now, Igor."

"This is what I mean." Audrey sighed. "That cat gets more attention than your last boyfriend."

"This cat is better to cuddle with than my last boyfriend," Gretchen said cheerfully. "And you're going to be late to work."

Audrey sighed again and adjusted her dark gray jacket, then picked an imaginary piece of lint off her matching skirt. "You're going to be fine?"

"Igor and I will be just fine."

She rolled her eyes and pulled out her phone, jiggling it in her sister's direction. "Call me if you need me. And keep your phone on you so I can check you via text."

"I'm twenty-six, Audrey. I can handle myself."

"You're in your pajamas, talking to your cat. Forgive me if I feel a moment of doubt. It's like you're turning into the crazy cat lady before my eyes."

"Am not. Igor and I are having a month-long slumber party," Gretchen said, holding the cat in front of her and making a kissy face at him because she knew it'd drive sensible Audrey bananas. "Isn't that right, Igor-Wigor?"

"God, you and that cat." She waved a hand. "It's no wonder you're eternally single. I'm out of here."

"Text ya later," Gretchen said, and moved the cat's paw up and down in a facsimile of a wave. She laughed to herself when Audrey shut the door to the bedroom behind her, her sigh of sisterly annoyance still echoing in the hallway. "I'm thinking she's not fond of you as a roomie, Igor."

The cat said nothing and simply blinked up at her.

Gretchen sighed and placed him on the bed. "Okay, so Audrey might be right about the whole me-still-in-pajamas-talking-to-a-cat-is-pathetic thing. And given that I'm still talking to you, she might also have a point about the eternally single thing."

It wasn't that Gretchen ran into a lot of spectacularly eligible men in her line of work. The only people she knew in publishing were female, as it was a female-dominated business, and when she wasn't doing job-related networking, she was more or less at home, working on her latest manuscript.

And sometimes she didn't change out of her pajamas for days, which was kind of gross and not something that a boyfriend would approve of. So it was a good thing that she was single. Single let her hit her deadlines.

Well, theoretically. Since she wasn't good at hitting those either, she really had no excuse.

She waited a few minutes, listening to her stomach growl, and then glanced over at the clock. Audrey had to be well on her way to work by now. *Good.* Gretchen rolled off the bed, bounding up onto her feet and heading for the bedroom door. Having her sister around for the weekend was enjoyable for the first night, but after that it sort of made the weekend crawl by. She wanted to explore the house and poke around on her project at her leisure, but all Audrey wanted to do was work on PowerPoints and go through her work email, even on Saturday nights.

The girl needed a hobby. Of course, the odds of that happening were about as good as the odds of Gretchen getting a boyfriend.

She slipped out the door of her room and down the hall. There was no sound of vacuums today. Today they were cleaning the boathouse and greenhouse or something. No flood of maids to drop in on and say hello, since she didn't know where either the boathouse or greenhouse were. That meant that the only person around was Eldon, and he tended to avoid her.

This also meant that the north wing—Mr. Buchanan's wing—would likely be deserted.

Gretchen headed there, unable to help herself.

It was a crazy idea, but the more she entertained the thought of apologizing to Mr. Buchanan, the more she wanted to do it. Her spying was going to hang in the air between them, and she didn't want to spend the next thirty days hiding from him—or having him retreat at the sight of her.

They needed to deal with it like adults. Adults saw nudity all the time. Penises? No big deal. She wanted to apologize and make this next month as smooth as possible, since they'd be living together.

Unfortunately for her, his wing of the estate was *entirely* deserted. She spent a good half hour knocking on doors, only to come to that maddening conclusion. This place was a maze, and it would be near impossible to find the owner unless she knew where to look for him.

Disgruntled—and a bit hungry—Gretchen headed to the kitchens in the north wing, since it was the only one stocked. Even here, the place was immaculate. Not a crumb marred the gorgeous granite countertops, and the fridge and pantry were brimming with all kinds of delicious things that she was itching to bake with. It wasn't her kitchen so she wouldn't touch anything that she didn't have permission to. Though it killed her not to rummage through the pantry and start baking, she made herself a simple sandwich out of some of the fresh bread left out on the counter (she'd come back later for Igor's food), washed her knife and plate once she was done, and then wrapped the sandwich in a paper towel and walked the halls as she ate, musing to herself about her surroundings.

As she finished her sandwich, she strolled past a long corridor of windows and almost missed the sight of Mr. Buchanan in the gardens. His tall figure cut a dark form against the naked rosebushes. She moved to the window to watch him, and she noticed that he seemed to be inspecting the bushes. They looked pretty dead to her, but maybe they weren't supposed to be? Intrigued, Gretchen hunted for a door that led outside.

Five minutes later, she was slogging through the light dusting of snow in a pair of boots that she'd found in the mudroom. Her flannel pajamas were warm enough for the indoors, but the bitter winter wind cut right through them. For a brief moment, she pondered heading back to her room to dress in something other than pajamas, but in that time, the mysterious Mr. Buchanan might disappear on her again.

And she desperately needed to talk to him.

Her footsteps crunched loudly as she walked, and she crossed her arms over her chest, heading toward him with determination. He didn't seem to have noticed her yet, so she studied him from behind. She'd seen him previously, of course, but not clothed, and he looked different, somehow. Rich guys didn't need to work hard to get chicks. She always suspected that more often they looked like pasty nerds rather than soldiers. But this man was definitely of the latter variety, however. His shoulders were thick and burly underneath the tan jacket he wore, and his entire frame seemed built for muscle. He wasn't short either, which was nice. Not that she was interested in those sorts of things. She just wanted to apologize for ogling his junk.

He turned around even as she was considering his nicely formed behind, and her face flushed bright red. She was forever going to be caught leering at him, wasn't she?

Mr. Buchanan stared at her for a long moment, frozen. Then color began to dot his cheeks. It made the scars on his face stand out even more, like jagged talons of white cutting across his tanned skin.

He also looked like he was torn between running for cover or choking her with the length of rope he held.

"Hi there." She tried to keep her tone cheerful and nonchalant. "I thought I'd come out and say hi."

His eyes narrowed warily, and she was reminded for a moment of a wounded animal. That piercing gaze moved up and down her form, noting her pajamas. "Are you drunk?" he asked abruptly.

"No," she said, drawing out that one syllable. Okay, so the pajamas weren't making the best first—um, second—impression. "I'm friendly. I saw you out here and wanted to talk."

His face darkened into a scowl, the scars at the corner of his mouth twisting his entire face into an ugly grimace. He turned away. "I have nothing to say to you."

So this wasn't going well. When he began to stalk away at a pace more rapid than she could sustain in her oversized borrowed boots, she panicked. "Your penis!" she called out. "I saw it!"

He stopped in his tracks and turned to give her an incredulous look.

She stomped after him, nearly losing her balance in a snowdrift. "It's true," she said, struggling to stand upright. "I was snooping and I saw you naked. All of you. Really naked. That's why you won't talk to me, isn't it?" When he began to scowl again, she continued. "I mean, you can sit here and pretend you don't want to talk to me, but we both know it's totally awkward because I saw your dick before I saw your face."

His scowl seemed to turn even blacker, making the scars livid on his face.

Oh shit, his *scars*. He thought she was insulting his face. "I, uh, didn't mean it like that. Damn, I'm much better at banter when it's on the page." Gretchen trailed after him when he began to walk away again. "Can we try this again?" She assumed a cheerful expression and made her voice two octaves higher. "Hi there! I'm Gretchen, and I'm working on ghostwriting the project in your library. I'm only going to be here for a month, but I hope we can be friends."

And she thrust her hand out.

He stopped, stared down at her hand for a moment, and then looked back at her. "I trust you'll stay out of my way for the next month, then."

Ouch. She couldn't help the flinch that crossed her face. "I guess I will."

He gave a curt nod. "See that you do. I'm a very busy man." Winding the length of rope around his arm, he continued back toward the house.

Gretchen watched him leave, frustrated and a little embarrassed at herself. *Not exactly a smooth conversationalist there, Gretch. Did you hope to wow him with your witty "Your penis, I saw it!" Did you really think that would break the ice?*

"Seems to work for Astronaut Bill and Uranea," she muttered to herself. Then, shivering and rubbing her arms, she headed back to the manor house.

So much for apologizing to the owner of the place.

————

Hunter ripped his snow boots off and tossed them down in the mudroom, discarding his gardening gloves and the rope he'd brought inside. She was heading for the mudroom, too, and he needed to get out of there. Tearing down the hall, he headed for the one place he could truly relax and think—his greenhouse.

God, he'd fucked it all up again.

He headed down the covered garden path that led to the side of the manor house and his private greenhouse. He walked in and the humidity hit him, as well as the perfume of the roses. Immediately, his pounding heart began to calm. He moved to his table of tools and picked up his favorite pruning shears and then moved to inspect his roses. As he knelt and began to prune away the dead leaves, his thoughts whirled with the bizarre, abrupt encounter.

She'd come out to talk to him.

Him. She'd wanted to talk to *him*. Part of Hunter had been thrilled at the thought, but the larger part of him—the scarred, wounded part—had lashed out. She'd seen him naked. Commented on his face. Pointed out quite bluntly that she'd seen his cock.

It had almost seemed like she'd wanted to break the ice and was having a hard time spitting it out.

And what had he done? He'd snapped at her and tried to chase her off. To her credit, she hadn't been deterred until he'd more or less told her to stay out of his way for the entire month.

Hunter gritted his teeth, viciously snapping a browned leaf off a wilting Gemini tea rose.

He didn't want her to avoid him. He wanted to see her. Watch her work. Talk to her. Have her turn that odd sense of humor on him. And instead, he'd driven her away.

Fuck. Why did he always freeze up around women? Hell, around people in general. Eldon was the only one who didn't make him stiffen with alarm. And she'd been so lovely and . . . odd. He thought back to the sight of her, standing in his snowy garden in Eldon's borrowed boots and ratty flannel pajamas that outlined the hard tips of her nipples when the breeze had blown her shirt a certain way.

That had made him panic as much as anything, even as it made him hard with need. Hunter groaned and pressed a hand to his cock, willing his erection to go away. He'd give in to the need later, in the privacy of his room. He'd dream about that spill of messy red hair, her pale skin, and the way her mouth made a perfect little bow when she was startled. And then he'd dream of that bow of a mouth descending on his cock, licking the head—

. . . we both know it's totally awkward because I saw your dick ever before I saw your face.

Yeah, that fucking killed his boner.

Hunter shook his head to clear his thoughts, forcing

himself to concentrate on the maintenance of his roses. Some people read or painted to calm their minds but Hunter liked tending to his roses. He grew all varieties, but his favorites were the showy hybrid tea roses that were so delicate in their constitution and yet so incredibly beautiful and fragrant when coaxed into blooming. He ran his fingers over a velvety petal of a Cajun Moon, his exterior calm despite his roiling thoughts.

He'd more or less demanded that she leave him alone. He didn't want that. How could he fix it? Demand that Eldon prepare a candlelight dinner and then insist that she show up? Act as if he said nothing to her at all? Better yet, act as if they'd never even met and start fresh?

She'd think he was crazy if he did. Well, more than she already thought.

There was no good answer to this. He thought for a long moment, touching a petal of a blooming Blue Girl. The rose was lovely, the color a cross between pewter and baby blue. He wondered if her eyes were the same color. They'd been pale, making her entire face seem almost too pale in color, and overly round. But he liked that about her. It made her seem less . . . perfect.

With careful fingers, he cut the blue rose and trimmed the thorns off the stem. He'd have to apologize. He wasn't good at that sort of thing, but perhaps a rose would say more than he could.

————————

When Gretchen showered and dressed, she headed for the library. No sense in avoiding it for any longer—she had to start on the project. Her spirits were a bit low after that morning's encounter, but at least she'd tried. Now when they avoided each other, she'd know it was because he wanted it that way, not because he was embarrassed.

Shame. It'd make this month lonely.

The desk set aside for her use had been opened when

she entered the quiet library. To her surprise, there was a beautiful pale blue rose, freshly cut, laying on a silver tray. A small folded note lay under it.

She picked up the note and opened it, scanning the contents.

I was rude. I apologize. Eldon cooks dinner at seven every night. Tonight, I will be eating in the red dining room if you wish to attend. Pajamas optional.

It was signed with a scribbly *HB*.

And she smiled.

FIVE

⌒

Gretchen showed up to dinner five minutes early, a bit on edge. It was silly to be nervous, of course. It was just dinner with a man who, for all intents and purposes, didn't seem to like her very much. She supposed that she still felt a bit of guilt about their rather nude-ish meeting. It was her fault she'd embarrassed him, after all. And since he was the only shot she had of any company while she was staying here, she very much wanted things to be calm and easy between them.

She'd brushed her hair back into a clean ponytail instead of her regular messy bun, but she wore no makeup and dressed in her track pants and a long-sleeved T-shirt. It was just dinner with someone that she wanted to be a friend. Dressing up would make it weird.

Still, when she knocked on the door (after getting directions from Eldon earlier that day) and entered the red dining room, she was surprised to see Mr. Buchanan open the door for her. He was dressed in a crisp suit jacket, and his hair was smoothed against his scalp.

"Were we supposed to dress up?" Gretchen offered him a smile as she stepped into the room. "I admit that I thought of this as a work trip so I wore my usual writing clothes. Sorry if I'm a bit underdressed."

"It's fine," he said abruptly. "You are sufficient."

She laughed, trying to ease the mood. "Sufficient? I bet you say that to all the girls."

He looked flustered, and he turned away, shutting the door behind her with a bit more force than it needed. *Good Lord.* Here she was just trying to be funny and he acted as if he had ants in his pants. He'd been the one to invite her to dinner. "Thank you for the rose," she told him, crossing her arms over her chest and moving around the room to get a look at the furnishings. That seemed safer than looking at her dinner companion, who looked as if he might fall to pieces if he caught her staring at him.

And to be honest, she was practically twitching with the need to watch him. She'd been distracted in the gardens since it had been so cold and their conversation had gone badly. She wanted to stare at his fascinating face and figure out how it had ended up the way it had. He was covered in scars on one side of his face—deep, almost pitted scars that held a story in them. She was very curious about that story.

But since he seemed to be skittish, she pretended to look at the art on the walls of the red dining room. She could see why the room was called that, for rather obvious reasons. The walls were a flat, dark red, and the paintings on the walls were of still life scenes that contained quite a bit of red. This one was of a bouquet of roses, that one of apples. It was all very . . . red. She imagined it would be rather blinding if the lights were up fully, but fortunately—or not—the room was lit only by two candelabras in the center of the long wood table.

If Mr. Buchanan weren't acting so very weird, she'd think that between the rose and the candlelight that this was a date of some kind, except his manner seemed to say the exact opposite.

"Blue Girl," he said abruptly, moving to the far end of the table and pulling out a chair.

"What?" She turned to look at him.

He averted his gaze, as if not wanting to meet her eyes, and gestured at the chair that he'd held out for her. "The rose I sent you. It's called Blue Girl."

Gretchen took a step forward, noticing that when she did, he subtly shifted to one side, unconsciously moving to ensure that the good side of his face remained in her sights. Interesting. "I see. It's a lovely rose. I thought it was more purple than blue, though."

"It is. Very hard to get a true blue color from roses. Most soil is not acidic enough." His tone was brusque, as if explaining things to a fool.

"Ah." She sat down at the table and he pushed in her chair for her, then moved to her right. She noticed he didn't sit at the far end of the table but moved to the center of the right side, sitting at a ninety-degree angle from her. To hide his face again? She couldn't see the scars on the right side when he sat there. The only thing she could see was a clean, crisp profile.

He was handsome enough, she supposed. His jaw was square and strong, his features regular. His nose was slightly larger than beautiful and, on most men it would have overwhelmed his features. On him, it just looked . . . commanding. His eyes were narrow and dark, and his mouth was thin, as if he never smiled.

Of course, then when he turned slightly to the side, she saw the reason for his serious mien. The scars that covered the right side of his face were hideous. They marked the smooth rise of cheekbone and marred the strong lines of his chin. He was careful to keep his face angled away from her, but she recalled long gouges of scarring that crisscrossed his entire face. His brow was striated with white scars, and the scarring even went into his hairline.

She wondered what had happened that would have caused such scarring.

He glanced up and noticed her watching him. He dropped the silverware he was holding, and it clanged to the tabletop with a bang.

"My apologies," he said.

"No problem," she told him, a little curious at his mannerisms. *Was he . . . nervous?* "Sorry I didn't dress up. I figured this wasn't a date, so you know . . ." The words trailed off and for a moment, she felt a little uncomfortable. What if he viewed this as a date?

"Of course not," he said. And as if to prove her wrong, he gave his napkin a rough snap of the linen and placed it in his lap. "I simply wore a jacket because it was pleasing to me to dress well."

Well, so much for that, she thought. She couldn't tell if his words were intended to put her at ease or put her in her place. Actually, it was never easy to tell with him.

Mr. Buchanan reached over to a bottle of opened wine. "Would you like some?"

"Are you just trying to get me liquored up?" she teased. He stiffened.

"That was a joke," she told him quickly. Wow, he really didn't know how to interpret her humor, did he? "I'd love a drink." Gretchen extended her empty glass toward him, still watching him. His fingers were long and skilled, and he poured the glass with remarkable grace. If she hadn't seen him drop his knife earlier, she would have never suspected him of such a thing. He finished pouring and tilted the bottle back with a practiced flourish, not spilling an ounce.

His manners were beautiful, even if his words were abrupt.

The candles flickered as she sipped her wine and he

began to pour his own glass. She wondered for a moment if the candlelight was for ambiance or to hide his scars. If it was for the latter, it was a bad idea—the flickering light made his scars that much more hideous with the shadows. And again, she found herself wondering about them.

"I'm Gretchen," she offered when he finished pouring. "I don't know that we ever had a formal introduction."

"We did not," he said in a crisp voice. "I find it hard to introduce myself when I am naked and unawares."

Her mouth dropped a little at that, and it was on the tip of her tongue to offer another apology when he glanced over at her, and she realized . . . that was a joke. Was he waiting for her to laugh? Or respond?

"Yes, I do imagine it's quite hard when a madwoman approaches you in the gardens shouting about how she saw your penis," Gretchen offered back. "I can understand how that's not much of an icebreaker."

She tried to gauge his reaction, curious. Would he get upset again, or would he be a bit more at ease now that they were sitting and talking?

To her disappointment, he showed no reaction. Instead, he nudged a covered silver plate closer to the two of them. "I'm Hunter. Buchanan."

"I figured it was Buchanan," she said. "Unless you were related to Eldon and you had the real Buchanan locked away in the attic."

He snorted, though there was no smile on that grim face. "Eldon is my assistant and butler."

"Clearly you hired him for his sparkling personality," Gretchen said.

Hunter glanced over at her, still expressionless.

She grimaced, taking another swig of her wine. *Faux pas again?* "Sorry. I'm not trying to be unpleasant. He just wasn't very . . . welcoming when I arrived. I'm sure he's quite capable as an assistant."

He pulled the lid off the tray, revealing a pale white

pasta. It looked as if it had been cooked hours ago, and the noodles were limp, the sauce clumpy.

"Eldon is very protective of the estate. He is not fond of visitors."

"I gathered that," she said lightly.

He gave her a solemn look. "Was he cruel to you? Should I speak to him?"

"Oh, no." Gretchen extended her plate toward Hunter, since he seemed to be serving. "I was just surprised, that's all. So it's just you and him in this big house?"

"Not at all," Hunter said, taking the serving ware and spooning out some of the rather awful-looking pasta onto Gretchen's plate.

"Oh?"

"The cleaning crew is here most days. I assume Eldon told you the schedule?"

She took her plate back from him and tried not to look repulsed by the noodly mass on her plate. Maybe he'd cooked it himself, though? Could she insult him by asking about it? She decided it was time for a little white lie.

"This looks delicious," she told him, adjusting her napkin in her lap and waiting for him to spoon out his own portion.

"Eldon is an adequate cook," Hunter said.

"Well if that isn't a ringing endorsement, I don't know what is."

He gave her another curious look, but still did not crack a smile.

She waited for him to take a bite, and when he didn't fall over, choking, she took a tentative bite herself. The food was every bit as awful as it looked. The sauce was congealed, the noodles overcooked, and the entire thing was cold. She forced herself to swallow, her gaze on Hunter. How could he sit there and eat this mess?

Sufficient cook, indeed.

He glanced over at her. "Is everything all right?" Tension seemed to suddenly vibrate through his body.

Gretchen forced a bright smile to her face. "Great, thank you."

Hunter grunted and turned back to his food, eating quietly and methodically.

Well, this was definitely one of the oddest dinners she'd ever had. She was seated in one of many dining rooms at the biggest house she'd ever set foot into, and the food was worse than anything she'd ever tasted. Worse than that, the room was unnervingly quiet, and she wondered if Hunter even knew how to make small talk. Or did he even have to? She imagined he had people falling all over themselves to talk to him.

Another thought bothered her. He was a man who seemed to value his privacy. Perhaps spending dinner with her wasn't very pleasurable for him and he was only doing it out of politeness? Ouch.

She toyed with the noodles on her plate.

He paused again, setting down his fork and knife. "Something is bothering you."

"No, really, I'm fine."

His gaze hardened, as if disapproving of her obvious lie. "It's not necessary for you to humor me with dinner. If you wish to go, please go."

Oh, great. Now he thought she didn't want to be here with him? She shook her head and shoved another forkful of the hideous pasta into her mouth to prove that she did want to be there. Immediately, her gag reflex kicked in and she choked. Grabbing her napkin, she spit the gluey wad into it. "Sorry about that. I don't think I can eat this."

He looked down at his plate, surprised. "Do you not like Italian?"

"Don't you have a cook?" she blurted out. "I mean, you're rich. You can afford a cook, right?"

He frowned at her, then put his napkin down on the table. "Eldon's cooking is sufficient."

"I can't eat it," she told him. "It's not you. Trust me. I

just . . . I'll gag if I have to pretend to like another mouthful."

"You already gagged," he pointed out.

She wished he would smile so she could tell if he was joking or not. "Yeah, I did. Thank God this dinner party is only for two, right?"

"Is the wine acceptable?"

She nodded and chugged the rest of her glass, determined to wash away the taste of Eldon's cooking. "It's very quiet here, too. I find that unnerving."

"Quiet?" He tilted his head, regarding her as if the idea were foreign to him. "Do you not like the quiet?"

"I live in SoHo," she told him, and held out her glass for him to refill. "There are cars on the street at all hours, and noisy neighbors, and people going up and down the stairs of my walkup. It's never quiet. You never feel isolated and alone like you do here. I guess I'm just not used to it."

"I see."

She had no idea what he meant by that. "Your house is gorgeous, though. Please don't take it as a slight against this place."

"I don't." He looked over at her, and she realized that, for the majority of their dinner, he'd taken great care not to look at her.

"Well, I appreciate you letting me stay here, regardless."

"But you do not like it here."

"How can anyone not like it here? It's like a castle."

"Castles are not pleasant for those in the dungeons."

"Well, if my room is a dungeon, it's the most enjoyable dungeon I've ever stayed in. Seriously, it's fine." She took another sip of her wine. "I can't believe I'm insulting the grandest house I've ever stayed in."

"Perhaps it is not the house," he began slowly. "But the lack of company?"

Gretchen smiled gratefully at him. "That's probably it, yes."

"What about your cat?"

"Well, Igor's not much of a conversationalist," she teased.

He got that funny expression on his face again that made her think he was blushing. "I meant you could keep him with you."

"Oh. That's very nice of you. I worry he might get lost, though. My room's larger than my apartment."

"If he gets lost, I will help you find him," he said gravely.

She pictured that—the stuffy billionaire on hands and knees, calling her hairless cat—and stifled another smile. "You're very kind."

"Would you . . ." He paused again. "Would you like to meet again for dinner tomorrow night?"

A smile curved her mouth. He'd sounded so utterly reluctant saying that, and yet . . . she didn't think he disliked her. She didn't know what he thought of her. "You don't sound excited by the prospect."

"It is you who should not be excited. Eldon will be cooking again."

She laughed. "Can he make a sandwich?"

His expression seemed to thaw a little, though he still did not smile. "He can make a mean sandwich, yes."

"Then dinner sounds terrific."

One Week Later

Gretchen stared at the thirtieth letter and contemplated burning the entire trunk of them. "Seriously, Igor, I don't see how a project like this could be so mind-numbingly dull."

The cat didn't get up from his spot under the lamp, basking in the glow of the artificial light. He didn't even stir.

She sighed, carefully placing the letter back in the trunk and stripping off her plastic gloves. At least it was close to dinnertime. Strange how the project she'd been so excited about had turned out to be a total snooze-fest, and the billionaire she'd initially thought to avoid turned out to be the highlight of her day.

Over the past week, Gretchen had woken up early, dressed (well, sometimes), and headed to the library to dutifully work on the project. Each letter was opened up, attached to a specialized clipboard with delicate care, and then transcribed. There were better ways to do such things, as she'd pointed out to Eldon at least once, but he seemed very against her ideas. When she was finished with cataloging the letters, she'd be able to move on to the next phase of the project, which involved turning all her notes into some cohesive sort of storyline that would make a novel.

Of course, that was going to be a bit trickier than she'd anticipated. The letters were boring as hell. Written in a tight, crabby script, Ms. Lulabelle Vargas droned on and on to a Mister Benedict Benthwick about the weather in Rochester. Or how the family vacationed for the summer in Jersey. Sometimes she commented on flowers in her father's gardens or the upcoming Christmas Eve ball that seemed eons away. Sometimes she commented on her fashionable new neighbor, down to the number of bows the woman wore in her bonnet (thirty-nine).

Finishing seemed eons away for Gretchen, too. She'd gone through plenty of the letters and they'd only gotten to September of 1872. She still had most of the trunk to go through. By the time she got through all the letters, she'd know the weather patterns for the entire time period, the neighbor's wardrobe, and she'd probably want to jump off the balcony from the sheer monotony of it all.

And because the letters were so incredibly dull it was

taking her a damn long time to work through them. She had a month to catalog the hundreds of letters. She'd gone through thirty in the last week. At this rate, she'd be done by, well . . . she thought of upcoming holidays and cringed.

Her agent would kill her if she blew an important deadline like this one. Not only was she behind on her Astronaut Bill deadline, but now this one? It wasn't looking good.

"We'll just have to buckle down, Igor," she told the cat, reaching out to scratch behind his enormous triangle-shaped ears. "I'll come back after dinner and then we'll pick up round two. Sound good?"

The cat ignored her.

Figured. She'd only been at this big, empty house for a week and already she was talking to the cat. Again. "I don't know how Hunter does it," she muttered to herself. Give her another week or two and she'd probably be talking to the furniture.

She scooped up her cat and returned to her room, straightening up before dinner. It was just casual between friends, of course, but for some reason, Hunter continually dressed in jackets and nice clothing, and so she'd started to do the same, since she felt weird sitting next to him in sweatpants.

Last night, she'd shown up in a plain green dress, and his eyes had gleamed with appreciation. She'd felt a little . . . pleased at that. Unfortunately she'd only packed two dresses, and those at Audrey's insistence. She'd never expected to actually have an occasion to wear them. Go figure. Tonight she dressed in her dark gray sweaterdress that had a large cowl-neck and clung to her curves. Audrey had insisted on her bringing it but she normally didn't have an opportunity to wear it. Tonight, she could have kissed fussy Audrey in appreciation of her forethought.

Gretchen pulled her hair into a simple upsweep, washed her hands free of dust from the letters and, on a whim, headed back to the library.

Every day, a new rose was left on her desk. Whether it was politeness on Hunter's part or something else, there was always a new rose. Considering that it was winter outside, she suspected he had them ordered in. They were always unique and different from the last one, though. Today's rose was a delicate white on the inside and a dark pink at the edges of the petals.

She wasn't quite sure what the roses meant. Just a polite gesture from a lonely man? She liked to think otherwise. Maybe he was as quietly fascinated with her as she was with him. There was something about Hunter that called to her. His sharp mind? His flawless physique? His scarred face and tortured eyes? She didn't know, but she couldn't get him out of her head. He was so different from all the other men she'd ever met. He fascinated her.

Let's face it, Gretch. You have it bad for him.

She snapped the rose stem and tucked it behind one ear, then winced. A tiny bead of blood welled on her fingertip and she sucked it clean, searching for the hidden thorn. Figured that she'd be pricked the moment she tried to look pretty. Still sucking on her finger, she headed down to dinner.

Hunter was at the red dining room, waiting for her. He didn't smile at the sight of her—she was coming to expect that—but his gaze moved over her in a way that made her definitely think he'd noticed her dress and approved of it.

"Good evening," he said, as stiff and formal as ever.

"Hi to you, too," she told him, grinning. Somehow just seeing him always made her day a little more fascinating. "Have a good day?"

"It was—"

"Sufficient?" she interrupted cheekily. She'd noticed something about him over the last week. He never mentioned things in a positive sense. If she asked him how his day was, his answer would be neutral, guarded. If she asked him if he'd liked dinner, it would be equally neutral.

It became a game to her to see if she could goad him into a response—one way or another.

"Indeed," he said in a dry voice that was almost amused. Almost. "How are the letters coming?"

"They're coming," she said in a bright singsong voice that masked her utter dislike for the project thus far. Not that she could tell Hunter that, since the publisher had handpicked her for this job. "Nice weather we're having, isn't it?"

He grunted.

She laughed, shaking her head as he pulled her chair out for her. "Before I leave this place, Hunter Buchanan, I'm going to get you to admit that you're having a good day and that the weather is nice. Not everything has to be shades of gray."

He ignored her teasing, pushing in her chair as she sat. "I see you received your rose today."

"I did. What's this one called?" She touched a hand to the flower behind her ear.

"Gypsy Carnival."

"I love it."

"Do you?" He stilled, as if hardly daring to breathe.

Gretchen nodded. "Well, it's not quite my favorite so far. I liked the first one the best. The blue one."

"Blue Girl. I remember." He looked so very serious, so intense.

"I liked it best, though they're all incredibly lovely. Your taste is impeccable."

Another grunt of acknowledgement.

Tonight's dinner was more sandwiches. After her first complaint, they'd had sandwiches every night. It wasn't thrilling food, but at least she could eat it. She just went to dinner for the company, anyhow. If she wanted decent food, she cooked it herself when she was bored, and then dined on leftovers. She never touched Eldon's cooking. Hunter might have thought Eldon was sufficient at cooking but she thought he was terrible. Why a billionaire didn't hire a cook, she didn't understand.

Hunter was an enigma, and she was growing increasingly fascinated by him. She'd never met anyone quite as remote as him.

To her surprise, he picked up her hand and examined her red fingertip. "You hurt yourself."

"It's nothing." She studied his fingers on her skin, and she noticed the scars were on the back of his hand, too. He seemed to be missing a finger as well, which she had never noticed before now. Had he lost it in the accident?

"You should be careful." His gaze moved over her face and, to Gretchen's surprise, he was leaning so low that she could scent his aftershave. A hot rush of pleasure coursed through her. Odd that she would be attracted to this man. She knew nothing about him because he never shared anything of himself at their companionable dinners.

But was it because he refused to? Or because he didn't know how?

Greatly daring, Gretchen pulled her hand from his and regarded him. His face was carefully angled away from her once more. "May I ask you something personal?"

"I suppose." His tone had gone flat, wary.

"How did your . . . injuries happen?"

He jerked to his feet, and Gretchen knew she'd made a mistake.

"I'm sorry I asked. I just . . ."

Her words trailed off as he headed for the door. *Well, shit.* She must have touched on the one thing that could break through that icy veneer. She'd wanted him to show a reaction, after all. She'd gotten one.

He paused at the doorway, as if struggling with something internally. Then, he turned and gave her a look so cold that she shivered. "You want to know about my scars? Why I'm as ugly as I am?"

"I didn't mean—"

"My secret is not a secret. Ask anyone and they'll tell you. You can find it in all the newspapers, too. When I was ten, I was kidnapped from boarding school and held for ransom. The fools thought that because my father was incredibly wealthy, that he'd pay anything for his only heir." His laugh was cold, bitter, his expression bleak. "They did not know my father well. My father didn't give two shits about me. He didn't care about leaving a legacy. He just wanted to see how much money he could acquire before he died. I was simply an inconvenience. When he'd heard I'd been kidnapped, the first thing he wanted to know was how much they wanted. And when he heard the price, he refused to pay it."

Her lips parted in shock.

"They kept me on a boat for a week. As the days passed, I knew my father wasn't sending anyone for me, so I planned my escape. I thought it'd be easy to jump over-board and swim to shore. So I did, except when I went over the side, I hit the propeller. It destroyed my face and my arm and tore up my chest." He held up his hand. "I almost lost all these fingers, but instead I only lost one. I nearly died."

Holy shit. Her jaw dropped.

"I suppose I should be considered lucky. The propeller was moving at a very low speed and it only destroyed half of me." The cynicism in his voice made her ache. "The kidnappers panicked as soon as they saw the blood in the water and tried to get away. A nearby fisherman saw me go overboard and swam out to save me. He is why I lived." Hunter turned away. "Now you know. Never ask me again."

And he shut the door.

Their tentative friendship had just taken one massive, ugly step backward. Gretchen sighed and tossed the limp sandwich back onto the plate, her appetite gone.

Anger and despair raged inside of Hunter. He tore down the halls of Buchanan Manor, knocking over priceless vases and statues as he passed them. He needed something—anything—to quell this helpless rage he was feeling.

She'd asked about his face. Wanted to know why he was so hideous. She couldn't see past the scars despite her pretty words.

And it made him furious, even as it made him feel black with despair.

Why was he nothing to her but a ravaged face? Why was she just like everyone else? Why could she not ignore them and focus on the man underneath?

He slammed a hand into a delicate Chinese ginger jar, pleased when it launched off the end table and smacked into the wall. *Good.* Now it was as shattered as he felt inside.

How could he possibly explain to another person the event that had destroyed his life? Waking up in the arms of strangers as a young boy? The horror and fear he'd felt as they'd held a gun to his head and transported him to the boat? The emptiness he'd felt when days had passed and no ransom was forthcoming? Could they possibly have known that his father couldn't have cared less that he had a son? That he couldn't be bothered to deal with the child who had killed his beloved wife in childbirth? The grim determination he'd felt when he'd realized he'd have to save himself, and launched over the side of the boat . . . only to meet a fate worse than death when he hit the propeller?

It had destroyed his life, reshaped him like a crucible.

There was no one to trust. Better to be alone and safe, secure and unharmed. He could count on no one to care for him, save for those he paid. He grasped the delicate doily the vase had been sitting upon and fought the urge to rip it into shreds.

He would always be alone. No matter how much he

hoped otherwise, it was just another reminder that he was unlovable. No one would ever see past his face.

A throat cleared.

Hunter turned. Eldon was in the doorway. He coolly surveyed the destruction Hunter had left behind him—the shattered glass covering the hallway, the destroyed priceless vases. He said nothing, simply waited.

Hunter ran a hand down his face, suddenly weary. "Send the cleaning crew in this wing tomorrow."

"Of course."

"That'll be all." Hunter turned, heading toward his room. He'd change and work out his aggression in his private gym. A few rounds with the punching bag, some shadowboxing, some weight lifting, and maybe he'd be tired enough that it wouldn't matter.

"Shall I send her away, Mr. Buchanan?" Eldon's quietly worded question made him stop in his tracks.

Did he want that? He could say the word and she'd be out of the house within the hour. No more questions. No more wide-eyed inquiries about his scars. Just him and utter silence once more.

He thought of Gretchen's lovely face, her laughing eyes and her outrageous sense of humor. Her curves in the dress she'd worn tonight. The way her entire face lit up when she smiled, which was often.

He still wanted her. Still wanted to be around her, wanted to bask in her playful smiles and teasing comments.

"No," he said abruptly. "She stays."

"I see."

"Thank you, Eldon." He walked down the hallway and shut the door to his room.

———

Gretchen set her alarm for sunrise. She had a plan, and today she was going to put it into action.

When it went off the next morning, she jumped out of

bed, slid into her favorite yoga pants, and dragged her hair into a messy ponytail. She tossed down a can of food for Igor, kissed his head, and bounded out the door in her slippers, heading to the library.

Hopefully she was early enough.

To her relief, the library was empty when she entered, and the customary flower and note inviting her to dinner were not present. That meant Eldon had not arrived yet. Perfect.

She sat down at the letters and began to work, glancing at the door repeatedly. Excitement was making her twitchy, and it was hard to settle down into the latest letter. They were so incredibly dry. Lula wrote to someone named Ben over and over again, and Ben never wrote back. It was so boring to read, like a one-sided conversation. Like she cared about household life a hundred and thirty-odd years ago? Like readers would?

When she finished transcribing the latest description of what bushes were flowering and how many times the neighbor had visited Lulabelle, she carefully folded the letter back into the yellowed envelope and replaced it in its spot in the trunk. Yawning, she pulled out the next letter and glanced at the date.

Three months had passed since the prior letter. Huh. She glanced down at the trunk, then back at the letter. Were they out of order? She flipped through the envelopes, but sure enough, there was a three-month gap between letters.

My dearest Benedict,

So much has changed since we last wrote.

Yeah, Gretchen thought to herself. Like winter into spring. Not exciting.

I cannot believe we are to be parted once more. The three months we spent together were Heaven on earth. I wake up in the morning, wanting to feel your form next to mine, but you are gone. My hands slide into my pantaloons and I must touch myself, trying to remember the feel of your mouth against my most delicate of female parts.

Gretchen's eyes widened. *Holy shit,* That was . . . graphic. "Lulabelle, you little Victorian sexpot, you."

My father is very against our marriage, as you know. However, I cannot help but think that if he knew of the carnal ways that we had tasted each other, the hours we had spent in each other's arms, that perhaps he would relent. Still, I shall keep our secret as you have instructed.

Tell me when you will return to me and, until then, imagine my hands where yours should be.

All my love,
Lula

Well now. Things had just gotten a bit more interesting. Curious, Gretchen reached for the next letter and was surprised to see a masculine handwriting. Benedict had actually written Lulabelle back. Interesting. All the prior letters had been penned by one hand—Lula to Benedict.

Lovely flower,

It shall only be a few months that we are to be parted. You know that I cannot marry you as long as my fortune is no more than that of a beggar's. Your father will never look upon me as a proper suitor for you

*unless I become more successful. Give my business
time to take off, beloved, and we shall soon be together.*

*Your letter to me fired my loins and my imagination.
My body aches to sink deep into yours once more, to
feel your plump thighs wrapping around my waist as
I move deep inside you. I know what we write is scandalous, but I do not care. If we cannot be together in
person, let us be together in spirit. I know my mind is
filled of thoughts of your mouth upon my maleness. It
is an image burned into my mind.*

*Write me again,
Your Ben*

*Wow. So Lula gave old Ben a blowjob? She is a total vixen.
Good for her.* Gretchen pulled out the next letter, fascinated, and began to open it. The project had taken on new
life with these latest letters, and now she couldn't seem to
read them fast enough. They were dirty and wrong—
terribly wrong considering they were dating back to the
Victorian period, but man, were they juicy.

For the first time, she tried to picture the duo. Lulabelle
would have been dressed in some sort of frothy concoction
of a dress befitting the times. Her appearance was never
mentioned, other than she was concerned with fashion.

She pictured Benedict like she did Hunter, though. Tall,
serious, and deliciously, wickedly scarred. Wounded inside
and out. Maybe that was why he'd never written Lula back
until now. Maybe she'd reached out to him over that three-
month break and crashed through his barriers, and now
he'd let her in.

*I know my mind is filled of thoughts of your mouth upon
my maleness*, Benedict had written.

Gretchen suddenly envisioned herself, kneeling in front
of Hunter, taking his cock in her mouth and working it as
his hand knotted in her hair. Warmth pulsed through her

body and she resisted the urge to fan herself with one of the delicate letters. *Whew.*

The door to the library opened and Gretchen jumped in her chair, whirling around.

Eldon stood there, looking just as surprised as she was. Of course, Gretchen couldn't stop blushing now that she'd been more or less caught reading the letters. Not that she wasn't supposed to be reading them, of course. It was just that they were . . . dirty. And it made her feel weird to be seen reading them. Did Eldon or Hunter have any idea how incredibly graphic the letters were? Was that why they'd wanted someone to transcribe them?

"You're here early," Eldon said, his voice disapproving. He held a tray in his hands.

She waved a letter at him. "Thought I'd get a head start on things. Don't bother making me breakfast, by the way. I made my own."

"I did not make you breakfast," he said flatly, as if it were the last thing he'd planned.

"Yeah, I guessed." He never made her breakfast.

Eldon moved into the library and set the tray down on the nearest end table. On her tray was the rose of the day, singularly beautiful and crisp, the bud just beginning to unfurl. Today's color was a red so deep that it almost seemed like velvet.

To her disappointment, there was no note from Hunter inviting her to dinner. That was fine. She wouldn't let him retreat away from her. She had plans.

When Eldon straightened, he turned to leave.

"Wait," Gretchen said, jumping to her feet. She grabbed the folded paper on the edge of the desk that she'd written this morning and held it out to him. "Can you please give this to Hunter?"

Eldon eyed it, and then her. Ever so reluctantly, he reached out and took the paper from her.

Gretchen kept the smile on her face, though inside she

was a bit gleeful at his capitulation. He'd taken her note. "It's very important that he gets it as soon as possible," she told Eldon, trying to seem innocent.

To her dismay, Eldon flipped open her note and read it aloud. "Dear Hunter, I would very much appreciate it if you would join me for dinner tonight in the kitchen. Nothing fancy, but I promise you I'm a much better cook than Eldon. Sincerely, Gretchen."

All right, that was embarrassing.

The butler's mouth pursed unpleasantly as he finished the letter. "I don't see anything urgent in this."

"Yeah, well, it wasn't for you," Gretchen said, crossing her arms over her chest. "Just deliver it, all right?"

"Shall I bring back a response?"

"Nah," Gretchen told him. "I'll know tonight if he shows up or not."

"Very well." He refolded the letter she'd given him and left the room, shutting the door behind him.

Gretchen counted to ten slowly, waiting, and then crept to the door. Her slippers muffled her footsteps, and she ever so slowly eased open the library door, glancing down the hall.

Eldon turned a corner and vanished.

Excellent. With quiet steps, Gretchen tiptoed down the hall after him, keeping her distance. If Eldon did as he promised, he'd deliver that letter to Hunter. She could always wait for him to arrive tonight and apologize then, but Gretchen liked to be on the offensive, and what better way than to get things ironed out than to confront the man herself?

Of course, she couldn't confront him if she didn't know where he was. Which was why her plan to follow Eldon was perfect. She would be able to see Hunter's reaction and find out where he was all at once.

Gretchen trailed a good distance behind Eldon, creeping quietly through the echoing halls of Buchanan Manor. It was a good thing for a change, she thought, that the place was so empty. No one would be there to tattle on her for stalking the butler.

Sure enough, he turned down the wing that she'd come to think of as Hunter's wing and continued all the way down the hall. Once there, he opened a door and disappeared inside. She followed behind him and was surprised to see that the door led to a glass-covered walkway through the gardens.

Where was this going?

She followed him down the covered path, noting the snowdrifts against the glass. The path itself was cool enough that her breath frosted, but nothing like the wintry cold outside. The room ended in a small mudroom that had steps up to double doors. Through the glass, she could see a vaulted glass roof outside, the windows damp with condensation.

A greenhouse?

Of course, Gretchen realized, glancing around the mudroom. Of course he had a greenhouse. It was likely full of the roses he'd been gifting her with this last week. It had seemed odd but charming that he'd carefully selected one different rose every day. Now she knew he was plucking them from his own gardens.

How fascinating. There were layers to Hunter she was just beginning to discover.

The double doors hung open, and she could hear the faint sound of voices in the other room. She glanced around, but there were only a few jackets hanging on a peg in the shadows of the mudroom and a mix of boots lined up against the wall. Not much for her to hide behind so she wouldn't be discovered.

"She left you this note," she could barely hear Eldon saying. His voice seemed to drip scorn. Jeez. What had she ever done to him? Then again, she had not been nice about his cooking in the note. *Guess he's sensitive about that.*

There was a long moment of silence. Then, a quiet, "Thank you, Eldon. That'll be all."

"Very well," Eldon said in that same stiff voice. "I shall return to my duties, unless you'd like for me to carry your response back to her?"

"No thank you. I'm going to think on it."

Think on it? Gretchen scowled to herself. What exactly was there to think on? Had she truly hurt his feelings that much just by asking about his face? She'd simply been curious about a friend. No more, no less. She'd had no idea he'd be so touchy.

Before she could think about it more, there was the sound of footsteps. A swell of alarm pulsed through Gretchen, and she darted behind one of the hanging coats in the mudroom, squeezing her eyes shut in the hopes that Eldon wouldn't notice her lurking in the shadows. If he did, it'd be totally awkward.

She kept her eyes squeezed tight as she heard the soft sound of the doors closing, and then footsteps walking away.

Not caught. Whew.

After a few moments had passed and she was sure that Eldon would not return, Gretchen slipped out from under the jackets and crept toward the doors. She carefully turned the doorknob of one and eased it open a crack, peeking inside.

Greenery exploded into view—the jade of fresh leaves, the smell of turned soil, and the thick perfume of roses. Everywhere she could see brilliantly colored roses set against the thick verdant shrubs. There had to be hundreds of roses in the greenhouse. How amazing.

Standing nearby was Hunter. He wore no jacket, and the collar of his starched shirt was loose, the sleeves rolled up to his elbows. He wore a pair of gardening gloves, pruning shears in one hand. His gaze was on the nearby table . . . and the note she'd asked Eldon to deliver. He hadn't noticed her.

She'd nearly shied away at the sight of him, thinking

she'd be caught, but there was something so vulnerable about his face that she couldn't help but stare.

He continued to read the note, his gaze flicking over it over and over again, as if memorizing its contents. And his face? He had such a naked, hopeful longing in his eyes that it made her heart ache. Was that longing for . . . her? Then why did he push her away at every turn?

It didn't make sense. None of it did.

But she did know that if she caught Hunter unawares again, he wouldn't be pleased. So she carefully eased the door shut again, waited a moment, and then knocked loudly.

"Enter," she heard Hunter call out.

She opened the door, a careful, easy smile on her face. "Surprise."

He did indeed look startled to see her. The note was gone, as if put away, and he stood there in the midst of the greenery, a solitary figure. "What are you doing here?"

"Nice to see you, too. Can I come in?"

The wary look returned to his face. "Of course."

She stepped inside the greenhouse, immediately noticing the damp, warm feel of the air and the thick scent of roses and fresh dirt. Her gaze moved over the blooming bushes, and she leaned down to scent a familiar one. "Gypsy Carnival, right?"

"Correct."

She smiled at him and straightened. "I thought you were ordering flowers to send to me. You grow all of them?"

The wariness in his gaze reduced a little, and he gave her a quick nod. "Gardening is my hobby. I enjoy roses the most." He gestured at the greenhouse, thick with flowers. "This is where I come to get away from things."

That could have been accusatory, but she chose to ignore it. "It's marvelous," she said, moving past him and strolling down one of the aisles to look at the neatly lined-up rows of roses. "You're really good at this—the roses look better than anything I've ever gotten from a florist." She leaned down to sniff one that had an open yellow bloom the size of her hand. "Do you do anything with them?"

"Do?"

"Yes. Do you sell them to a local florist or something? You have so many."

He walked behind her a few steps, his gaze on her instead of the roses. "I . . . sometimes I have Eldon show them. And sometimes I cross them, to try and see if I can create a new variety. But I mostly like growing them."

She glanced at him over her shoulder and smiled. "I would have never pictured a big, strong guy like you as a gardener."

He blushed, his gaze skidding away from her again, a sure sign that he was embarrassed. "I enjoy plants," he said simply. "They are far easier to understand than people."

"Most people are assholes," she said bluntly. "I think that's why I prefer writing. Or baking."

His mouth twitched and, for a hopeful moment, she thought he might smile, but it was quickly contained again. "Did you come out here to discuss the merits of books versus roses?"

"Actually, no." She straightened and turned to face him. "I wanted to come out here and ask you if you were going to come to dinner tonight."

"I . . ." His voice died and his gaze slid away again. "Perhaps."

"Oh, come on," she said softly. "I can tell you all about my day. It's been most interesting." Her voice had taken on a soft, almost sexy purr.

The effect on Hunter was startling. His gaze flew back to her, his eyes wide, one eyebrow lifting as if to voice the question that he wouldn't.

She took a step closer to him, gratified when he didn't

back away. "You know all those letters I've been transcribing? It seems that my two historical figures had a rather torrid love affair."

He said nothing. His attention was frozen on her face, and she saw that strange mixture of fear and longing flicker through his eyes again.

Feeling bolder, Gretchen slid a bit closer to him, her voice husky. "What's even better is that they describe, in rather blatant, sexual detail, what they want to do to each other. Isn't that . . . interesting?"

Hunter's lips parted, and Gretchen thought for a moment that he might break the distance between them and drag her against him in a wild kiss. Her pulse fluttered with excitement at the thought, and she found she desperately wanted Hunter to kiss her. Tongue the hell out of her mouth and toss her down into the dirt and claim her. She wanted to see that reserve of his shatter.

"What do you think?" she prompted.

"I . . ."

"Yes?"

He bolted away, turning his back to her. As she stood there, all soft and full of need for him, he stormed across the room and began to jerk on a pair of ugly, thick gardening gloves. "I'd like for you to leave."

Disappointment crushed her fledgling desire. She sighed heavily and rolled her eyes at his retreat. "So I take it dinner's off?"

"I . . . no. I will think about it." But he wouldn't look over at her.

"Suit yourself," she said softly. "I'm off to go read more letters. I hope to see you tonight." She sauntered out of the greenhouse before he could say anything else.

He was an utterly frustrating and confusing man. She knew he wanted her. She'd seen the desire in his eyes. The need. He wasn't married or dating anyone. She wasn't either.

So why was he fighting this so very hard? It didn't make sense.

Was it possible he just didn't like her? That was depressing to think about. Gretchen sighed and returned to the library, discouraged and unhappy.

She worked quietly for hours, cataloging letters and reading through them. Engrossed in her project, she didn't notice that someone had entered the room until the door clicked shut again. Her head lifted, and her gaze settled on a tray that had been left on a table across the room.

It was a vase filled with roses. Every single one she'd casually touched this morning while in his greenhouse had been cut and placed in a gorgeous crystal vase. Unable to help herself, Gretchen moved to the roses and leaned over to take in their scent.

A note was on the table.

I will be there.

Gretchen smiled to herself. Maybe Hunter was interested after all.

———

"It sounds like he likes you," Audrey told her over the phone. "But it sounds like he's shy."

"You think so?" Gretchen dragged one of her T-shirts out of the closet and winced at how ratty it looked. Why hadn't she brought more dresses? "He's just so hard to predict. I can't forget how he freaked out when I asked him about his face."

"Maybe he's just a loner. I mean, he's friends with Logan and his buddies, but out of all of them, he's the most remote. Doesn't attend any parties they give or anything."

"He's definitely a loner," Gretchen agreed. "But there's something so incredibly . . . remote about him. Most loners seem happy to be by themselves. He just seems a bit lost."

"Yeah, Logan says that he's not the friendliest guy, but

he's very true once he lets someone in. He's always very polite to me, though."

She'd forgotten the fact that Audrey's boss was friends with Hunter. "I didn't think he ever left this house." She thought of what he'd told her—the kidnapping. His utter loneliness. The way that the staff kept to assigned wings so as not to "bother" him.

Gretchen had never met someone quite so alone as him. It made him strangely vulnerable despite his icy demeanor, and it fascinated her as much as it made her want to touch him. Show him that he wasn't alone and unlovable.

"Of course he leaves his house, Gretch. He has a billion-dollar real estate empire."

"Yeah, but does he have to do anything for that other than just, I don't know, own property?"

Audrey giggled. "You really have no idea how billion-aires work, do you?"

"I don't want to know, honestly. All that money just seems like a lot of hassle." She pulled a plain black sweater out of the closet and held it against her. A bit worn, but it'd have to do. "So did Logan tell you about his past? The thing with the scars and the kidnapping?"

"Nope. No one talks about it, apparently. No one except you."

"Yeah, me and my big mouth." She tossed the sweater down on the bed, and it landed on a curled-up Igor, who meowed in resentment. "I guess I shouldn't have asked. But I was curious."

"Well, leave your curiosity at the door. From what I can remember from meeting him, he doesn't like it if people so much as look at him the wrong way."

"Jeez, Audrey, exactly how many times have you met this guy?"

"A handful of times. Like I said, he's one of Logan's closest friends."

"And you never thought to give your sister the cliff notes rundown on the man?"

"Well gee, Gretchen, I didn't think you'd want to bang the guy."

She sighed deeply. "Is it weird that I'm finding the scars sexy?"

"Yes," Audrey said flatly. "They're not cute scars, Gretch. They're disfiguring."

"Yeah, but they have a story. He has a story. I like that about him. I just can't figure him out."

"Have you considered that he might be a virgin?"

"What? He's not a virgin."

"Why does that seem so crazy?" Audrey snorted. "You said he blushes, right? And doesn't look you in the eye? And that he was scarred at an early age?"

"Yes, but—"

"You think he's going to get a lot of ladies with a play-book like that?"

"But he has to be close to thirty, if not already thirty. I can't believe he'd still be a virgin. Can't you hire hookers for that sort of thing?"

"Gross, Gretchen. That's just gross."

"I know, but we were both thinking it." Gretchen stared into her reflection in the mirror, considering. Was the reason why Hunter kept shying away from any sort of flirtiness that she tossed his way because he didn't know how? Because he was a virgin?

That seemed weird, and yet . . . the more she thought about it, the more it made sense. He'd been kidnapped when he was ten. Something like that would probably leave him with trust issues and emotional scars, not to mention the physical scars. He'd freaked out when she'd seen him naked. And he'd freaked out again when she'd come close to kissing him. He'd also froze like a deer in headlights when she'd flirted with him.

And he'd stared at her note like it was the thing he

wanted most in the world. "You might be on to something, Audrey."

"Of course I am," her sister said smugly. "The question is, what are you going to do about it?"

"You mean, hold him down and take his virginity?"

"No! Yuck! Gretchen, that's a visual I did not want."

"You brought it up. What do you mean, what am I going to do about it?"

"I mean that the man's skittish as hell. If he's a virgin, you're going to have a hell of a time getting him to come on to you."

"So I'll come on to *him*."

"But you said he retreats every time you try to get intimate. Perhaps he doesn't want you to come on to him. Maybe he wants to be the aggressor and you're not giving him a chance? Is there a way you can level the playing field?"

Gretchen thought for a moment and became a little depressed. The playing field hadn't been level since she'd seen him naked that very first day. There was no way to recover from that. "I'm not sure."

"He might be off balance and afraid to make a move if he thinks you're sexually experienced and he's not. Can you pretend to be a virgin?" Audrey sounded amused at the thought.

"Har de har. I just need to think about it."

"About pretending to be a virgin?"

"No. About leveling the playing field." And somehow getting Hunter to forget that she'd seen him in the natural state.

"Good luck, whatever you do."

Gretchen hung up the phone and chewed on her lip. She looked into the mirror and played with her wet hair, still dripping from the shower. Dress sexy? Nah. She didn't have the right equipment. It was like Audrey said: Hunter would be off balance around her and continue to be off balance unless she did something to "level the playing field" as her sister had claimed. So that was what she needed to do—get them on equal ground. Somehow. She'd seen him naked, though.

An impulsive idea flashed through her mind and she immediately shut it down, hugging her robe closed. He'd run for sure if she did that.

There was a knock at her door.

Gretchen adjusted the belt on her robe and went to the door, but didn't open it. "Who is it?"

"I . . . me. Hunter. Buchanan."

As if there would be a dozen other Hunters at her door. Biting back her smile, Gretchen opened the door and glanced out at him. "Hi there."

He was dressed in a black suit, a black shirt underneath, and a dark gray tie. His hair was impeccably smoothed into a part and he carried sunglasses in his hand. Behind him, a large man easily seven feet tall stood behind him, dressed in equally dark clothing and wearing his sunglasses. Gretchen had never seen him, and alarm immediately rose. "Is everything okay?"

"Everything's fine," Hunter said. He glanced backward at the man behind him and gave a brief nod. "Leave us."

The man nodded and headed down the hall, his back to them. Gretchen peered out the door, watching him. Then she looked at Hunter. "Who's that?" she whispered.

"My bodyguard."

"I see. So you're ditching me tonight?"

Two spots of color flushed in his pale cheeks. "That's not what I . . . that is, I—"

"I guessed it as soon as I saw the suit. Though I admit, you do clean up nice. I'm a little sad the suit isn't for me." Not that she'd ever seen him wear anything but suits, but her flirty words seemed to be working. He was definitely blushing.

His gaze moved, darting about the room, looking

anywhere but at her. "I came to give you my apologies. I can't make it to dinner tonight. A business meeting was scheduled and I find that I cannot move it."

"No worries." Gretchen twirled one of the ends of her robe. "Thanks for letting me know, though."

He shifted on his feet, and then tugged at his collar, seemingly more uncomfortable by the moment. "I would, however, like if we were to meet for dinner tomorrow night instead."

"Tomorrow's fine."

"Good." His voice was curt. "Very good. Good. That's . . ."

"Good?" she offered. He was adorable.

He gave her another scathing look, but Gretchen only smiled. She was starting to realize his defense mechanisms. God, why had she not seen this before? Suddenly it was so obvious . . . and so sexy that she drove him so crazy.

She took a step forward, wanting to tease him a little. "May I?" She gestured at his tie.

He looked down at it, frowning.

"It's crooked," she lied, moving forward and pretending to adjust the tie. It was more or less an excuse to move into his arms and see how he'd react.

He stiffened, but didn't move away.

She took that as an encouraging sign and continued to adjust his tie. Then she smoothed a hand down the front of it, noting the hard muscle underneath. "All better."

Hunter's attention was definitely on her now, and she noticed the look in his eyes was hungry. It emboldened her and made her think of her outrageous idea from earlier.

"Hunter?"

"Hmm?" He seemed distracted, almost dazed.

She reached for the loose collar of her robe and pulled it open. Stepping back, she flashed him her breasts.

He stared, frozen in place.

"Now we're even," she told him lightly. "The field is leveled. Enjoy your meeting tonight."

And she closed her robe and sauntered back into her room, grinning the entire time.

SIX

⌒◠

One week later

The trouble with a flirt battle was that both parties had to actively participate. Both parties had to know *how* to actually flirt.

And Gretchen had been flirting her head off, but she was getting nowhere fast.

It wasn't that Hunter wasn't interested. If anything, he seemed more interested than ever. But when she teased, he froze up. When she coyly suggested things, he shut down.

When she'd made him dinner, he'd stared at her in silence, and her attempts at conversation had fallen completely flat. Her pleasure at showing him her cooking had been deflated by the fact that he'd looked as if he'd wanted to escape the room.

And yet . . . she continued to get roses every day. Delicate, scented blooms that were thoughtfully selected for her, along with a note inviting her to dinner. She'd declined it once or twice, just to see how he'd react.

He hadn't reacted at all. And that had been even more frustrating.

She'd tried being sexy. In fact, she'd offered to help him in the greenhouse one day and had unbuttoned her shirt, declaring herself overheated and exposing a lot of skin. All she'd gotten was an abrupt suggestion that she take a shower and him turning away.

Not exactly the reaction she'd wanted. She was utterly mystified. How could she break through to him? She supposed she could state it baldly. *I'd really like it if you and I did a little mutual exploring. I'll even go first.*

But she was enjoying the challenge. And screaming out that she desired him seemed almost like a cop out. Plus, he'd probably run for the hills.

Virgins were so much trouble.

The letters weren't helping things, either. Now that things had escalated between Lula and Benedict, they weren't holding back at all. Letter after letter went into great detail of what Lula would do to Benedict with her mouth, and how she'd please him. He'd write pages back to her, describing how he'd like to lay her down under the trees, spread her petals wide, and lick her nectar clean. By the time she finished a day of the letters, Gretchen was squirming and overheated, her imagination on fire. She kept picturing Hunter as Benedict, and herself as Lula. Each graphic description left her breathing hard and her panties wet.

There had to be a way to get through to Hunter.

———

It was during one of their frequent dinners that Gretchen found a chink in Hunter's icy armor.

Her phone rang while they were in the midst of a quiet conversation. Surprised, Gretchen picked up her phone and gave an apologetic look to Hunter. "I should take this."

She rarely got calls out of the blue, so any sort of call

concerned her. Especially if it was coming from Cooper's Cuppa.

"Hello?"

"Gretch? It's me."

She glanced down the table at Hunter, who seemed to be staring at a painting on the wall and trying very hard not to listen in on her phone conversation. "Hey Coop. What's up?"

"I was calling to, well, check on you. See how you're doing."

"Oh, I'm fine," she said brightly. "The project's coming along really well. I might even finish early."

Hunter accidentally sent his knife skidding, the silverware clanking.

"That's great news," Cooper said enthusiastically. "I've really missed seeing you."

"I've missed seeing you, too." She watched as Hunter picked up his knife and gripped it, his knuckles white. "It's weird being away from everyone," she added to defuse the statement and make it friendly instead of romantic.

"When you come back, I . . . I think I'd like for us to have a nice talk."

Her mouth went dry and Gretchen panicked. "Oh, Coop. I just . . . I don't know. Can't we just let things go as they do?" Her gaze slid back to Hunter, who was still staring at the painting. "Can I call you back some other time? Now's really not great."

"Oh, of course. I just . . . you know. Wanted to tell you that I missed you. That's all." His sad puppy voice grated on her nerves.

"I'll see you when I get back," she said, and hung up. Picking up her napkin, she folded it in her lap again. "Sorry about that."

"Boyfriend?" he asked, and the word was almost a growl.

Gretchen's eyes widened. That was . . . interesting. It was almost a reaction. Should she push harder or lay off?

She decided to push a little harder. "A male friend. He misses me."

"Then perhaps it's a good thing that you're finishing early," he said abruptly. He stood, tossing his napkin to the table. "I won't keep you from your work any longer."

"Oh, but—"

Hunter turned and stalked out.

Gretchen sighed heavily. Good Lord, but the man was prickly. She sat at the table a moment longer, toying with the casserole on her plate. She didn't want to leave things like that. Didn't want Hunter spending the evening all annoyed and frustrated. She'd had her share of frustrated evenings herself lately.

Tossing her napkin down on the table next to his, she stood up and pocketed her phone, determined to find Hunter and talk to him.

She headed to his wing of the house first, but all the doors were shut, and no one responded to her knocking. He was either not there, or simply not answering. Before she'd give up, she'd try one more place.

Hugging her sweater close, Gretchen headed down the long walk to the greenhouse. There was a light inside, and one of the doors was eased open just a crack. Curious and a bit nosy despite herself, she moved forward and peered through the crack.

He was across the room, standing near one of the beams that kept the arched roof of the greenhouse aloft. Hunter's back was to her, one hand clenched above his head and resting on the beam, the other against his side. His entire form seemed curiously tense, his head bent forward as if he were struggling with something.

She bit her lip. *Damn.* Surely he wasn't that upset over a phone call? Hell, that would be uncomfortable in the extreme. What did she do now? Gretchen stepped inside, just as he tilted his head back, and she caught sight of his face, which was full of tension. The hand at his side jerked a bit more.

And she realized he was masturbating.

Gretchen froze for a moment, shocked. He'd retreated out of anger—or jealousy—and she'd expected to see him seething as he pruned his roses. She'd expected to argue with him, cajole him to see her side, and maybe they'd walk away on better terms.

She'd never imagined that she'd catch him pleasuring himself.

It shocked her senses as much as it aroused her. She felt herself grow slick with excitement, and she barely resisted the urge to stroke herself between her own legs in response to his movements. She moved forward, her steps quiet as she carefully shut the greenhouse door behind her and approached him. He hadn't noticed her yet. His shoulders seemed to be aching with tension and need, his entire form tense.

She moved forward and lightly touched his shoulder, heat coursing through her.

He jerked around, startled. Hunter's eyes were wide, his pupils dilated with need, the scars on his face flaring white against the red of his cheeks. His hand was still curled around his cock, and he stood there for a moment, as if too shocked to move.

And then he began to pull away from her.

"No," she whispered. "Don't."

Her fingers curled in his jacket and she held him there. He seemed frozen in place, like a wild animal caught by the barest of tethers. One wrong move and he'd snap, retreating. She didn't want that. She wanted to touch him.

Her hand slid down to cover his, where he grasped his cock. "Is this for me?"

His mouth parted slightly, but no words came out.

"I think it is," she said softly. "May I touch you?" She knelt before him, not caring that she was kneeling in the slightly damp, slightly muddy path in the center of the greenhouse. All she knew was that she wanted to touch him—to pleasure him. To give him something that would blow his mind.

She really, really wanted to blow his mind.

Once she was kneeling, she slid her other hand up his thigh, her gaze moving up to his face. He seemed paralyzed in a rictus of yearning and . . . fear? Of what? The scars were livid against the high color in his face, the slashes marring the beauty of his features.

Very slowly, she uncurled his fingers from around his cock, releasing his grip. "I want to get a look at you," she told him in a low voice. "It makes me wet just thinking about this. I remember seeing you, naked and gleaming from the shower, though you weren't as big then as you are today." She ran a finger down the length of him, from root to tip, idly exploring.

Pre-cum slid down the head of his cock in response to her touch, and Gretchen sighed with pleasure.

"You're very big. I like that. I imagine when I take you in my throat, it's going to be hard to take you deep, isn't it? I'm going to have to work to fit all of you." Her fingers brushed against his sac, then she clasped the base of his cock, measuring its girth. "You'll have to be patient with me."

And she leaned in and swiped the slick head of his cock with her tongue.

A full body tremble moved through him, and she noticed the hand at his side clenched into a fist. Gretchen looked up at Hunter. "Do you want me to stop? Or can I keep exploring you?"

"I . . . no. Keep . . . going." His words sounded almost strangled, the tension on his face incredible.

"Good," she purred, giving his cock a stroke of her hand, squeezing in a mimic of his jerky earlier motions. She heard his sharp intake of breath and was pleased.

And because she wanted to torment him a little more, she leaned in even more and put her mouth on the head of his cock again, sucking the large tip of it into her mouth.

She swirled her tongue around the crown, enjoying the salty, pleasing taste of him and the way his hand spasmed at his side in response.

Gretchen flicked her tongue over the slit and worked her hand against the base again, gazing up at Hunter. "I love touching you. Tastes so good. Do you want to touch me?"

"I . . ." His hand clenched again.

"It's okay," she told him in a soft voice. "Maybe this time I'll just touch you." She took him into her mouth again, rubbing her tongue against the vein along the bottom of his cock and taking him deeper into her mouth, then pulling back.

Suddenly, his hand was in her hair and he groaned, his fingers tightening in her hair. *Oh, yes.* Gretchen felt wetness flood her panties in a fresh wave, and she moaned at his touch.

He flinched and pulled away.

She released him from her mouth and shook her head. "I like it when you touch me. Show me what you want. Please, Hunter."

And she let her lips rest against the head of his cock, looking up at him and waiting.

The look in his eyes was a mixture of frenzied longing and . . . something else. Anxiety? She wanted to make that look go away, but it would take time. For some reason, sex made the man skittish. She'd have to be patient.

And she waited.

Ever so slowly, his hand moved back to her hair, all the while his cock pulsed in her hand. His pulse was beating so strong she could feel it through his hot skin. Then he gave her head a subtle nudge forward.

He wanted her to take him deep.

She parted her lips, letting the head of his cock push into her mouth. He groaned again and pushed her head forward with more force.

She took him deep into her mouth, but she hadn't been

stroking his ego; he was big and thick, and she couldn't take him to the root, not at first. Slowly, she worked him deeper, relaxing her jaw and letting each stroke push a little more, until he was hitting the back of her throat and her lips were meeting her hand, which was still curled at the base of his cock.

Hunter's entire body began to tremble again and he bit out a curse. He tugged on her hair, trying to pull her backward. "I . . . no. Gretchen . . ."

He was going to come; she knew as much based on the tension in his body and the way he struggled for control. And she wanted to let him know it was okay. So she moaned again and sank deeper onto him, relaxing her jaw to take him deeper.

"Ah!" His hand tightened in her hair, and then she felt his hot come filling her throat. She ignored his efforts to pull away, digging her fingers into his slacks and holding him there until he'd finished.

He panted above her and, with a shudder, the tension left his body.

Gretchen released him, swallowing again, her own body wired with need. It wouldn't happen tonight, she suspected. It would be too much for him to take in. Tonight was all about Hunter.

His fingers slowly released her hair from their stranglehold and then he reached out and caressed her cheek.

"I . . ." he began.

She got to her feet, nearly swaying with how much she wanted him. Her core ached, her pulse throbbing with need. She forced herself to ignore it. "Don't overthink it, Hunter. Just enjoy it."

"Gretchen." The way he said her name was so husky that it made her wet all over again.

She bit her lip and brushed her fingers over his mouth, careful to avoid the scar that tugged down the one side. "Good night, Hunter."

And she turned around and left.

It was the most difficult walk she'd ever done. She wanted to run back to him, bend over the nearest table and present him with her slick, aching sex, demanding that he take her. But Hunter was skittish. He'd bolt if she overwhelmed him.

There was something that filled him with anxiety and some sort of idea that he was hideous—his scars, probably. It was something that had affected him so much that he chased most people out of his life, lived in a big lonely house with no one but a grouchy butler, and avoided the world.

She'd take her time with him. It was important to her to show him how delicious he was and how wonderful sex could be.

And so she'd be patient. Or try to, anyhow.

Goddamn.

Hunter leaned against the pole in the greenhouse, his entire body feeling wrung out.

Had he imagined it all? That had to be it. Surely reality didn't hold a place where someone as beautiful and sexy as Gretchen approached him in his greenhouse while he'd jerked on his cock, desperate with need for her. Reality didn't include scenes like that. Nor did it have her kneeling in front of him, taking him in her mouth and finishing for him.

It did not have her moaning with her own pleasure as she took him into her throat.

He groaned, his mind full of images of her.

He'd never expected that in a million years. He was still shaken to his core by her.

That phone call at dinner had aroused something in him that he was unfamiliar with—jealousy. She'd gotten a phone call from a man, and white-hot agony had pierced his mind. He wanted her. He didn't want that stranger she was so friendly with to have her.

Gretchen was his.

And before tonight, he'd have cast aside that idea. She didn't want a scarred, lonely man. She deserved someone as lively and full of life as she was.

And yet tonight, she'd touched him. She'd taken him into her mouth and pleasured him. And when he'd tried to pull away, she'd insisted on finishing him.

His cock grew hard again, just thinking about her. Automatically, he took himself in his hand, stroking as he closed his eyes.

He'd been blown away by the sight of her gorgeous breasts the other day when she'd flashed him. He allowed that visual to mix in with his erotic thoughts of her now. Her breasts were full, with small, rosy nipples. He pictured her naked as she knelt in front of him, the tips brushing against his skin as she took his cock in her mouth. Groaning, he fisted his cock harder.

At the thought of her beautiful lips parting to take him, the tip of her tongue flicking over the head, he came with a shout, spraying his cum on the path before him. Drained, Hunter collapsed to his knees, staring at his greenhouse.

He'd never picture it quite the same way ever again. Never be able to come here without seeing her kneeling in front of him.

It was his first sexual experience with someone else. And it had been flat-out amazing. He didn't know what had possessed Gretchen to give such a gift to him, but he'd treasure it always.

———

Hunter dressed with care for dinner the next night. He'd spent the last day in turmoil, his world upended by his interlude with Gretchen.

He'd worked out until his skin dripped with sweat, then headed to the showers. But the showers made him think of Gretchen and how she'd discovered him naked. So he'd jerked off and then jerked off again when he thought of her, easing her robe open.

If she knew he was a virgin, she'd be appalled. Someone as open and forthright with her sexuality as Gretchen would laugh at him. So he needed to be relaxed at dinner. Act as if nothing had changed between them.

And yet he picked her a rose with extra care. He'd liked seeing one of his flowers behind her ear the other night. Perhaps he'd get to put this one on her, run his fingers along the delicate shell of her ear, tuck it into her red hair . . .

Throw her down on the table and fuck the hell out of her, make her give those wild, sexy little moans again.

Hunter shook his head, willing the visual out of his mind and for his cock to go down. He took a few moments to compose himself, then entered the dining room they used for their meetings.

It was empty.

She'd called off dinner. She was embarrassed by what she'd done. Disappointment flashed through him, and Hunter moved to the table, picking up the note there.

Dinner's running late. I'm in the kitchens. G.

Immediately, he headed for the kitchens, hope putting a spring in his step. She wasn't avoiding him, then. He adjusted his collar, finding it rather warm in the house, and played with the cuffs of his shirt as he entered the kitchen, rose in hand.

He didn't see her at first. The delicious scent of baking bread filled the air, but he could see no one. His gaze scanned the kitchen and disappointment flared again.

Then Hunter noticed her bent over, her lovely ass flexing as she pulled something out of the oven. He immediately went hard again, longing tearing through him.

God, he wanted her.

"Oh! Hey," Gretchen said, turning and closing the door to the oven with her foot. "Sorry about this. I thought the roast would be ready in a half hour, but it's still looking a little pinker than I'd like, so we need to give it a bit more time. That's why I'm still in here." She set the bread pan on the counter and smiled at him. "Hope you don't mind filling up on bread and appetizers until it's done."

He gave a brief, jerky nod, unable to take his eyes off her smiling face.

"Is that for me?"

"What?" He glanced down and noticed he was still clutching the pale yellow rose he'd picked for her. "Yes," he said, internally wincing at the brusque tone of his voice.

"The bud's tight on this one," she said, pulling off her oven mitts and taking the flower from him. She lifted it to her nose and closed her eyes, giving a slight groan of pleasure that made him tense with anticipation all over again. "Smells wonderful."

"Yes," he said again. He didn't know what else to say. He was mesmerized by her.

As he watched, she lifted the rose and brushed the rosebud against her full lower lip. "Soft."

His cock jerked. The way she'd moved it against her lips made him think of yesterday. Oh, fuck.

She opened her eyes and smiled at him. "Ready for dinner?"

"I . . ." He couldn't go anywhere. Not with this aching hard-on. Couldn't sit with her and pretend that he wasn't ready to spill in his pants. "No. I must go."

And before she could protest, he walked out of the kitchen.

Like a fucking coward. A fucking coward who needed an ice-cold shower to get his cock back under control.

———

Gretchen was getting frustrated.

She sighed and flopped down on the couch in the library, glaring up at the blue mural on the ceiling.

She'd thought their little interlude in the greenhouse

would make him open up to her a bit more. Get him to bend a bit. She wanted more from him. Last night, she'd dreamed of kissing him for hours. Nothing else but just sitting in each other's arms, exploring each other's lips as if not a care in the world.

She wanted that. She wanted to kiss Hunter, and so much more.

But she hadn't seen him for two days. She'd invited him to dinner and he'd declined. Was he done with her now that she'd gone down on him?

It didn't make sense. Every instinct she had about men—and she'd dated around quite a bit during her college days—told her that Audrey had nailed it and he was a virgin. It explained his reactions perfectly, his wariness any time she came on to him.

And despite his virginity, he still wanted her. It was obvious in every look he sent her way.

So why was he avoiding her?

Maybe he was uncomfortable with approaching her and asking for more? Should she be bold and come right out with it? Put his hand on her breast and her hand on his cock and say, "I want this"?

Sighing, she picked up another letter and skimmed it. "Good God, these two are horny little buggers," she muttered to herself, reading yet another description of Ben licking at Lula's perfect feminine petals. The letters had been arousing at first, but with her own frustrations in the relationship department, they just became excruciating. It was no fun to read about someone else having incredible sex when she couldn't even get Hunter to kiss her.

She folded up a letter and tossed it aside. Hell, she needed to get Hunter in here to read some of these letters. Then maybe he'd be just as worked up as her.

Gretchen stared down at the folded letter on the table. That was it.

Perfect.

Get Hunter in here. Somehow get him to read a letter. Then, her reluctant virgin would be putty in her hands.

A wicked smile curved her mouth.

She penned a quick note and folded it, then rang the bell pull. Five minutes later, Eldon arrived.

He gave her a sour look. "What may I help you with?"

Gretchen held the note out to him. "Can you please give this to Hunter?"

Eldon looked down at the note. With a disapproving sniff, he took it in his hand. "More commentary about my cooking?"

"Nope. I'm inviting Hunter in for some research help."

Eldon raised an eyebrow. "I am sure Mr. Buchanan would prefer not to be disturbed with such requests. If you need assistance, you are to come to me."

Yick. The thought of having Eldon assist made her want to throw up her cookies. Thank god he had no idea what he'd just suggested. "No, I'm pretty sure he'd prefer to help me with this on his own. Anyhow, can you just give him the note?"

"Very well." Man, she didn't think one person could stuff that much disapproval in two words, but she was wrong.

Eldon disappeared down the hall and Gretchen watched the door, a bundle of nerves. After five minutes had passed and no one showed up, she began to feel silly. Of course he wouldn't come the instant she summoned him. He could have been busy. She returned to the letters, pulling out a few that would be likely candidates for her seduction scenario, and began to type in the next letter in sequence.

There was a knock at the door some time later.

Gretchen looked up just as the door opened. Hunter stood there in the doorway, his frame poker-stiff as ever, his face inscrutable. He wore a dark navy dress shirt, the collar slightly open. His hair was damp, as if he'd just gotten out of the shower, the ends curling, and she wanted to touch it.

He cleared his throat and then focused his gaze in her direction—but not on her. "Is there a problem?"

"Yes. You won't look at me."

He looked startled at that, his gaze flying to her. "I—"

"It's okay," she interrupted, getting to her feet and picking up the stack of letters she'd set aside. "I wasn't trying to make you uncomfortable. I just know that you always look away when you're uneasy. You've been avoiding me since the greenhouse."

He said nothing, but she watched the red rise in his cheeks.

"Look, Hunter, I apologize if my actions made you uncomfortable. I want us to be friends. We can still be friends, can't we?" She forced herself to keep her expression as innocent as possible.

"Friends," he bit out after a long moment. "Of course."

"Great. I thought I'd ask you, friend to friend, if you could help me with my project a little."

He shut the door behind him, stepping into the room a bit further. "Of course."

She smiled and extended the stack of carefully folded letters to him. "Perfect. I'm trying to transcribe this in a way that'll be interesting to readers, and I'm having trouble with the dynamics."

Hunter picked up the first letter and began to open it. "Dynamics?"

She laid her hand over the letters—so he couldn't read them too early and bolt—and gestured at the couch. "Shall we sit?"

She half-expected him to decline, but after a moment's hesitation, he followed. Discreetly, she glanced at his crotch. He was already hard with wanting her, unable to control himself. In that moment, she *loved* his virginity.

Gretchen slid a little closer to Hunter, leaning over his arm and pressing her breast against him, pretending interest in the letters she'd handed him. "I think if we're able to act out some of the things that are described, it'll be easier for me to write them. I'm a visual learner, after all."

"I see." His gaze moved toward her, and then he glanced away as if burned.

She noticed he was careful to keep his good side of his face toward her, and a little part of her heart ached to see that. Did he truly think he was so hideous that he needed to hide who he was? The scars were not beautiful, but they were fascinating. They made him different.

She liked different.

"Shall we start, then?" She reached for the first letter and brushed her breast against his arm again, her nipple hardening at the contact. Gretchen had to stifle a moan of pleasure. He was so big, hard, and warm against her and he smelled divine. Hell, give her a few more minutes of this torture and she'd be rubbing up against him like a cat in heat. "Why don't I read the first one? You can read the next."

"Very well," Hunter said. She noticed his gaze had moved from the letters to her breasts.

Gretchen cleared her throat politely, unfolded the first letter, and then peeked over at him. "There is a man and a woman mentioned in this letter. I'll be Lula, and I'd appreciate it if you can be Ben for me."

He gave a quick nod.

"*My dearest Ben,*" Gretchen began in a soft voice. "*It has been thirty days since we last saw each other. How languidly time passes when I am not in your arms. How achingly slow the sun moves through the skies, and the days cycle into evening. The nights are the hardest for me.*" She peeked up at him again, but he hadn't moved away. Encouraged, she continued. "*It seems the darkest hours are our time, my love. Last night I had a dream of our most recent party together. I remember that you found me in the dark. You put your hand on mine and guided it to your lips.*"

A hint of a frown touched Hunter's mouth, bunching the scars on his cheek. He reached for her hand. Fascinated, she was so distracted by his touch she almost missed the graze of his mouth over her knuckles, and she felt heat flash through her anew.

Gretchen's voice grew a little shaky as she read on. *"Then, it was like you changed your mind on what you wished to do to me. You took my hand and raised it over my head, pinning it there. I remembered that you held me down on the sofa and your weight settled over me."*

Hunter stiffened against her, and Gretchen thought he would refuse her. Then he laced his fingers in hers and lifted her hand over her head. In a swift move that left her breathless, he pushed her down to the couch, his weight settling over her and between her legs.

His face was close enough to kiss, his breath brushing against her skin. His gaze moved over her face, and Gretchen felt a hint of nerves.

He studied her. "Was this a plan to get me to touch you?" he asked softly. His thumb caressed her wrist, his eyes boring into hers.

"Who, me?" She gave him an innocent look. "I just wanted you to help me act through some of the letters."

"Mmmhmmm."

She shifted her hips, wriggling underneath him a little until she felt his cock cradled against her hips. A sigh of pure pleasure escaped her. "I might have had a slight ulterior motive. Slight."

His thumb continued to stroke her wrist and he said nothing. Just that small motion was driving her wild. With his weight settled between her legs and that small touch teasing her, she definitely understood Lula's sentiments.

"What comes next?" he asked huskily.

"Let me see," she whispered, distracted when his hand began to slide down her thigh. *"My pantaloons are damp with arousal just thinking of your touch. I think of your lips grazing over my skin. How you'd rip my clothing away and bury your face into my feminine petals, determined to make me cry out with delight. You would taste me and please me even as your hands reached up to caress my breasts."* Gretchen fanned her face with the letter. "Whew. Sounds wild."

He ignored her chatter, carefully sliding his hand away from her wrist and moving it down her torso. He hovered for a moment over her breast and then, ever so slowly, laid his palm against her breast through her shirt. His thumb grazed over her nipple and she sucked in a breath, surprised at how good that felt.

Hunter looked down at her breasts, his own breathing speeding in time with hers. Very gently, he circled his cupped hand on her breast, kneading the flesh and catching the nipple between his fingers and plucking at it.

She whimpered, biting her lip and angry at herself for making noise. The look on his face was so incredibly intense that she hated to interrupt—she didn't want him to stop, not for anything.

He continued to caress her breast and whispered, "What did the letter say again?"

"Um." She forced her gaze away from him. His fingers were playing on one of her nipples, coaxing it into an even stiffer peak, and her pulse was pounding at the junction of her thighs. She rocked her hips slightly as she shifted to read the letter again, enjoying the feel of his cock pressed against her pussy. She forced herself to focus on the letter. *"I think of your lips grazing over my skin."*

"Lips on skin?" He lifted his hand off her breast and began to slowly push up her shirt, seemingly gaining confidence with every moment that passed. He pushed her shirt up around her neck, exposing her bra cups and her belly. He looked down at her in wonder and ran the backs of his fingers over her bare skin, then leaned in to kiss the swell of her breast.

She moaned in response. "That feels so good, Hunter. More."

He licked her flesh, pushing aside the cup of her bra and revealing her aching nipple. "Does he lick her here?"

"I'm sure he does," Gretchen breathed.

When he leaned close, she arched her back and offered her nipple to him.

He groaned, moving down to take it into his mouth, sucking lightly on her flesh. He ran his tongue over her nipple and whispered, "Tell me what to do—what pleases you."

"Just keep doing that," she told him, running her fingers through his hair. She let the letter flutter to the ground, no longer interested in it. Her eyes fluttered closed and she lost herself to the sensation of his mouth on her skin. "God, Hunter, you feel incredible against me."

"Rip your clothing," he breathed, and it took her a moment to realize that he was quoting the letter. "Bury my face into your feminine petals."

His hands were suddenly frantic, tugging at her yoga pants and sliding them down her hips.

She lifted her hips to assist, excited. "Yes. Hunter, yes."

He tore her pants down her thighs, exposing her flesh. Before she could direct him to do anything, he pushed her thighs apart, stretching the fabric around her knees, and buried his face in her aching flesh.

Gretchen gasped, startled at the sudden move. She'd been thinking she'd have to convince him to touch her, but now that it was all laid out in the open, he'd dove upon her like a starving man.

"Ah, fuck," Hunter moaned, and she felt his breath on her pussy. His tongue stroked out and licked her lightly, and then he groaned again. "You taste so good."

Dear sweet heaven, his mouth on her felt incredible. "Yes. Keep touching me." Her hands moved to his hair, holding him there.

"Tell me how," he growled, sending shivers through her body.

"My clit," she breathed. "Put your tongue there."

He did, and she almost came off the couch. Sensation flared through her body and she dug her fingernails into his scalp, desperate for the pleasure he offered. "More."

The licks he gave her were rough and untrained, but there was something raw and delicious about his enthusiasm. She'd wanted this—and him—for what seemed like so very long. When he flicked his tongue against her clit and then circled it, she shuddered in response. "Oooh, you're good at that."

To her surprise, he stiffened against her. Alarm bells went off in her mind, but before she could encourage him again, he sat up and dragged away from her, breathing hard.

Gretchen opened her eyes, blinking up at him, still throbbing with need. "What's wrong?"

The look on his face was tortured. His hand moved over the front of his pants, rubbing the length of his cock through the fabric and then jerking away again. "I . . . can't."

"You can't?" She gave him a mock pout. "Please, Hunter. You were so good at that."

He groaned again, dragging a hand down his face. "It's not you. It's just . . . I . . ." He clenched his fists and remained silent.

He what? Wouldn't last? At the moment, she didn't care. She just wanted his mouth back on her again, enthusiastically licking away. "You won't touch me? Don't you like touching me?"

Hunter gave her such a tortured look that her breath caught in her throat. "Love touching you."

"Did you feel how wet I was?" she asked him. "I need to come so badly. Won't you touch me?"

He didn't move.

It was time for plan B. Her fingers slid to the slick heat of her pussy. "If you won't finish me, I guess I'll have to do it myself, won't I?"

She heard his sucked-in breath. His gaze riveted on her, lustful and full of need all at once. Encouraged, she slid one fingertip in lazy circles around her clit, shivering when it sent a bolt of pleasure through her body. He watched her as if fascinated, and his hand rubbed against the hard length straining at the front of his pants.

"Touch yourself for me," she breathed, dipping a finger into the wet well of her sex and then spreading the moisture around her clit, wetting it. Faster and faster, she glided her finger in circles around it, biting her lip as she spiraled closer to her climax.

She should have felt awkward lying on a couch with her pants tangled below her knees, legs spread wide as she stroked herself to orgasm. But the gaze of the man sitting across from her on the couch had her riveted. She wanted to do this for him. To show him how much pleasure he'd given her.

"Touch yourself, Hunter. I'm so close." She slid her other hand between her legs, spreading the lips of her pussy to show him just how wet she was.

She watched with pleasure as he unzipped his pants, shoving them down and then quickly followed them with his underwear, releasing his cock. The head was flushed a deep red with need, slick with pre-cum. He stroked it once, his motions jerky.

She paused in her self-pleasure, fascinated by his hand working his shaft. *God, he was beautiful.*

"Don't stop," Hunter commanded, his voice ragged. "Need . . . to see it."

"I won't," she promised, and began to touch herself again. She watched him stroke and jerk at his cock even as she continued to play with her clit. "I wish it was your mouth on me," she told him. "Your cock deep inside me." And she dipped a finger into her sex.

He groaned again, his face contorting. Hot cum jetted out of him, spraying across her belly. The look on his face was so full of exquisite pleasure that she felt her own body pulse with pleasure. Working her fingers faster over her clit, she came a moment later, hard and messy, her eyes tightly shut.

When she opened them a short time later, the room was empty. Hunter had retreated again.

Well, that wasn't so surprising. Gretchen smiled to herself and touched a finger to the cum he'd left on her skin. She had a feeling that Hunter wouldn't be avoiding her much anymore.

Things were going rather well, she thought.

SEVEN

Hunter lay in bed, staring at the ceiling, his body stiff with need.

Over and over, he played that scene in the library through in his mind. Gretchen's innocent question as she asked him to help her with a project. Her breast pressing against his arm, and the way his cock immediately responded. Her soft red hair moving over her shoulders as she tilted her head, watching him.

The amazement he'd felt when she'd began to read the lewd letters out loud, asking him to act them out.

He'd put his hand on her breast and nearly shattered, the pleasure had been so intense. She hadn't been repulsed by his touch, either. Instead, she'd encouraged it, moving her hips in little motions under him until he'd dared enough to strip her pants down her thighs and taste her.

He'd been lost in that moment. He was totally and completely hers.

Except . . . he'd felt too much too soon. He knew his control wasn't what it should be, and he'd tensed, suddenly afraid of showing his inexperience. She'd pouted a little, but had ended up surprising him all over again, touching herself and inviting him to touch himself in response.

When he'd set this project in motion, he'd hoped to merely spend time with her. Be around her and let his glimpses of her fuel his longings. He'd never hoped for as much as he'd gotten this afternoon.

She wasn't repulsed by his scars. She hadn't flinched away from his scarred hand and missing finger. He touched his cheek. She hadn't backed away when he reached for her. If anything, she'd seemed . . . eager for his touch. As if it had been what she'd been waiting for all along.

And he'd been unable to give her what she wanted. She'd wanted to be fucked but he'd pulled off her like a green schoolboy and jerked his cock instead. Shame mixed with hunger and he sat up in bed, frustrated.

His dick was already hard again. Just the merest thought of Gretchen and he went wild with need.

He wanted to see her again. That afternoon, he'd left her on the couch, sated. Was she hurt by his abandonment? Angry? As frustrated as he was? It was suddenly important to him that he talk to her and explain himself. The thought of telling her about his inexperience made his throat go dry, but she deserved to know. It wasn't her who was the problem; it was him. And he didn't want her to go another moment thinking that there was something wrong with her.

Hunter jumped out of bed and tossed on a robe, loosely tying it as he headed down the dark hallways of Buchanan Manor. She'd think he was crazy. Completely crazy. But he needed to talk to her.

A short time later, he stood in front of her room, hesitating. Her door was shut, no light shining underneath. She was asleep. Should he stay? Go? Gathering his courage, he knocked softly, and when there was no response, knocked louder.

Gretchen arrived at the door a moment later, rubbing her

eyes sleepily. She was dressed in an oversized T-shirt and panties. Her long, curvy legs were bare. "Mmm, Hunter? What's going on?"

She was mouthwatering. Soft, sleepy, and gorgeous. The T-shirt slipped off one shoulder, baring her skin, and he couldn't wait any longer.

Hunter moved forward, grasped her by the shoulders, and kissed her.

Gretchen stiffened against him and that horrible, horrible fear crashed through him—fear that she wasn't attracted to him, fear that she'd be repulsed by his touch, fear that she'd turn him away. But then she pushed into his arms with enthusiasm, sliding her hands around the back of his neck and kissing him.

It was his first kiss. He realized after she softened in his arms that he had no idea what to do. He'd never kissed anyone before. What if he fucked this up? What if—

Gretchen's tongue slicked out and licked the tight seam of his mouth.

Ah, fuck. Fuck, fuck, fuck. That was the most amazing thing he'd ever felt. The tip of her tongue might as well have been licking his cock, for it shot a jolt straight there. Hunter groaned, unable to help himself.

She touched the seam of his mouth again with her tongue, and he parted his lips, fascinated by the aggressive lead she'd taken. Immediately, Gretchen's tongue swept into his mouth, stroking against his in a coaxing move that made him harden with need.

"Gretchen," he breathed against her lips. His cock ached so badly for her that he couldn't think straight, was losing track of what he'd arrived here to do. "I—we need to talk."

Her warm, delicious figure suddenly pulled away. "Talk? That sounds bad." She tilted her head up at him and gave him a teasing look. "Are you coming here to break up with me?"

"No." He wanted to crawl between her legs and settle there again. He wanted to touch her all over. Caress her. Kiss her more. Kiss her for hours. "I just . . . there are things that need to be said between us."

"That sounds very serious. Why don't you come to bed and tell me? It's cold out here." She gave a small shiver, and he noticed her nipples were hard, poking against the thin fabric of her sleep shirt.

The sight made him nearly spend right there. Hunter scrubbed a hand down his face as Gretchen took his hand and led him to the bed. She crawled under the covers and then held them open for him, inviting him in.

The most beautiful, desirable woman he'd ever seen was inviting him to her bed. Damn, he was a lucky son of a bitch.

Hunter hesitated but then slid into bed next to her, feeling stiff and uncomfortable and awkward. He didn't belong here. Any moment she'd tug his robe open, see that the scars covering one half of his face also went down his side, and be repulsed. She'd pull away and then he'd be left wallowing in his own humiliated fury.

To his surprise, Gretchen reached over and turned off the lamp, setting the room in darkness. "Better?" she asked softly. "You seem uneasy."

He was. He was tense as hell and kept waiting for her to come to her senses and realize he wasn't handsome. "The lights off is better for you," he bit out. "Less to see."

Her warm chuckle in the dark made his cock jump, and he nearly groaned aloud when her hair brushed against his shoulder. Gretchen's fingers touched his chest, lightly trailing along his chest hair. "I like the way you look."

"Don't lie to me," he said harshly, a stab of anger flaring through him. He kept his fists clenched at his side, though he wanted nothing more than to touch her. "I know what I look like."

"I do, too," she said easily, and those teasing fingers

trailed down his stomach, lightly swirling at his belly button. "You have dark hair and a strong nose, and scars on one side of your face. You're taller than me, have big arms, and you turn your cheek aside when possible, like you're trying to shield the world from your face."

The breath left him. Stunned, he said nothing for a long moment, waiting. Waiting for her to say something. When she remained quiet, he struggled for something to say, to make her feel the depth of his struggle. "People flinch when they look at me. They turn away when they see my face."

"People are assholes," she said, and he felt her shoulders lift as if she were giving a tiny shrug. "You're a gorgeous, intelligent man . . . with a few scars."

Her finger dipped into his belly button, distracting him from the angry protest about to spill forth. She wasn't listening to him. She didn't understand what it was like to be the one who everyone looked away from. To turn people's stomach with a look of your face.

To be so utterly alone in the world.

Of course, he was having a hard time thinking about being alone while she played with his navel, her fragrant hair brushing against his cheek.

"Won't you touch me?" she whispered back to him. "You seem so stiff and angry."

He ached with his need to touch her. Ached. But something held him back. Fear of . . . what? Rejection? Seeing that look of loathing on her face that he'd seen so many times?

"I don't know how to do this, Gretchen."

"Hmm?" The teasing lilt was back in her voice. "Don't know how to touch me?"

"No," he said harshly, hating the word even as he spit it out. "I've never . . . I don't . . ."

"That's all right, Hunter."

"It's not," he said roughly, reaching out and daring to touch a lock of her hair that was tickling his chest. It was soft and silky, and his mind immediately filled with images of her hair sliding all over him, her naked body following. His cock reared, and he bit his lip to keep from spilling with need. "It's . . . not . . . okay."

"I know you're a virgin, Hunter. I guessed as much. You were so young when you were hurt, I just assumed . . ."

An ironic twist flexed his mouth. Of course she knew. He was fucking obvious as hell. "I just wanted you to know that it's not you. It's me. It's all me, and if I push you away it's because I don't know how to pull you close. I'm not . . . I'm not good with people."

"I'm not, either," she said in an easy voice. "I don't know if you've noticed, but I tend to blurt out the first thing I'm thinking."

"I like that about you," he told her honestly. "I like everything about you."

"Mmm." She sounded pleased.

Encouraged, he closed his eyes and rubbed that strand of hair, imagining the deep red spilling across his palm. "I can't stop thinking about you, Gretchen. I want to touch you all over. Explore you. Give you pleasure like I'm supposed to, but every time you touch me, I just . . . lose it."

"Hair trigger?" she said with a chuckle.

A knot of humiliation burned in his throat. He remained silent.

"Hunter. It's okay. I don't mind," she said softly. "Is it me? Am I too forward for you?"

"No. I like you forward. It's just . . ." He struggled to find the right words to say. For the first time, he wished the room weren't so dark so he could see her face, see the expression in her beautiful eyes.

"Do you want to explore me? I don't mind."

He went silent. *What exactly was she offering?*

"Here," she said in a low voice, moving his hand to her wrist. She then reached behind her and placed her hand on the headboard. "I'll put my hands here and I won't move them. You can touch me how you like, and I promise not to touch you back. We'll go as slow as you need to. I promise."

His breathing grew rapid. Hunter remained still, and when she didn't move a muscle, he sat up, wishing he could see her in the darkness. But he didn't want to turn the light on, not yet. He didn't want to see her flinch. "What should I—what do you want?"

"Whatever you like. I'm here for the taking." Her voice was sultry and still contained that delicious hint of fun that made Gretchen so very intoxicating to his senses. "This is your game. You're in charge."

It took him a long moment before he reached out on the bed . . . and discovered a smooth knee. He caressed it, marveling at the feel of her skin.

"You can go higher, you know. Nothing bites."

"I know. I'm just . . . enjoying." This was his first time to ever touch a woman and truly explore her. He wanted to savor the moment.

He'd never thought he'd have this. Even in his younger years, when he'd ached with need for a simple touch, he'd never considered hiring an escort for sex. To pay a woman to suck his cock and then watch her flinch when she saw him? No, paying for sex seemed like the worst of both worlds.

And yet Gretchen had offered herself to him. His hand trailed higher, caressing her thigh.

"Now we're getting somewhere," she said, her voice light but with a hint of a tremble in it.

"Are you . . . nervous?"

"I'm mostly excited," she said, and he could hear the breathless quality of her voice. "Full of anticipation. My belly—and other parts of me—are tingling with it. I've been trying to get you to touch me for a week now."

He knew. He just hadn't had the courage until she'd more or less seduced him in the library. His exploring hand shifted upward and hit the edge of her shirt. He fisted it, drawing the material away from her body, imagining the material pulled taut against her breasts, outlining her nipples.

Nipples that he had *carte blanche* to touch. Another surge of need rose through him, and he felt pre-cum sliding down the head of his cock, soaking the front of his boxers. Any minute now, he'd lose control. He had to pace himself.

Breathing deeply to calm his body, Hunter forced himself to relax.

"If you want to take that shirt off me, you're going to have to do it on your own. I can't help you, remember?" He heard the sound of her fingers drumming on the wood of the headboard as a reminder.

"I thought I was in charge here?" he bit back.

"You are. I'm just bossy even if I'm supposed to be all submissive," she said, her voice saucy. "You can always spank me for being bad, if you want."

He groaned at the visual. "Gretchen, please. I need to keep control."

"Oh, of course. I'm sorry." She didn't sound sorry in the slightest. "I'll just lay here and be quiet. All silent and needy and half-naked, but very willing to be fully naked if given the opportunity."

His hand clenched tighter on the shirt, feeling the old fabric give a little. "What if I ripped this off you?"

Her breath caught in her throat. "That would be extremely naughty of you. I'm game."

Hunter tugged harder at the fabric and heard a satisfying rip, as well as Gretchen's intake of breath, followed by a mischievous giggle. Then he was holding the loose fabric in his hand and he tossed it aside.

"You going to rip my panties next?"

He flexed his hand, feeling her thigh next to his on the large bed. He didn't remember what her panties looked like. They'd been swallowed up by the oversized shirt. His mind was suddenly full of mental images of Gretchen in sexy panties, an image he liked very much. "Are they sexy?"

"Mmm, not really. They're boy shorts with a bit of lace. I wasn't really coming here expecting to get laid, so I didn't pack my best."

"I . . . don't know what boy shorts are."

"Then yes, they're incredibly, ultra sexy."

"Then I shouldn't rip them." He was starting to get the hang of her teasing. In the darkness, it was a bit easier. Maybe she'd known that, and that was why she'd insisted on the lights being off.

He reached for her on the bed and, after a bit of awkward fumbling, touched a soft material that crossed over her thighs. He hooked his fingers into the waistband and began to drag them downward, his mind full of thoughts of earlier this afternoon, when he'd done the same thing and buried his face between her legs.

She'd liked that. God, he'd liked it also, but he had to pace himself. Had to. He intended on making this last long enough for him to get his fill. He might never have such an opportunity again. So he slid them down her legs and tossed them onto the floor.

His mind was suddenly filled with images of Gretchen, stretched out and naked on the bed. For him. His cock was rock hard in his boxers. She'd said he could explore her. Would it count as exploring if he ripped off his own boxers and sank deep inside her? No. She'd given him permission to touch. No more, no less. He'd take that and be grateful.

"You're quiet," she said.

"Just thinking."

"Uh-oh. Good thinking or bad thinking?"

"Thinking about you. Good thinking."

"Sexy thinking, I hope."

"Thinking about where to touch you next."

"Wellllll," she drawled. "I'm told my feet are quite ugly. I'd advise against heading in that direction."

"Nothing on you is ugly," he said, meaning it. He'd change nothing about her.

"Perhaps you did not see my feet," she said, amused.

He reached for her foot, determined to prove her wrong, and cupped her heel. He was immediately distracted by the size of her foot. She was small in comparison to him. His thumb ran along the underside of her foot, and then he slid his fingers over the arch. "Feels lovely to me."

She shivered underneath his touch. "Your fingers are ticklish."

"Should I stop?"

"No. It's not a bad ticklish. Just . . . makes me shiver."

Hunter felt an insane urge to lean in and kiss the top of her foot. *Would her skin be soft there?* He leaned in and brushed his lips over it to find out.

Her breath whooshed. A soft moan touched his ears. "Oh, okay. That feels pretty good."

His fingers slid up her calf, exploring her skin. "You're very soft, Gretchen."

"Mmm, yeah. I'm pretty soft all over, I hear. All those hours at the computer and stuff. It doesn't exactly lend itself to tons of muscles. Gardening seems to be working for you, though. That's one amazing six-pack I saw when you got out of the shower."

Her endless chatter was light and irreverent, and he suspected she was keeping up a steady stream of conversation to keep him at ease. It was working, too. He chuckled. "I don't just garden, you know. I have a gym and I work out daily."

He felt her shift, and she was suddenly sitting up in the bed. Her hands reached out, patting his shoulders in the darkness. "Holy crap, Hunter. Did you just laugh?" Her searching fingers touched his cheek. "I'm so bummed. I finally got you to laugh and I didn't get to see it."

Hunter stilled under her touch. Her fingers were touching his scarred cheek. The urge to push her hands away was strong, and he had to fight to remain still.

Her fingers hesitated on him. "Does this bother you? My touch?"

Yes, he wanted to say. He forced himself to swallow and answer instead, "Go ahead."

Her fingers lightly touched his cheek again, tracing the line of his jaw, and then moving over the crease of one of his deepest scars. She continued, moving to his mouth and where the line of it extended unevenly. It'd been reconstructed during surgery, and he knew it twisted his smile. That was one of many reasons why he never did smile.

"I don't find you ugly, Hunter. No one who knew you could." Her voice was achingly soft. "If anything, I'm grateful that you have these scars, because they saved you for me—for this moment in time. And that's a little selfish of me, isn't it? And yet I can't help but feel that way."

His heart ached with the sweetness of her words. Hunter reached for her, cupping Gretchen's cheek in his hand and drawing her forward. He wanted to kiss her. Their noses mashed together awkwardly, and he heard her giggle. He didn't care. He liked that nothing was ever serious to her—it made him feel like there was less pressure on him to be perfect, to do this right. His Gretchen wouldn't mind.

Hunter's mouth slanted over hers, his lips placed in haphazard fashion against her own. It didn't matter—she still tasted sweet, her lips soft. This time he was the aggressor, sucking on her lower lip until she parted her mouth, and then he stroked his tongue inside.

She moaned, and her tongue met his. Her hands curled in his hair, and she pressed her body up against him, even as they continued to kiss. Her nipples scraped against his chest, and his breath exploded in a rush.

She gasped, pulling back from him. "Too much?"

He groaned. It had almost been. Pressing a hand to his forehead, he took a moment to recover. Her fingers stroked and petted him, trying to comfort. Instead, it was just driving him crazier. He pried one of her hands off him and kissed her palm. "Isn't this supposed to be on the headboard?"

"Oooh, right. I got distracted." She laughed. "Guess you'll have to spank me, huh?" The bed bounced, and her leg brushed against his. She'd flipped onto her stomach. After a moment, she announced, "Hands are now back in place. Do with me as you will."

"I'm not going to spank you." Though his hands itched to touch her ass.

"You're no fun."

And she was entirely too much fun, he thought to himself. His hands moved to her thigh and he trailed up her leg, then brushed over the fullness of her ass.

She made a pleased noise. "Mmmm. Keep going."

He groaned at the sheer pleasure of being able to touch her. Both hands went to her ass and he cupped it, kneading her soft flesh. His cock ached so fucking much now that it was painful, but he couldn't seem to stop touching her. Nor could he resist sliding a finger between her cheeks and exploring her. He found the wet heat of her sex . . . and she was soaked.

The change in her was immediate. Gretchen moaned and pushed back against his fingers, and one slid deep inside her. Oh, God, she was so hot and wet. Her inner muscles clenched around his finger, and he imagined his cock being squeezed by those muscles and—

With a groan, he came. Hot cum splashed inside his boxers—fuck, he was still in his goddamn boxers—and he withdrew from her to clutch at himself in dismay. He'd tried so hard to keep control and he'd ruined this.

She made a noise of protest as he pulled away. "Hunter?"

He rolled off the bed, humiliated. *Damn it.* He'd fucked this up. The front of his boxers clung to him with the evidence of his shame.

"Hunter? Where are you? Please don't leave." Her voice was soft.

"I . . . I can't stay. I . . ." He couldn't bring himself to say the words. *I came all over myself like a boy.*

"But your touch feels so good. And I ache so bad." He heard the blankets rustle. "Won't you come touch me?"

"Gretchen," he said harshly. "I . . . need to clean up." There. Now he'd admitted it and she would leave him alone.

"After you clean up, will you come back and finish touching me?"

Astonishment made him turn, even though it was dark and he couldn't see her face. Wasn't she embarrassed by his lack of control? "You still want me to touch you?"

"Hey, you got yours. I want to get mine."

"But that's not how this works. I wanted to make it good for you."

"And I intend on you making it good for me," she said. "No sense in us stopping now if we're having fun. And I thought we were having fun."

"Some of us were having too much fun," he said wryly, her good humor restoring his.

"Oh, my God, did you just make a joke? I should leave you in the dark all the time."

"Very funny."

"I know. I'm full of sparkling humor. Sparkling humor and soft, soft skin that you need to come over here and touch."

He heard the bedsheets rustle again. "I think there's a stack of towels on the chair by the fireplace. Fix yourself up and come back to me. I'm just going to wait right here."

Hunter found the stack of towels and stripped off his boxers, then wiped himself off. He still felt a little foolish, but then Gretchen made a needy little moan and his attention riveted back to her.

"Are you coming back?" she asked.

He approached the bed, extending a hand forward once he crossed the room. His hand encountered Gretchen's upraised flank since she'd changed positions on the bed.

Skimming a hand over her, he mentally pictured her new pose—she was now kneeling on the bed, her ass raised in the air, knees spread. Asking—no, begging—for him to touch her.

Hunter groaned.

"Touch me, Hunter. Use your fingers on me."

He didn't want to use his fingers—he wanted to use his mouth and taste her sweetness again. He pushed forward, leaning in to skim his lips over her buttock, enjoying her quick, noisy intake of breath. He wanted more of a response from her, wanted her to lose control like he had.

It had suddenly become his new goal.

Hunter nipped at her hip, and she gave a squeak of surprise. That was better. He let his lips trail over her skin, moving toward his goal. He felt her body tense with anticipation when he leaned her forward and skimmed his fingers between her legs, searching for that wet heat he'd felt before.

He knew he'd touched the right spot when he felt that slick clench of muscles in response and felt her entire body jump. Gretchen moaned his name, sounding breathless and wild. He moved his mouth to where his fingers had found her hot core, and he brushed his tongue up against it, tasting her. She tasted wet and tart with need; it was a taste he wanted on his tongue forever.

A shudder racked through Gretchen, and he brushed his tongue against her skin again, seeking her heat.

"Oh, God." She jerked against him. "Right there. Oh, keep going." She quivered against him as he continued to work her pussy with his tongue, stroking inside her and flicking at her sex. She rocked against him wildly, and his fingers dug into her flesh, his excitement building with hers.

"More, Hunter," she breathed. "I need more."

He stabbed his tongue into her, pressing forward with every stroke, until she was whimpering against him and little quivers were rocking through her body.

"My clit, baby," she instructed him. "Get my clit for me, baby."

Her excitement had ignited his cock—already he was rock hard again. He wouldn't last long, either. With every quiver and moan she made, he felt a shudder of desire rock through him as well. But he wanted to make sure she came before he lost his control again.

He did as she'd instructed, reaching between her legs and finding the slick folds of her sex from the front. He slid his fingertips between them, searching for her clit. Her sharp cry echoed in the room the moment he made contact, and she writhed against him. The sound she made was incoherent with need.

And hell, he wanted more of that. So he rubbed her clit between his fingers and worked it even as he continued to tongue her pussy, lapping up her juices.

She made a throaty cry and then gave a full-body shudder, racked with tremors. New moisture flooded against his mouth, and he groaned in response, his own pleasure rocketing forth.

He'd made her come so hard. It was the most incredible feeling in the fucking world. He pulled away while she panted, trying to get her breath back, and lightly kissed her buttock. She'd given him a gift tonight.

And he'd come in his boxers and now on the side of her blankets. *Hell.* He was just a fucking mess. He pulled away and grabbed another towel.

Still a goddamn virgin. He couldn't even wait to be inside her to finish.

"Mmmm, Hunter?" she called after him a moment later, sounding sated. "You're not leaving, are you?"

He'd actually contemplated just that. "I'm not . . . I fucked this up."

"Fucked it up how?"

He was silent.

"Hunter, if it's because you're still a virgin, don't worry about it. We'll take our time. I'm kind of enjoying endless amounts of foreplay." She chuckled to herself. "You didn't bring a condom with you tonight, did you?"

"No," he admitted.

"Well, then, there's no sense in hating on yourself, is there? No glove, no love. It's probably a good thing that we never got further than the heavy petting. Now, come on." He heard her pat the mattress. "I kind of felt like cuddling, if you're game."

Spend the rest of the evening with his hands on her naked body? She didn't even have to ask. He finished toweling himself clean again and then reapproached the bed. He tossed the now-messy blanket off the side, hesitated a moment, then took a deep breath and slid under the sheet next to her.

She immediately moved forward and tucked her arms around him, laying her cheek on his chest again.

"That was incredible," she told him in a soft voice. "Thank you."

"I should be thanking you," he said gruffly.

"Mmm, I don't know. You have a very talented mouth." She yawned. "Don't sneak away on me again, okay?"

He ran his fingers through her hair, thinking that this was quite possibly the best place in the universe to be. "I won't."

When Hunter woke up, he thought it had all been a dream. Exploring and touching Gretchen, making her writhe with desire. The way she'd been so open and sexual with him.

The tousled hair on the pillow next to him told him that this was reality.

Hunter reached out and brushed a lock off her face, watching her sleep with a feeling in his chest that was something close to gratitude but more like . . . elation.

God, he loved touching her. Being with her. There was no one on earth more wonderful than Gretchen. The fact that this gorgeous woman would let him touch her—hell, wanted to be touched by him—was a miracle.

He wanted to do something for her. His first instinct was to go and trim every one of his roses and shower her with them. But he gave her roses every day. It wouldn't be special enough.

He needed more. He'd have to give this some thought.

She mumbled something in her sleep and rolled over in the bed, her red hair spreading over her pillow. He longed to touch her again, but she was sleeping so peacefully that he didn't want to disturb her. He'd get up and work out instead. Maybe when he was done, she'd be awake and they could spend some time together.

Now he sounded like a ridiculous, lovesick fool. But for some reason, he didn't mind it.

They still hadn't slept together—not really, not officially. He was still a virgin. But Gretchen hadn't minded. *We'll take our time*, she'd told him. *There's no rush.*

He'd woken up with a stiff cock and raging need for her. He suspected that he was going to wake up like that from now on—desperate with the need to bury himself inside her. He wouldn't, though. Not while she was sleeping and didn't have the opportunity to tell him no.

Hunter rolled over in bed. He drew back immediately. "What the fuck—"

A hideous creature was staring at him, all wrinkly face, large golden eyes, and triangular ears. A skinny, naked tail swished back and forth on the nightstand like a piece of rope flicking in the wind.

"Mmm?" At his side, Gretchen stirred, and then she chuckled. "I see you met Igor."

He stared at the creature. "This is your cat?"

"It is."

"He's naked."

She laughed, and her hand slid over his stomach, caressing his skin. "That makes three of us, then."

His cock reared in response to her touch, and Hunter groaned. "Gretchen, don't—"

"Don't touch you? Did someone wake up with morning wood?" Her sense of humor seemed to be alive and well this morning. She lifted the blanket up and peeked underneath, then gave a long, gusty sigh of pleasure. "Mmm, you sure did."

"Can you blame me?" God, she was gorgeous. That naked skin, that beautiful hair that was spilling all over her shoulders, the blankets just barely covering her breasts from his view. He wanted to touch her, his hands flexing with the need of it.

"So it's my fault?" She shook her head, a coy smile touching her lips. "Guess I should take care of it for you, shouldn't I?"

And before he could even utter anything, she disappeared under the blankets.

Hunter stiffened, surprise locking him into place.

A warm hand clasped the base of his cock and a hot mouth moved over the head. He felt Gretchen's tongue swirl over it and he collapsed against the pillows. "Gretchen, I . . . oh, fuck. You're amazing. So amazing."

"I know," she murmured, her words muffled. And then she took him deep into her mouth and began to suck.

God, she was the most amazing woman. He groaned again as she began to work his cock, his hands fisting in the blankets. He wanted to reach down and touch her, but he didn't want to disturb her. Not when she was doing something so incredibly perfect. Her mouth was like heaven on his cock.

He glanced over at the nightstand, suddenly disturbed that her cat might be watching him get a blowjob, but it was gone. Thank God for that.

She sucked him harder, and he couldn't resist a little thrust into her mouth, his hips pushing up. That small movement reminded him that he wasn't going to last, and he told her that. True to form, Gretchen didn't move away from him. Instead, she redoubled her efforts, taking him deep in her throat and making little noises of pleasure from under the blanket, as if she loved nothing more than to suck on him.

That image, combined with the feel of her on his cock and the tickle of her long hair on his skin, sent him over far too quickly. He came with a shout of her name.

She came up from under the blankets with an impish look on her face. "Just a little something to start the day off right."

"The day started off right when I woke up and saw you."

Her face softened and she smiled at him, then poked him with a finger. "Keep saying stuff like that and it's going to be very hard to get rid of me."

That was fine with him. He had no intention of ever letting her go.

Gretchen's pleasant, relaxed mood disappeared the moment she went into the library to work. She'd left her phone on the secretary last night and saw that she'd received several voice messages since she'd last checked it.

The first one was from her agent asking if she had finished the Astronaut Bill manuscript. The publisher was waiting on it and getting very upset. If she didn't turn it in within the next week, the book would have to be pushed and the publication schedule—including her payments— would be juggled. Kat needed Gretchen to call back ASAP.

She deleted it.

The next message was from her apartment manager. Rent was due two days ago and they hadn't received her check. Had she forgotten?

She hadn't. She just didn't have the money yet. She'd signed the contract for this project, but the check still had not come in. Frustrating, but nothing she could do about it except call her landlord and explain that she could mail them a check, but they couldn't cash it until she was paid. They wouldn't be keen on it, but they knew she was a writer and that payments were few and far between. She'd had to make arrangements like that before.

The third message was from Cooper. Gretchen listened to it with a growing feeling of dread. The message was friendly and pleasant. Cooper wanted to know how her project was going and that he was looking forward to seeing her again, and did she possibly want to get together this weekend just to hang out and catch up?

She deleted that message, too, and barely resisted burying her face in her hands. The situation with Cooper was a sticky one. He was a friend—a good friend—and had been since college. Unfortunately, he was more like the wimpy little brother she never had, rather than the strong, silent, almost lonely type that she seemed to fall for.

Gretchen put her phone down and thought dreamily about Hunter. Last night had been . . . delicious. The endless foreplay was fun, but she had a craving ache deep within that told her that she wanted more. Time to tell Hunter to buy some condoms. She wondered how he'd like that. Her virgin billionaire didn't seem to like to go out in public and she suspected the scars were the reason why. He'd probably just delegate the task to Eldon.

And Eldon would disapprove. He disapproved of everything.

The phone rang as she held it, and Gretchen picked up the call automatically. "Hello?"

"Gretchen, honey, tell me you're hitting send on that Astronaut Bill manuscript as we speak?"

She winced. "Hey, Kat. And um, it's not done. I still need another week or two."

"Gretch! You told me you'd have it done in a week . . . two weeks ago."

"I know. This other project has been a little more . . . time consuming than I thought it would be." There was that, and the fact that she spent every spare moment trying to seduce the owner of the house she was staying in. But Hunter was just so deliciously bleak and fascinating. She couldn't stay away from him. Was he in his greenhouse even now, selecting a rose while thinking of her? Why did that make her panties instantly wet just to think about?

"Well, can't you put the project aside for a few days and finish this other one? Just have Bill shag Uranus in her anus and send it off."

"Uranea and the publisher would freak out if I threw in butt sex."

"Whatever, and the publisher's freaking out right now because you're grossly overdue. Gretchen, they're going to fire you if you don't get this book in. I'm your agent. I'm supposed to tell you when you're doing bad career moves, right? This is a bad one. Very bad. Can you just sit down and hammer out a few chapters for me? Please?" Kat's voice turned wheedling. "So I don't have to make an ugly phone call about how my favorite client didn't hit her deadline again?"

Gretchen pulled her laptop open and sighed. "I'm pulling up the document as we speak, Kat. I promise."

"Good. Think you can send it to me by tomorrow?"

"Ummm."

"I'll take that as a yes. Don't tell me otherwise."

"Okay."

"Since I have you on the phone, I did have a chat with Preston." Kat paused for dramatic effect.

Gretchen racked her brain for a moment. "Preston Stewart's the editor for the new publisher, right? What was the name again?"

"That's him. Bellefleur Publishing."

"Uh-huh. Did they ask for me because the Astronaut Bill stuff is pulp and I'm used to writing in some sex?"

"Huh? What does that have to do with anything?"

"The letters. Does he know these are dirty letters?"

Kat spluttered. "Say what?"

"I'm serious! The trunk is full of letters between a gal named Lula and her boyfriend, Ben. It took years for them to be together, and so apparently they spent all that time in-between visits sending dirty recaps to each other. Want me to read you a page?"

"Dirty letters? Are you sure?"

Gretchen picked up the letter on the top of the pile. "My dearest Ben. I woke up this morning, my woman's flesh aching with need for you. I dreamed that you were deep inside me, your rod—"

"Okay, okay!" Kat laughed wildly. "Oh, man. Well, that's going to be a wicked cool marketing angle, that's for sure."

"If you say so," Gretchen said, amused. "Apparently these two lovebirds went to a lot of Victorian house parties and used every excuse to sneak off and make out while there. They're kind of creative with things. It's rather inspiring."

"I'll say. Anyhow, back to Preston. He's super excited about your book, too. How's it feel to be a lead title, kiddo?"

"I . . . haven't given it much thought."

"You haven't?" Kat gasped. "What's going on with you, Gretchen?"

"I've been, um, distracted. I met a guy."

"A guy? Audrey told me all about that horrible butler. Don't tell me you fell for him?"

"Jeez, Kat, when did you talk to Audrey?"

"We went for lunch the other day. I had some books for her to pick up for the charity and we ended up going out for drinkies."

"I think I need to widen my social circle," Gretchen muttered. "And no, I didn't fall for the butler. But I just might be kinda-sorta shagging his boss."

"You what? The billionaire?"

Count on Kat to be fascinated by the amount of money

he had instead of asking anything about him. Gretchen rolled her eyes. "He's different, Kat. I like him."

"Of course you like him. He's rich!"

"Can we talk about something other than how much he makes?"

"Sure. What kind of car does he drive?"

"Not funny. I like him because he's different, not because he's rich."

"I'm just teasing you, Gretchen. It's good that you met someone. I just wish he wasn't directly tied to the job you're doing. As your agent, that makes me a little uncomfortable."

"It's not like he's actually involved in the project," Gretchen told her. "He just happens to own the house the letters were found in."

"Very, very dirty letters. You sure you're not getting inspired by these dirty letters?"

"Give me a little credit?"

"Just a little. I'd like to meet this guy."

"We're just fooling around, Kat. It's not like this is anything official."

"I don't care. I still want to meet him. Maybe he has a sexy younger brother."

"He's an only child. But I'll see what I can do about getting some friends together. This house would be a great place to entertain." Though, the thought of entertaining would probably drive Eldon to drink.

Kat squealed. "Oooh, maybe we can do a Victorian house party! We can invite your editor so he can get excited about the progress you're making on the book."

"I don't know—"

"And the publicist! And a photographer. Think of the angle we can spin on things to get some in-house excitement."

"I don't know if the owner of the house is going to be particularly excited about this. He's pretty reclusive. And by pretty, I mean completely."

"So, you can just take him into a closet and play Seven Minutes in Heaven or something. Victorian house party coming up! So where's my invite?"

Gretchen sighed. "Let me work on him, Kat."

"Tell him it'll be good for your career. You need as much in-house support as you can get."

"We'll see." But for some reason she was thinking less about her career and more about dragging Hunter into a closet and rocking his socks off. A smile curved her mouth. Maybe this party thing wasn't such a bad idea after all.

———

"Oh, Astronaut Bill, what can we do? The universe is doomed for sure. The solarship with the cargo full of super-plutonium is headed straight for the galaxy warp. If we can't get on board somehow, it'll cut across space and head straight for the planet of my people, Vifraxa. Billions will be doomed." She wiped unhappy tears from her shining blue eyes. "You must find a way to save them."

Bill's strong hands clenched on the railing of the deck. He turned and stared at his captain's chair, furious. "We'll find a way to stop them." He snapped his fingers. "I have it! All we need to do is—"

Is . . .

———

Gretchen drummed her fingers, waiting for an idea—however stupid—to come to her.

And waited.

And waited.

Damn it. Nothing. She consulted the outline she'd turned in to her publisher. The storyline with the Vifraxans in danger was a new one and not included. *Damn it, damn it.*

She was stuck. She supposed she could backtrack a few

chapters and delete the subplot and move back to the original storyline, but if she did, she'd lose an entire day's worth of work.

She continued to drum her fingers, thinking. The trunk of letters lay open, waiting for her to turn to them, but she'd promised Kat that she'd try and knock out the rest of Astronaut Bill. Her gaze swung to her purse, where her phone hung out of one side.

An idea wormed its way into her head. Even though she knew she shouldn't, Gretchen pulled her purse into her lap and began to dig through its contents.

A few minutes later, she had what she was looking for, and smiled. In the corner of one back pocket was an individually wrapped condom. Expiration date? Not until next year.

Hot damn.

She tucked it into the pocket of her favorite yoga pants and bounded out of the library.

Perhaps it was time to take a quick break and see what Hunter was up to.

———

To her surprise, he wasn't in the greenhouse. It was empty, the roses blooming in the heavy, warm moisture-laden air. Gretchen turned around and headed to his room, knocking on the door. Not there, either.

She knew he had a gym on the premises, but not where it was. The house was too large for her to spend all day exploring. Frustrated, Gretchen spotted a phone on a table at the far end of the hall and headed for it. She picked up the receiver, and then paused.

She had no idea what Hunter's phone number was. Actually, she didn't know all that much about him other than the basics: He was lonely, he was scarred, and she loved to make him blush.

All right then, she'd learn more about him . . . right

after she seduced him. Again. It wasn't her fault, she told herself. The man was just completely seduce-able and utterly delicious. She couldn't help herself. Even now, her fingers itched to curl into one of those starchy collars on his shirts and rip it open so she could slide a hand inside and touch his hot skin.

Her mouth watered just thinking about it. Gretchen stared at the receiver and sighed. She was going to have to do the inevitable, it seemed. With a sour frown, she hit zero to dial her least favorite person in the world.

Eldon answered on the third ring. Instead of hello, he said, "What are you doing in the north wing?"

"Hello to you, too. I'm looking for Hunter. He's not in his room and not in the greenhouse. Any idea where he would be?"

"I'm not his keeper."

She snorted to herself. *You think you are.* "I know you're not. Can't you just tell me where he is?"

"Why?"

"I'm going to go deflower him." She smiled to herself at the butler's outraged splutter. "Hey, you asked. Now, seriously, where is he?"

"You're a vile young woman."

"Yeah, well, you're kind of a dick yourself." When he spluttered again, she sighed. "Look, Eldon, I just want to spend some time with your boss. I don't think he'd be keen on you keeping information from me. You may not like me, but he does. So spill the beans or I'm going to tell him you're trying to keep us apart."

There was a long moment of silence on the other end of the phone. Then he said, "Did you look in his office?"

It sounded like Eldon was spitting the words out of his mouth as if they tasted bad. "No, where's his office at?"

"Second floor, west wing. Third door on right." He hung up.

"Grumpy, grumpy," she said to herself, hanging up the

receiver. With a cheerful saunter, she headed for the west wing and went up the stairs. The door to his office was easy enough to find—there were not many doors in the West Wing, which meant that these were large rooms instead of the hall where she slept, a long corridor full of doors that were guest rooms.

She hesitated in front of the door and then knocked.

"Enter," Hunter called from within.

Bingo.

Gretchen opened the door halfway and slid inside, shutting it behind her. There was a lock on the door and she turned it. *Good.* She didn't want Eldon barging in on them.

Hunter's office was surprising to her. While the rest of the house was decorated in a Victorian, almost Rococo ornate elegance, the office was spare and gray. The walls were painted a pale, wintry shade. Photos of buildings of every kind and shape covered the walls. An enormous TV on the far end of the room was turned to a financial channel, and the ticker moved quietly across the screen, the volume down. To the left of Hunter's desk was an entire panel of windows that overlooked the gardens. There was a long, curving balcony there, and she imagined that he stepped outside in the summer to look over his beautiful, blooming plants.

The most surprising thing to her was that Hunter's desk faced the far wall . . . and an enormous mirror. How very odd. She wouldn't have thought Hunter, of all people, would work facing a mirror.

He looked up as she closed the door, glancing at her in the mirror, desk phone in hand. Confusion showed on his face. "Gretchen?"

"Hey. You busy?"

He set the phone down in the cradle and turned his chair to face her. "Just have a few meetings today I can't reschedule. What are you doing here?"

She took a few steps forward, her hips swaying. Her

hand went to the corner of his desk and she ran a finger along the edge of the wood. "I thought I'd come by and devirgin you."

His brows furrowed together. "What?"

"Your virginity—I've come to take it." She pulled the condom from her pocket and held it aloft like a trophy. "Unless you're not interested, of course."

"What happened to going slow?" His face was thunderstruck, his gaze darting to the condom she held tucked between two fingers.

That wasn't a no. Gretchen moved forward, pressing her knee between his legs on the chair and sliding forward until her breasts were in his face. "I promise to go slow, if that makes you feel any better?"

"Gretchen—"

"The way I figure it is that we've been going about this all wrong. I thought taking it nice and slow would make you feel more comfortable, but now I'm thinking we should treat this like ripping off a Band-Aid—make it rough and fast so you won't overthink things." She removed her knee and slid down until her elbows were resting on his knees. His cock was already getting hard in his slacks, tenting the front. "Parts of you are interested at least."

"All of me is interested, Gretchen," he said, his voice hoarse. "But I have a conference call in two minutes and I can't reschedule it."

"Mmm." She trailed a finger over his groin. "I can stick around, you know. I promise to be quiet."

"I won't be able to concentrate—"

She put a finger to her lips, smiling, even as his phone rang.

With a muttered oath, he grabbed her and spun her around, dragging her ass down to his lap. He pulled his chair in, tucking their legs under the desk, and grabbed the phone. "Hunter Buchanan here."

Gretchen wiggled slightly in his lap, keeping quiet. His

cock was already hard underneath her ass, and getting harder by the minute. His thighs were thick and rather strong, and she liked that, she decided, tucking her legs over his knees to spread her ass cheeks a bit more. She leaned forward on his desk and gave a bit of a wiggle again, so her pussy would rub up against his cock.

Immediately, Hunter reached past her and hit the mute button on his phone. He groaned, his free hand going to her hip. "Don't move like that. Please."

"I'll be good," she promised in a voice that told him she'd be anything but.

He clicked off mute, giving her a warning look. "No, I'm here. Go on."

Gretchen propped her chin up on her hands, glancing around at Hunter's desk while he discussed a property acquisition with whoever else was on the line. His hand remained at her hip, his thumb lightly rubbing back and forth as he talked. It was hard to be still, especially when she could feel the thick length of him nestled against her pussy, but the conversation seemed to be an important one—they were discussing how many millions of dollars to offer for a shopping mall—and so she tried not to disturb him.

His desk was rather austere. Most people had small trinkets or personal possessions on their desks to mark them as theirs. Gretchen's desk at home was covered with knick-knacks, postcards of exotic places, and a stack of unpaid bills. Hunter's desk was spotlessly clean, and the only photo he had on his desk was of yet another building that she didn't recognize. He sure did like pictures of buildings. On one corner of the desk was a single rose—matching the one he'd given her that day—in a slim crystal vase. Since he wasn't using his computer, she tapped his mouse to get rid of the screen saver and glanced at his desktop. Jeez, he hadn't even changed it from the factory setting. Boring. She opened his Internet browser and looked for a desktop wallpaper that would suit him, and ended up picking something that was a gorgeous shot of roses sparkling with dew. There. At least that was something.

She glanced over at the mirror, studying it. It didn't make sense that a man as concerned with his appearance would want a big full-length mirror directly in front of his desk. "Why the mirror?" she whispered.

He tilted the phone away from his mouth so only she could hear his response. "So I never forget who—and what—I am."

"That's depressing," she told him, and then rolled her eyes when he shushed her. "You know who does that? Emo people."

"Uh-huh," Hunter said, but his response wasn't for her. His fingers had moved slightly up her waistband and had moved to her skin. He now grazed her skin over and over as he alternately talked and listened. "How many inspectors did you send out?"

That small touch on her skin was driving her crazy. Gretchen leaned forward on his desk, glancing up in the mirror. Hunter's gaze was on her, his focus intense. He had the phone to his ear, but it was clear his attention was riveted to her. She felt her pulse begin to thrum with excitement, and she gave her thighs a little squeeze to see his reaction.

His eyes widened and he tilted his head back against his chair, as if trying to keep control. "Mmmhmm."

She could hear the strain in his voice even as he answered the person on the other end of the phone.

"Go on."

She was pretty sure he hadn't been talking to her, but she decided to feign ignorance. Gretchen glanced across the desk at the mirror on the far wall and decided to take the teasing in another direction. She pulled her shirt over her head, tossed it on the ground, and cupped her breasts through her bra.

He pushed forward, pinning her against the desk as he

reached for the mute button again. "You're not playing fair, Gretchen."

"You told me to go on," she said, tweaking her nipples.

"Goddamn it." His gaze was riveted on her breasts. "I'm going to have to fight fire with fire, aren't I?"

"I wish you would," she breathed, excited at the prospect.

His hand on her hip moved forward, between her legs, his gaze on her in the mirror.

She arched her back, letting him know that he was heading in the right direction, and spread her legs a little wider on his lap.

"I'm a very busy man," he said in a husky voice, the phone still on mute. "I can't afford these distractions."

"Of course not," she said innocently.

His hand slipped into her panties, his fingers seeking out her wet heat. He groaned when his fingers touched her pussy. "You're soaked already."

"Thinking about you gets me hot," she said, teasing one bra strap down her shoulder. "Can't help myself."

Hunter's fingers caressed her folds, exploring her. One fingertip grazed her clit, and she was unable to keep herself from crying out in response.

He jerked forward, cradling the phone against his ear, his other hand still trapped in her panties and pushing against her flesh. He released the mute button and growled into the phone, "I'm going to have to drop off the call. Someone send me the meeting minutes."

And he hung up. The look on his face was hard and almost forbidding. "You're derailing my plans, Gretchen."

She kept the smile pinned to her face, though she couldn't tell if he was furious at her or not. "You derailed mine. I kept thinking about you and couldn't get any work done."

And she gave one of her breasts a squeeze just to distract him.

"Clearly you need a taste of your own medicine." His

fingers moved across her clit again, and she jerked in his lap, that little touch sending skitters of pleasure through her body.

"Is this your idea of punishment?" Her laugh was breathless with need.

"Actually, I just want to touch you," he whispered in her ear. His hand moved to cover hers over her breast, and his fingers danced against her clit.

She shifted her hips to push him to the exact spot that would send her wild with pleasure, since his seeking fingers kept coming close but weren't quite there. "Then touch me all you want."

And she rolled her hips against him, bearing down against his cock.

He groaned, his hand tightening against her breast. His fingers began to move rapidly against her clit, stroking back and forth in slick little motions that made her breath hitch in her throat. "Gretchen, I don't know how long I'll last with you on my lap like this."

"Then maybe we should get that condom on you," she agreed breathlessly. "And then I can get back on your lap after you put it on."

He pushed his chair backward so they were no longer pinned to his desk.

Gretchen got off his lap and produced the condom again, kneeling between his legs in front of his chair. His cock seemed enormous, the tent in his pants straining, and she sighed blissfully at the sight. Her hands pulled at his belt, ready to put the condom on him.

He stopped her, his hand covering hers. "I can do this. I want you to get naked."

So very authoritative. She shivered, standing up and tugging at the laced waistband of her yoga pants. Gretchen pulled the knot free, then shimmied the pants down her legs, letting them drop to the ground. She'd worn her cutest pair of panties today—hot pink silk with little black bows at the hips.

They, too, went to the ground.

His belt quickly followed, and then he was dragging his pants down his hips, along with his boxers. His cock jutted into the air, and she licked her lips with the sight of it. A moment later, he was smoothing the condom down the length of it, and then he turned his eyes aching with need on her.

"Sit down again," he told her, the tightness in his throat her only indication of his nerves.

She unhooked her bra and tossed it to the ground, then slid in front of him. She turned to face the desk, her bare ass presented to him. And then, slowly, Gretchen sat back down on his lap, his cock a hot bar of iron pressing against her backside.

"Take me inside you, Gretchen."

She lifted her hips and positioned him at her entrance. When she looked in the mirror, she saw his gaze was not on her, but on the spot where their two bodies would join. He wanted to watch his cock sink into her. The thought was a deliciously scandalous one, and she descended slowly, moving inch by inch to take him inside her.

He groaned, his fingers clutching her hips tightly as she began to work him into her. "Ah, fuck," he gritted. "You feel amazing."

She rolled her hips a little, taking him deeper, but moving slowly—he was thick and exquisite and she wanted to drag this out for both his pleasure and hers. Her gaze strayed to the mirror, fascinated by the fact that she got to watch his face. The scars on the side of his face stood out white against the flush of his skin, and his face seemed full of tension.

And then she'd taken him all the way into her, her legs straddling his, her ass against his stomach.

His forehead pressed to her back and he groaned again, loudly. "Never thought I'd feel anything so good, Gretchen. Never."

Her heart gave a little flip at the intensity in his voice. "The fun's just starting," she told him softly, and dug her hips in and rocked.

His hands clenched against her. "Ah!"

"Oh, Hunter. You're so deep inside me. That feels unbelievable."

"Gretchen," he breathed raggedly.

She began to work her hips, moving slowly over him in a subtle rocking motion. She leaned forward, bracing her arms against the desk, and began to bounce her hips on him, controlling the depth of each stroke.

He groaned again, and her eyes flew to him in the mirror. He was contorted in something curiously close to ecstasy, the look on his face so open and raw and exposed that it made her heart hurt a little. When had she ever had a lover look at her quite like that?

Never.

"Touch me, Hunter," she told him, continuing to work her hips over him. "I've got you. Just touch me."

To her surprise, he pulled her back against him, until her body was flush against his chest. His hands grasped her breasts tightly, and she cried out in pleasure when his fingers teased her nipples, her head lolling back against his shoulder.

He kissed her neck even as he continued to roll her nipples. The sensation was so overwhelming that she forgot to move her hips, until he thrust into her, hard. She gasped again.

"Damn," he groaned against her ear. "I think I like you being on top, but I want to be in charge for a bit."

"I'm all yours," she told him in a trembling voice.

He thrust hard again, and she whimpered, his fingers playing on her tight, aching nipples.

"Lean forward," he told her in a voice rough with desire. "On the desk."

Excitement pulsed through her, sending another wave

of slickness through her sex. She bit her lip and tilted forward until she had her stomach pressed against the edge of the desk.

"Forward more," he told her, rolling his chair back a few steps.

Their bodies parted, and she whimpered a protest at the loss of his cock deep inside her. But she leaned forward onto the cold, smooth surface of his desk, obedient.

She felt him come up behind her, and she tilted her head so she could watch them in the mirror. Hunter's large body was positioned behind hers, and he pulled her thighs apart, stroking his fingers over her slick pussy, as if seeking her entrance. She cried out at the touch.

Then, Hunter's cock was at her entrance and he thrust, hard. Gretchen's legs were pinned against the desk, her breasts pressed against the wood. He drove into her again, and the motion was so hard that the entire desk shook. She cried out his name again. Each thrust was rough with need, and he slammed into her at just the right angle that she could have sworn he was brushing against her G-spot. "Hunter," she cried. "Oh, God, keep doing that!"

His hand anchored on her shoulder, the other on her hip, and then he was slamming into her over and over again, his thrusts wild and undisciplined. She was being taken by a man out of control.

It was glorious. She'd never been fucked so hard.

Every time he pounded into her an involuntary groan of pleasure escaped her throat. She was so close and he hadn't even touched her clit. "Oh, God, Hunter, keep fucking me."

"So . . . damn . . . naughty," he told her between rough thrusts. "You're such a fucking tease, Gretchen."

"I am," she moaned. "I like teasing you. You like it, too."

He smacked her buttock in a light spank, and the crisp bite of pain mixed with pleasure was so startling that she sucked in a deep breath, her body tensing in surprise. She glanced up in the mirror and he seemed almost as surprised as her by his actions.

His hand quickly rubbed her buttock, as if soothing the smack away, and she lifted her hips again. "Need you, Hunter."

He obeyed. With his next thrust, she began to come, a soft, weak cry of protest escaping her throat. So fast. She hadn't wanted to come so fast. Ah, God, it was so incredibly good, though. Her nails dug into the wood of the table as he continued to pound into her and the orgasm wasn't stopping. He was hitting her so hard and so rough that she just kept coming and coming, her pussy spasming around him and it felt so incredible. She called his name over and over again. "Hunter! Hunter! Hunter!"

"I can feel you coming, Gretchen. Ah, damn it. You're so tight on my cock. God, I love that." He slammed in again and rocked deep, as if wanting to sink into her forever. "Fuck. Fuck."

"Yes," she moaned, still shuddering with the aftermath of her extended orgasm.

"*Fuck*," he bit out one last time, and then his fingers dug into her hips, hard. She looked up in the mirror and his lips were parted, teeth bared, mouth drawn back in an exaggerated grimace made alarming by the scars on his face. If it was on anyone else, it would have been frightening to see.

But it was Hunter, and his eyes were closed with ecstasy, his shoulders heaving with his breaths, and she thought he was the most gorgeous man in the world.

He rocked into her one last time, slowly, sweetly, as if reluctant to have things end. "Ah, Gretchen," he breathed, panting. "Ah, fuck me."

"Again?" she teased with a shaky breath. "Give a girl a moment."

He tugged her off the desk and collapsed back in his

chair, dragging her back into his lap. His mouth began to kiss her neck. "God, that was incredible."

"Mmmhmm, it sure was," she said, very pleased.

His fingers slid between her legs and began to tease her clit. "I don't want to stop touching you."

Her breath caught in her throat and she stiffened, half wanting to drag his fingers away from her and half wanting him to never stop. "We only have the one condom, Hunter."

"I'm still in you," he reminded her. "And after my shower, I'm ordering Eldon to get a box of a hundred condoms." His fingers continued to lightly play with her clit, spreading her thighs wide and continuing to slide back and forth, teasingly, slowly, over that sensitive bud of flesh.

"Oooh." She bit her lip, trying not to bear down against his hand and failing miserably. Oh, God, he was such a quick learner. "A hundred condoms? You're very optimistic about either my stamina or yours."

"Both," he said, and his teeth nibbled on her earlobe, sending shudders through her exhausted body. "I want you to come for me again. This time I want to watch." He took her leg and dragged it over the arm of his chair, leaving her spread wide for the mirror.

She shuddered, moaning. She looked in the mirror at her flushed sex wet with arousal, his fingers teasing and circling that small bud, his cock still buried deep inside her. Her nipples were hard and thrusting, her face contorted with pleasure.

He slid a finger down to the well of her pussy, where her heat still gripped him tight within her. He ran a finger in the wetness there, then dragged it back to her clit, circling it, his eyes watching her reaction avidly in the mirror.

She came again, the orgasm exploding through her in waves that seemed to coincide with his fingers grazing over and over on her sensitized clit. Gretchen cried out, the sound ridiculous and garbled with the intensity of her orgasm.

"Beautiful," he told her, and kissed her neck again.

And as they slid apart, Gretchen was wondering just exactly who had been seduced here. She'd come into the room expecting to throw him off, to seduce and tease her way into his virginal pants. Except that as soon as he'd gained a little confidence, he'd turned into a demon in the sack.

And holy hell, she was weak with desire . . . and she couldn't wait to do that again.

Forget Lula and Benedict. They had nothing on Hunter Buchanan.

EIGHT

After Gretchen had showered and taken a nap, she awoke with the realization that she'd completely forgotten to ask Hunter if he wanted to invite a few friends over.

She suspected it wouldn't be an easy topic to broach with him. There had to be a reason why this big, gorgeous house was empty of everyone but the owner and sour Eldon. Still, a party would be a good thing. She could introduce him to her friends, and she could put Kat's mind at ease about the situation.

And she could show him that the world wasn't full of people who wanted nothing more than to leer at his face and stare at him.

She suspected Hunter didn't leave the grounds much, just as she knew no one came to visit very often. Why he'd ever agreed to let her do the letters here, she had no idea, but she was grateful. It had brought them together, however briefly.

She'd have to approach the thought of a party with a lot of tact and subtlety.

Hunter wanted to do something for Gretchen, he decided as he ran off his tension on the treadmill.

She'd done so much for him—gave herself so freely and so sweetly—that he wanted to do something for her. But what? He was already giving her money through the book contract, and just handing a woman thousands of dollars after sleeping with her felt rather . . . crass. But money was the only thing he knew, other than property.

Property. Hunter debated it for a moment, then shook his head and kept running. Most of the properties acquired by the Buchanan family were extremely expensive investment properties. He doubted Gretchen would know what to do if he handed her a twenty-million-dollar flat in Manhattan or a shopping mall in Poughkeepsie. And she might panic at the amount of money. He didn't give a shit, but he suspected something like that might be alarming to a regular sort of person.

More roses? He gave her roses every day, though. It was part of their little ritual. He needed something that only he could give her. Something that would show her that he knew how she thought and what she would appreciate.

Something thoughtful.

Something that told her he loved her.

Because he was pretty sure he did. It was too soon to tell, and there was too much adrenaline rushing through his veins after sex to know that it wasn't just post-coitus giddiness.

But Gretchen was perfect for him. He wanted to show her that he was perfect for her, too. There had to be something.

Hunter continued running. He'd come up with something eventually.

Gretchen hadn't heard from Hunter all day. His schedule had been full of meetings, and despite her longing to spend time with him—which was ridiculous, really—he had to work, and she did, too.

Her morning rose had unfurled in its vase by dinnertime, and she leaned in and touched a velvety petal. Her work had been going slow, her thoughts distracted. Every single sexual act described in Victorian euphemism in the letters made her pulse race and her imagination automatically insert Hunter into her mental images.

It made working at a brisk pace near impossible. She had tight deadlines, so she couldn't afford the distraction, and yet . . .

A knock at the door made Gretchen jump. "Come in."

She turned just in time to see Hunter, and a smile curved her face. The smile disappeared a little when she caught sight of the somber suit he was dressed in as well as the bodyguard out in the hall. "Going out?"

"I have a . . . meeting." He grimaced, the lines of his scars stark on his face. "I don't know what time I'll be back."

"Oh. Well, that's disappointing." She gave him a playful mock-pout. "I guess I won't stay up and wait for you, then."

"Actually," Hunter said, moving into the room. He stood before her and lightly brushed the back of his hand over her cheek. "If you want to wait in my bed for me, I'd be happy to wake you up when I return."

"Mmmm." She leaned into his hand, and then lightly bit at the pad of his thumb. "We'll see."

Oh, who was she kidding? She'd totally be there.

Hunter's gaze seemed to brighten, though he didn't quite crack a smile. "I'll make it up to you."

"Actually," Gretchen began. "I wanted to talk to you about having a small get-together of some kind. My agent is really pushing for a small house party here, since it'd give me a good chance to spend time with my editor and tie in the project with the house." She winced at his expressionless face. "Feel free to tell me no. I know this is your house."

After a long moment, his finger brushed over her cheek again. "Would this please you?"

"Not if it makes you uncomfortable," she told him truthfully. "But it'd get my agent and my editor off my back for a while, which would be nice. I figured you could invite your friends, though. Maybe that'd make things less painful."

"I . . . am not good with strangers," he admitted.

"Is it because of your face?" When his cheeks began to flush red, she shook her head. "You don't have anything to be uncomfortable about. I find your scars incredibly sexy."

He gave her a scathing look. "My scars are not attractive, Gretchen."

"On anyone else they wouldn't be," she agreed, getting to her feet and wrapping her arms around his neck. She leaned in and traced her tongue along the jagged line that distorted the shape of his mouth. "But on you, they arouse me."

His hand slid to her ass and he gripped it tightly, then groaned low enough that only she could hear. "I can't miss this meeting, Gretchen. But you're making me want to leave early. If you want to have this party, it's fine with me."

"Are you sure?"

He leaned in and kissed her mouth, sucking on her lower lip in a way that made her quiver. Good God, where had he learned that? "As long as you're in my bed tonight when I come home, you can have as many parties as you want."

"I'll be there," she told him breathlessly, and collapsed in her chair when he gave her a scorching look and headed out the door.

Gretchen stared after him long after he'd disappeared, then glanced at the clock. How many hours until bedtime? Too many.

Reese threw his cards down on the table in disgust. "I'm out."

Hunter's mouth curved into one of his rare smiles, and he raked the chips on the table toward him. "You should have stayed."

Reese shook his head. "I can't read you tonight. You're being . . . weird."

"Weird?" Griffin's cultured voice cut through the smoky haze in the Brotherhood's meeting room. He put down his cigar and peered at Hunter. "Weird like how?"

"I don't know," Reese said bluntly. He tossed back his drink and then shook his head. "I can't put my finger on it. It's different."

"He's happy," Cade said.

All eyes turned to the blond man. Cade shrugged, grinning. "I've seen him smile twice tonight. He doesn't scowl when someone suggests something, and he's actually participated in every conversation and not all of it about business. He's happy."

At his side, Logan turned and stared at his friend.

Hunter ignored him, picking the cards up off the table and shuffling. He handed the deck over to Jonathan. "Your deal." He kept his voice gruff, even though he was pretty sure his face was burning with embarrassment. Was he that obvious?

He glanced over at Jonathan. The other man was chewing on his cigar, his brow creased as if something troubled him. He shuffled and then tossed a chip into the center pile. "Everyone ante up."

Jonathan didn't look in Hunter's direction. *Good.*

Hunter glanced over at Logan, his oldest friend. Logan was staring at him with a suspicious gaze.

"What?"

Logan's eyes narrowed. "What's going on?" He tossed

his chip into the center of the table and picked up a card that Jonathan threw his way. "Cade's right. You're downright cheerful."

He frowned at Logan. "You're one to talk. How's Brontë?"

A grin flashed across Logan's face. "In a state of crisis. She's trying to take classes and expand her reading charity at the same time." He picked another card up off the table and couldn't keep the satisfied grin off his face. "And she keeps complaining that I won't let her get any sleep."

Hunter's lips twitched with amusement. Brontë had a remarkably stubborn streak when it came to Logan's bulldozing ways, and it was a good thing. The tiny woman would never let him walk all over her like he did his business partners, and it was good to see Logan so completely confounded and besotted and happy.

"It's a woman, isn't it?" Logan said quietly to Hunter. "That redhead you asked Brontë about. Greta?"

"Gretchen," Hunter corrected, and then couldn't hide his smile. "She's the sister of your assistant."

"Audrey has a sister?" Logan looked surprised, then recognition dawned. "Ah, right, the one Brontë stayed with for a time. Brontë likes her quite a bit." His tone implied that anyone that Brontë liked, Logan approved of.

"She has two sisters," Cade added. "Daphne lives out in LA."

Hunter glanced at Cade. "You know them?"

Cade downed his drink, then shrugged. "Old family friends. We go back to childhood. You in on this hand?"

Hunter barely glanced at his cards, then tossed a few chips on the pile, feeling reckless. "Gretchen wants me to invite a few friends over," he admitted in a gruff voice. "A party of some kind."

"Does this mean we're all invited?" Reese asked with a cocky grin.

"No," Hunter said with a scowl.

Jonathan glanced at his cards, then folded. "I admit I'm curious to see this sister of Audrey's."

"You've seen one of them before," Cade replied easily. "Daphne Petty."

Hunter had no idea who that was, but Reese seemed impressed. "No way. Daphne Petty? The Daphne Petty? The one in the tabloids constantly?"

"Who's Daphne Petty?" Logan frowned, then looked over at Hunter as if he'd have the answers. Hunter shrugged.

"An old childhood friend of mine," Cade said. "And Audrey's twin. She's also—if rumor has it—heavily into drugs and alcohol, thanks to her career."

"Her career," Logan said blankly. "What career is this?"

"Singer. Pick up any magazine and you'll probably see her sloppy drunk on the cover," Reese said. "Holy crap. I never knew. Audrey looks nothing like her."

Cade grimaced in agreement. "I know. Daphne's not . . . well. Audrey's much healthier."

Hunter thought of Logan's extremely curvy assistant and drew a blank at her face. All he knew was that she wore her hair in a bun and she was brisk and efficient and didn't ask many questions.

She was nothing like Gretchen in that aspect, he thought with a hint of a smile touching his mouth again. Nosy, too-inquisitive Gretchen who didn't know the meaning of "mind your own business" if it bit her on the chin. But he kind of loved that about her.

"Ah, hell," Jonathan said in disgust. "He's grinning again. Whatever it is, he's got it bad."

"Now I'm definitely coming to this party," Reese said.

"You weren't invited," Hunter pointed out, glaring. The last person he wanted around Gretchen was Reese, the epitome of a ladies' man.

"You're in the Brotherhood, Hunter," Cade said with a slap on the back. "You know our rules. We're all invited. Even the obnoxious ones like Reese."

Hunter grunted in resignation. The teasing died back down again and they continued on for hours.

When they were ready to leave, Hunter pulled Logan aside. "I need your advice."

"Oh? On what?"

"On Gretchen. I want to do something for her. Something that shows her how much I appreciate her."

Logan gave him a wry smile. "Don't buy her a diner."

"What?"

"Nothing. Just something I did for Brontë that backfired in my face. What did you have in mind?"

"Something . . . thoughtful. Not jewelry. She's not a jewelry type."

"Well, you dodged a bullet there," Logan said. "Then again, jewelry makes it easy. Brontë's not much of a jewelry type, either. Gets mad every time I try to buy her a necklace. The trick is you have to find something that you can do for her that no one else can."

Hunter shook his head. "I don't know what that would be. Property? It's too much. Cars? Anyone can give her a car." He didn't share that he didn't want to give her a car because he was afraid she'd spend her days driving away from the house. He liked that she was stuck there with him.

"You said she likes books, right?"

"She's a ghostwriter."

Logan shrugged. "There's your answer. Something with books. Is she successful?"

Hunter considered this. "I don't know. She writes astronaut books or some such." It had seemed like an odd match to him—his silly, outspoken Gretchen writing overly masculine space pulp, but he didn't question it.

"So buy them. Buy all of them." Logan considered a new cigar, then put it down with a grimace. "I shouldn't smoke this. Brontë doesn't like the smell."

"Buy all of them?" Hunter asked.

"All the books. Get her on the bestseller list or some-thing. That would probably make her happy."

The more Hunter thought about it, the more he liked the idea. "I'll get Eldon on it right away."

———————

Hunter arrived home late that evening, his head slightly muzzy from cigar smoke and alcohol. He'd lost a fortune tonight at the table, but he couldn't stop grinning. For the first time, he was able to smile when Reese told one of his ridiculous stories about women. He'd simply ignored comments about his own relationship without feeling excluded by the group.

For the first time, he didn't feel like a freak amongst his friends—the scarred, lonely virgin.

Scarred, yes, but lonely and virgin? No longer.

He took off his tie and tossed it to the ground, then shrugged off his jacket even as he headed down the hall to his bedroom. His cock grew hard at the thought of Gretchen waiting for him in his bed. Gretchen, soft with sleep, her bright red hair spilling across his pillow. Would she be naked, waiting for him? Her legs slightly open? He imagined dipping his fingers between them and stroking her awake, thinking of the soft, aching cries she'd make when he touched her there.

Suddenly his pants were too constricting. He stripped off his clothes while moving steadily across his room to his bed.

The room was dark, but he knew—he just knew—that Gretchen would be there waiting for him. A faint light shone through the open window, and in the moonlight he could see a rumpled mess of covers in his normally immaculate bed. On one side of the bed, a small figure was curled up in sleep.

He moved toward the bed, heart aching at the sight. Such a wonderful, exquisite sight—he'd never thought to have so much. He thought he would always be alone, reviled. Now, he had a woman—such a perfect woman—waiting for him to come home so he could make love to her. Was life ever so sweet?

He noticed something shiny on the nightstand and moved to touch it. It was a crinkle of packets, and Hunter laughed. An entire strip of condoms had been left at the bedside. Wishful thinking indeed.

She sighed and he noticed she was wearing one of his shirts. *Ah.* His cock ached even harder at the sight. Hunter ripped one of the condoms out of the package and rolled it onto his cock, then moved to the edge of the bed.

Gretchen's legs were bare and smooth, gleaming pale in the moonlight. They were slightly parted as she slept, revealing the cleft of her ass. No panties. Was she wearing anything other than his shirt? He groaned at the thought.

She rolled over and faced him, rubbing her eyes. "Hunter? Is that you?"

"Gretchen." His voice was hoarse with need, even as he moved over her and began to kiss her jaw and throat. "I need you so badly."

She moaned lightly, her legs spreading underneath him. "I was having dirty dreams about you," she said. "Am I wet?"

He reached between her legs and groaned at the feeling of her. "Very wet."

"Then come inside me," she said in a soft, delicious voice.

Hunter didn't need further encouraging. His fingers searched for the slick, warm opening and dipped a finger in as if to reassure himself that she was ready for him. He positioned his cock there and sank deep, freezing at her sharp intake of breath.

"Ah, that's so good," she breathed. Her legs wrapped around his hips and locked behind him. "Fuck me hard, Hunter."

He groaned, her words making him frantic with need. He wouldn't be able to go slow. Not this time, not with her so sweetly willing. He thrust, rough and hard, and then couldn't stop himself. Over and over, he thrust into her, every rocking push forward shoving them across the bed. Her soft whimpers of pleasure became deep, wild cries, and her nails dug into his back.

"Hunter, oh, God, Hunter. Take me deep." She raised her hips and lifted her legs a little, pushing them higher up his sides. "Keep pushing forward."

He did, the force of his next thrust pushing her knees to her breasts.

She cried out in pleasure. "More!"

He did, giving her more. Every ounce of his being was determined to pound deep into her, to make it as good for her as it was for him—tight, hot, and oh so wet.

Her pussy seemed to shiver all around him, and then she cried out in surprise. "Oh! I'm coming!"

He exploded then, as if her orgasm had given him permission to release. With a sharp cry, Hunter came into her, clenching deep inside her pussy.

After a long moment of recovery, he rolled off her and stripped off the condom, tossing it into a nearby wastebasket. Then, he returned to the bed and pulled her close, unable to stop kissing her soft, perfect skin everywhere— the curve of her exposed shoulder, her neck, her hand, her dainty fingers.

"Mmm, did you miss me?" Gretchen asked sleepily, her backside snuggling up against his front. "It was a long evening without you."

"I hope you got a lot of work done," Hunter told her.

"Eh." She didn't sound enthusiastic.

"That's too bad," he told her, and bit lightly at her earlobe, a small move that he was starting to figure out that she enjoyed very much. Her sucked-in breath confirmed it. "I don't plan on letting you get much sleep tonight."

"Don't you?" she asked, her voice a mixture of playfulness and sleepiness. "Aren't you tired?"

"Not when I'm around you." His fingers slid to her

nipple and he caressed it, eliciting a moan from her. "You bring me back to life."

It was true. He felt alive when he was with her. Nothing else mattered anymore—his face, his loneliness—nothing. All that mattered was what Gretchen thought of him.

For the first time in his life, Hunter Buchanan was in love.

───────

Gretchen paced in the library, her hand pressed to her forehead. "No. I promise. I need my apartment. I really do. I'm just doing a project on location at the moment."

"Your rent is one week overdue, Ms. Petty," her landlord said into the phone. "And we haven't seen your check."

"What if I give you a check today?" Gretchen kept her voice bright and cheerful. "I'll call a taxi and head into the city. I'll give you a check and I can date it for next week. I should have my contract payment by then."

"Next week? Your rent was due last week."

"I know! But I have the payment. I can pay the rest of the entire year with my next check, which should be in any day now. I promise. I can get my agent on the line if you don't believe me, and she can confirm the dollar amount."

"Your contract with us states that rent is due on the first. Not when you get paid."

"I know. It's just—"

There was a knock at the library door and Eldon came in, giving her a dour look. "You have a guest."

"I . . . what?" She looked at him in surprise.

"A guest," he enunciated, exaggerating each syllable as if she were some sort of nitwit. "A visitor."

"Um, okay." Into the phone, she said, "Can I call you back in five minutes?"

Her landlord hung up.

Well, shit. Surely they couldn't change the locks in the next five minutes. She'd just call back after she got rid of whoever this was and explain that she could pay a big penalty fee if they'd just give her another week or so. Gretchen pocketed her phone and followed behind Eldon, who was already heading back down the hall.

Cooper stood in the front lobby of Buchanan Manor, a box in his hands. He was staring at the lofting ceilings and spiraling staircases of the entryway as if he'd just walked into a foreign land. It kicked her amusement into high gear. Had she looked as bug-eyed as he did when she'd walked in for the first time? How funny. "Cooper, what are you doing here?"

He lit up at the sight of her and set the box down. "Hey, Gretchen. There you are." He held his arms out for a hug.

She moved into them and patted his back, returning the hug awkwardly. At any other time, she would think nothing of his hug. Now that she knew he was in love with her? It made things . . . strange.

"Audrey said you were having a hard time with your project. She said you're behind on your deadline and was going to bring you a few things to help out. I told her I wasn't busy and I'd stop by, and I thought I'd bring you a little care package from the Cuppa while I was at it."

Had he held the hug for a little longer than was necessary or was she imagining things? Gretchen pulled out of his arms and smiled. "You're a good friend, Coop. Did you bring me the brownie fudge mocha latte flavoring I love?"

"Of course." He chuckled and picked up the box again, handing it to her. "You look great, by the way. How are you doing?"

"I'm awesome, of course," Gretchen said cheerfully, juggling the box. "You want to come hang out in the kitchen for a bit?"

"I wouldn't mind a coffee," he said, and took the box from her. "Here, let me get that for you."

She refused to release it, fighting annoyance. "I can carry my own boxes, Coop."

"Yes, but men carry things for ladies."

She snorted. "Who are you and what have you done with my friend?"

He laughed at her teasing, throwing his hands up. "Fair enough. At least I tried."

The box was deposited on the kitchen counter, and Gretchen put a pot of coffee on. When it was brewing and Cooper had taken a seat at one of the stools at the kitchen island, she opened the top of the box, peeking in. There were two smaller boxes inside, one with the Cooper's Cuppa logo. She reached for the other, glancing at Cooper. "This is from Audrey?"

He nodded, though he couldn't stop staring at their surroundings. "I can't believe you're staying here for an entire month. It's like a castle."

"Oh, I know," she said, setting the box down and pouring herself a cup of coffee. "Complete with creepy butler and everything."

"I swear this could be something out of a movie," he said with a grin. "Don't tell me. The owner's some *Phantom of the Opera*–style guy intent on sucking the blood of virgins."

Gretchen spit out her coffee, coughing.

Cooper immediately got up, slapping her on the back. "You okay?"

"Just . . . breathed . . . wrong," she said, coughing between words. It was kind of weird how close—and yet far away—Cooper had been with his guess.

After all, she was the one intent on the virgins around here.

With a weak smile, she opened the box Audrey had sent. Pink lace and black satin caught her eye and she immediately flipped it shut. Feigning ease, she pushed the box aside. "What did Audrey say she was sending me again?"

"Stress relievers, I think she said. Something to help

things along." He shrugged and sipped his coffee again. "She said you'd know what to do with it."

It was clear he hadn't looked in the box. "I have a pretty good idea, yeah." At his inquisitive look, she lied, "Bath salts."

"Ah. Girl stuff."

"Definitely girl stuff." And before she could giggle and ruin things, she pulled the other box out and pretended to sniff it. "I think I smell cookies."

He grinned.

She flipped open the lid and sighed with pleasure. "Two dozen? You shouldn't have."

"And some toffee dream bars underneath, just in case you want a little variety."

She pulled out the bags of cookies and smelled the bag of coffee beans that had been included. "You're awesome, Cooper. I'm sure these cookies aren't as good as mine, though."

"They should be. It's your recipe." He was watching her with a soft, adoring look on his face. "I've missed seeing you, Gretchen. The Cuppa isn't the same without your smiling face."

And he reached across the counter to place his hand over hers.

Damn. It seemed they couldn't even go a half hour anymore without things getting awkward. "Cooper . . ."

"I can't stop thinking about you, Gretchen."

"Cooper—"

"No, please, let me say this." His eyes were pleading. "It's time I said this."

The door to the kitchen opened. Hunter stalked in, a dashing figure in his neatly pressed, too-formal-for-around-the-house-but-he-wore-it-anyhow dark suit. He glowered at Cooper and his hand on Gretchen's, then moved to Gretchen's side and kissed her cheek, his arm sliding around her waist.

A very possessive, obvious gesture.

White-hot shock drained the blood from Cooper's face. He turned white, then went blood red with embarrassment, staring at Hunter. "I—"

"Introduce us, Gretchen," Hunter demanded, his gaze on Cooper even as he hovered possessively over her.

She ground her teeth. *Well, hell. This had just gotten ugly fast.* She slid her hand out from under Cooper's and gave him a soft, apologetic smile. "Cooper, this is . . . Hunter. He owns Buchanan Manor."

"Yes. The phantom intent on sucking the blood of virgins, I believe you said," Hunter stated coldly.

Cooper's face turned an alarming shade of purple. "Uh . . ."

"Thanks for bringing the box, Cooper." She shut it to give her hands something to do and so she could quit staring at the many shades of awkward that Cooper's face was turning. "This is going to be really helpful for my deadline."

"Of course. Anything you need, I'm here for you."

Hunter seemed to glower even more. "You don't need to be here for her. *I'm* here for her."

Gretchen inhaled sharply. This was going from bad to worse. "Since you're here, Cooper—"

"Actually, I was just about to leave." He got up hastily, the stool nearly falling over with his jerky movements.

"Oh, but I was wondering if you could take a check to my landlord—"

"He said he has to go," Hunter said darkly. "I'll take care of whatever you need, Gretchen." His gaze moved over Cooper again. "He knows that."

"I really should go," Cooper said. He gestured at the door.

"Eldon will show you out."

And the annoying butler was there a moment later, holding the door to the kitchen open. Cooper headed for it, but not before giving Gretchen a wounded look as he headed out the door.

"Thanks again, Cooper. You're a good friend," she called

as he was escorted out. When the door swung shut again, she buried her face in her hands. "Oh, God, that went really badly."

"Who was that?" Hunter asked, his voice stiff with fury.

"He's a friend of mine."

"He was trying to hit on you," Hunter bit out. "His hand was on yours."

"Not through any of my doing," she admitted. "I've been trying to figure out a way to let him down easy." She glanced at the kitchen door and felt a twinge of remorse. "Guess I don't have to worry about that anymore."

"You didn't tell him we were together?"

She tilted her head, giving Hunter an odd look. "Are we together, Hunter? You've never said and I didn't want to presume."

Shock crossed his face. "We had sex."

"We had really great sex, Hunter. And I love having sex with you. But it doesn't mean we're together."

The expression on his face looked shattered. "I . . . see."

Why was he so upset at that? She was trying to give him an easy out. *Here's some casual sex with no strings attached. You're welcome.* Why was he so offended then? Most guys would be thrilled.

He turned away, and she noticed he was carefully hiding the scarred side of his face.

It hit her, then.

The phantom intent on sucking the blood of virgins, I believe you said.

He'd heard that. And she'd simply sputtered. She hadn't defended him, or protested, and then to make matters worse, she'd just told him she wasn't in this for a relationship.

No wonder he was acting wounded. "Hunter. That wasn't what I meant."

"You don't have to explain yourself, Gretchen." His voice was stiff and cold. "Spare me your excuses."

"I'm not giving you excuses, you prickly jerk. I'm trying

to tell you that if you don't want to be with me, I understand. I'm not dumping you."

He said nothing.

"Hunter!" she exclaimed, moving to his side and wrapping her arm around his waist. "I like you. I like you a lot. But I didn't want to assume this was more than it was."

"You let Cooper assume."

"Cooper's been my friend for years, and he's my boss at the coffee shop I occasionally work at. I have to handle him with kid gloves, which isn't easy when he's trying to declare his love every five minutes. I'm not interested in him."

Hunter's dark eyes focused on her again, his gaze narrow and suspicious, as if he couldn't quite believe what she was saying. "Answer me truthfully, Gretchen. Are you interested in me?"

"Now that's a silly question," she teased, tugging on his jacket sleeve. When he didn't relax, she realized how deadly serious he was. No amount of teasing was going to ease this situation. And for a moment, Gretchen felt uneasy. Like she was stepping into raw territory. For some reason, it was very important that she not hurt Hunter. She didn't want to hurt him more than anything. "I like you more than I should," she admitted quietly. "Someone like you doesn't really belong with someone like me, but I can't seem to stop myself when I'm with you. I want to kiss you until you're blushing, and grab your ass every time I walk past, and do dirty, lascivious things to you."

The stiffness in his gaze receded a bit. He regarded her for a long moment, and then his hand tightened on her waist and he pulled her against him for a hard, breathless kiss.

"Someone like you is better than what someone like me deserves," he said gruffly.

She frowned a bit at that—she'd been talking about money and station in life. But it was clear he couldn't see past his face. "You shouldn't talk like that."

"I speak from experience, Gretchen. You're the only woman who's ever looked at me and not been revolted."

Her hand caressed his scarred cheek, and she brushed her thumb over his lower lip. "Shall I show you just how un-revolted I am by you?"

He growled low in his throat. "You should."

She glanced around at the empty kitchen, then grinned mischievously. "Does the door to this room lock?"

"No."

She shrugged and began to slide backward onto the kitchen island. "Then you'd better hope Eldon doesn't walk in on us."

NINE

"You're never going to believe this." Kat's voice bubbled with excitement. "It's wicked amazing."

Gretchen cradled the phone to her ear and continued typing, logging her current letter. The month was creeping past entirely too fast and she was barely halfway through the enormous trunk of letters. She kept getting distracted by Hunter, though who could blame her? A sexy, delicious man who constantly wanted sex and gave her great orgasms? Every job should come with such distractions.

Still, she was behind in her work and it wasn't going to get done unless she threw every free minute into it. "My landlord called you?"

"No. Though I did drop off that check. He was kind of pissy about it."

"We got the payment in for the contract?"

"Better."

"What's better than getting paid?"

"You know Astronaut Bill number forty-two? *Astronaut Bill and the Tragedy of Europa IV?*"

"That was the one with the rampant disease, right? Yeah, I hated that book." Gretchen wrinkled her nose. "The cover sucked and they made me write in a plotline where Bill cheats on Uranea because he thought she was dead and they needed sex in at least three chapters."

"It hit the *New York Times* Best Seller list."

Gretchen dropped the phone in shock. She stared at her computer screen for a moment, then scrambled to pick up the phone, where she could hear her agent laughing with glee. "You're joking."

"I'm not joking! You hit number thirty-four. That's the extended *New York Times* list, which isn't as great as the main list, but whatever."

"But . . . but . . . how?" Gretchen spluttered, thinking. "The majority of the sales are through truck stops and subscriptions. I sell hardly anything through retail outlets."

"Well, you sold a shit-ton last week," Kat said gleefully. "The team over at Incomparable Books is absolutely thrilled and they want you to do more Bill books. As many as you can work into your schedule this year. They don't even care that you're late on this other one. Isn't that awesome? Steady work!"

"Great," Gretchen echoed, suddenly feeling a little queasy.

"Sales is trying to figure out what the spike in sales came from, but they're super pleased. They say that if sales keep going the way they are, they might even add your name as a byline at some point." Kat sounded impressed. "Just think. You could write under your own name."

"Great," Gretchen said again.

"So how many Bill books do you think you can fit into your schedule this year? I told them you write fast. At least four, I think. What do you think?"

Four more Bill books, as fast as she could crank them out? Her stomach churned. "I'm not sure. Let me look at my calendar and I'll call you back, okay?"

"Will do," Kat chirped into the phone. "By the way, I

was going to send you flowers but I wasn't sure if it would be apropos since you're guesting over there. But I totally thought of flowers for you. I even bought some shoes in your honor."

"You're so thoughtful," Gretchen said wryly, laughing. "Call you back soon."

When she hung up the phone, she stared at her surroundings, uncomprehending. Then, the reality of it hit her and she burst into tears.

She felt . . . trapped. God, what was wrong with her? This should have made her happy. Before today, Incomparable Books had been on the verge of booting her from their stable of ghostwriters. She couldn't hit a deadline and her books weren't what the fans seemed to want. They wanted Bill having all kinds of sexist, ridiculous adventures and Gretchen had a hard time writing that. But with the success of this book, it meant steady paychecks. It meant success.

It meant she was locked into that misogynistic asshole Bill for the rest of the year, and possibly several years into the future. And she should have been thrilled.

But instead, she just wept.

It was there that Hunter found her, still on the couch and crying her eyes out. "Gretchen?"

She turned to glance at the doorway and absently dashed a bit of wetness from her cheek. "Hey." *Damn it.* Her nose sounded stuffy.

His eyes narrowed and he strode toward her, his fingers moving to lift her chin and tilt her face to him. "You're upset."

"It's nothing."

"I don't like seeing you upset. Tell me what it is that's bothering you."

She shook her head. It wasn't something Hunter would understand. "I'm fine. Really."

He looked as if he didn't believe her. "Is it something I can fix?"

A wry smile touched her mouth and she stood, moving

into his arms. She sighed with pleasure when he wrapped her in his embrace, and she rested her cheek against his chest. "I'm not entirely sure I understand why I'm upset, myself. So no, I can't ask you to help me fix it."

"A distraction, then?" Hunter murmured.

"Hmmm," she said, chuckling. "Now that has merit. What did you have in mind? What do you do to relax?"

"I don't know if you want to do what I do. I usually exercise or work in my greenhouse."

She made a face. "Yeah, that doesn't exactly sound like fun to me. Sorry."

"I think you're not giving it a fair chance. Come on." He wrapped an arm around her shoulders and steered her toward the library door.

Gretchen hesitated for a moment, then let him lead. She should have been working, but working was the last thing she wanted to do at the moment. It was part of the reason she was so unhappy.

They headed into the greenhouse, and Gretchen was immediately hit by the humidity and the perfume of the flowers. While it had its charm, she didn't share the fascination with plants that Hunter did. They were pretty, they were fragrant, but that was about it.

He took her hand and led her through the rows of green bushes. A hint of satisfaction was stamped across his proud features as they moved through the gardens.

"Are we here to pick me another rose?"

"Better."

"Two roses? You rebel, you."

"Better," he said again. "Which roses are your favorites?"

She ran her fingers along his sleeve. "The ones you give me."

"Do you like a particular color? Scent?"

She thought for a moment. "I liked the blue one you gave me the first day."

"What else?"

Gretchen thought for a moment. They were always lovely, which was why she was having a difficult time deciding. It was obvious that whatever this was, it meant something to him. He practically vibrated with enthusiasm. "Which one is your favorite?"

"For you?" He led her past a row of bright yellow blooms and knelt in front of a rosebush covered with red blooms. "This one. Papa Meilland. It makes me think of you every time I see it."

The flower's odd name meant nothing to her, but she knelt next to him, curious. "Why?"

"The petals are like velvet, the color a deep red like your hair, and no other rose that I own smells sweeter."

She smiled at him. "All very good reasons."

"It's also one of the more difficult ones to grow."

She snorted. "You calling me difficult?"

"It's a fragile flower. It looks beautiful and hardy, but even the smallest of ailments can bring it down. It reminds me that some things require a bit more thought and care." He smiled over at her, another one of his rare yet charming smiles. "It's a challenge, but there is no rose sweeter when it blossoms."

"That's beautiful, Hunter. Who knew you would get so poetic over flowers?"

"Not the roses," he said, giving her an intense look that made her toes curl a little.

"So what did you want to show me?"

"One of my passions is the hybridization of roses."

"Wow. Sounds . . . um, boring. I think."

He ignored her lack of enthusiasm, still stroking the soft petals of the red Papa Meilland rose in a way that made her panties damp. "I wanted to choose something you'd like. I'd like to create you a rose."

Now he had her interest. "Create me a rose?"

He got up and gestured at a nearby stone bench. She

followed him and was surprised when he sat in the center of it, leaving no room for her to sit. At her raised eyebrow, he gestured at his knee.

Ah, he liked it when she sat in his lap, did he? Gretchen smiled and gave an exaggerated wiggle as she slid into his embrace, her ass nestling against him.

"Hybridization," he said, brushing her hair off her shoulder and leaning in to kiss her through the fabric of her T-shirt. "Is how all the different varieties of hybrid tea roses are created. They've been bred and crossbred with each other for the best qualities—long stems, bright colors, lovely scents. I'd like to see if I can cross a rose just for you."

"I'm always game for a present," Gretchen teased. "So when do I get to see my rose?"

He chuckled, and she warmed. Was it her imagination or did he seem more quick to laugh and smile now? "These things take time. It's a slow process of pollination and experimentation. I'll have to take one of the Blue Girl roses—that's the one you liked—that's budding and force it open—"

"Pollination, experimentation, and forcing petals? Sounds kinky."

To her surprise, he reached across her front and lightly tweaked her nipple to shush her, sending a jolt of pleasure through her body. "You do that to prepare it for pollination from the other rose. They're covered to prevent them from being pollinated from another rose."

"Rose condoms. Gotcha."

He leaned in and nipped at her earlobe. His fingers continued to tease her nipples through her clothing, and she felt him hardening against her buttocks. "Do you always interrupt?"

"Yes. But don't let that stop you."

"I won't. Do you want to hear more?"

"Absolutely," she breathed. "This is as dirty as those letters I've been reading."

He chuckled again, which never failed to cause her to

squirm with pleasure. "We want the Papa Meilland to bloom and mature. Once it has, we take the pollen from the Papa Meilland and transfer it to the Blue Girl. We let the Blue Girl go to seed, collect those, and plant them to see what we've created."

"Hmm," she said, her voice breathy with distraction from his touch. "This isn't a fast hobby, is it."

"I'm a patient man."

"You think long term, don't you?" If what he was saying was true, it'd definitely be months—maybe even years—before her rose ever came to fruition. Would they even know each other by then? She'd be long gone.

For some reason, that sent a stab of unhappiness through her. She turned her face slightly, offering her lips for a kiss. She wanted to be taken hard and rough by him to forget all about her troubles.

But the kiss he pressed on her lips was light, soft, and tender, the barest brush of his mouth across hers. "I love you, Gretchen. Don't be sad."

He loved her? All breath escaped her lungs. She stared up at him in surprise. "Hunter, I . . . I don't know what to say."

"Don't say anything." His hands continued to caress her, moving all over her body, as if he couldn't get enough of her. "I've never met anyone like you. If I live to be a hundred, I'll never feel as deeply for anyone as I feel for you right now. You bring light and sunshine to my life. I'm not telling you that I love you to make you unhappy. I'm telling you thank you. Thank you for coming into my life."

She opened her mouth to speak, but was stopped when he pressed a finger to her lips.

"Don't say anything, Gretchen," he murmured. "I'm a practical man. I never thought to have a woman in my life, ever. I thought my face would turn off any woman worth having. I never thought I would be lucky enough to meet someone like you. I have no illusions as to what this means to you, but for me, it is the world."

She smiled softly at him and snuggled closer. "Sounds like fate's brought us together."

"Yes," he said, and his voice was curiously dry. "Fate."

———————

I love you most ardently, my dearest. It's becoming impossible for me to spend even a day without you. This is interminable, these endless partings between us. I ache to be with you. My love grows every moment of every hour, much like my passion for you. I—

Gretchen put the letter aside with a sigh. For some reason, reading the endless declarings of adoration and oversexed adulations of Lula and Ben was bothering her today. Maybe she'd woken up in a bad mood. She thought of the way that Hunter had woken her up that morning—with a kiss and his hand between her legs. Nah, that hadn't been it.

Maybe it was the rapidly mounting piles of work and her ever-approaching deadlines.

Or maybe it was because she felt like a jerk.

Lula and Ben were clearly in love. Wildly, passionately in love. Every day they wrote letters to the other, going on and on about how much they loved each other and wanted to be together. And last night, Hunter had declared his love for her.

And she'd sat there and stammered like an idiot.

It wasn't surprising that this had happened. They were spending a lot of time together. Pretty much every moment that one of them wasn't working, in fact. They were having an intense sexual relationship. And on top of that, she was Hunter's one and only sexual relationship. Of course her lovely, scarred virgin had fallen in love with her. The question was, why did that make her feel like an ass?

He'd told her that she didn't need to declare love for him.

She'd only known him for three weeks.

He was a man with Issues with a capital *I*.

And yet . . . he was really wonderful for her. He looked at her as if she were the smartest, funniest, sexiest woman he'd ever met. He listened to everything she said, laughed at all her jokes, and blushed when she deliberately tried to make him blush. Sex with Hunter was some of the best she'd ever had—and what he lacked in experience, he was more than making up for in enthusiasm and intensity. He always made sure that she came. He was rich, handsome, and devoted.

So what was her problem?

Gretchen fiddled with the letter, thinking. Her gaze moved to the rose on her desk—a Papa Meilland. She recognized the dark, velvety petals and her body flushed, remembering yesterday in the greenhouse.

It wasn't that she couldn't fall in love with Hunter. She could very well see herself falling for him.

So what was the problem, exactly? Nothing, except that now she felt like her love had a deadline. Hunter had declared and she had to make a decision. A declaration wasn't something you could leave hanging for months on end.

And Gretchen sucked at deadlines. They made her anxious and unhappy, as evidenced by her up-and-down publishing career. There was just something about other people's expectations that made her freeze in place, unable to function.

And that wasn't fair to Hunter.

Ergo, she was a jerk.

She put aside the letter, then studied her manuscript file of notes. Just from her transcripts, she had almost forty thousand words and two hundred letters between the two lovebirds. Really, that was more than enough for her to build her story around. Her editor didn't need every letter transcribed, after all; no one would read an eight-hundred-page epistolary novel. They'd faint if she turned that in.

To be honest, Gretchen had the work she needed. She could go home early instead of staying at Buchanan Manor for another week, get a week's start on her deadlines, and get that final chapter of Astronaut Bill and Uranea turned in.

But that idea didn't appeal much at all, and this time it wasn't just because of the sexist space adventurer. She wanted to stay another week and spend it in Hunter's arms.

"Hell, Igor. Now I've gone all moony, haven't I?" She reached over and idly scratched the cat's belly. Igor was curled up next to her laptop, his skinny frame pulled into a tight ball. He always wedged himself carefully against the left side of her laptop, where the fan blew warm air. She didn't mind it, though because she had company while she worked. "You just tell me if I'm being ridiculous, cat," she told him with another pat.

And since she was going to stay another week despite everything, she might as well continue reading letters and looking for super-juicy ones. She pulled out the next and began to scan it, almost bored by the endless florid sexual details of Ben and Lula's encounters.

Your games grow more and more scandalous, and more and more exciting, my beloved. Last Sunday's interlude still swirls in my mind. I've played Blind Man's Bluff many times before, but this was the first time I've played and made love.

Gretchen raised her eyebrows, a bit more interested. Sex in the middle of a parlor game? Kinky. This one was definite fodder for the book.

I was so surprised that you showed me the hidden passage in the library, darling. As many times as we've made love there, I pause and wonder if someone has perhaps spied on us. Surely not. How many could know about the secret panel you showed me? I wouldn't mind going back to that room by myself, but I don't remember which brick it was that you touched to make the room come alive. Do tell me, darling.

A secret passage? Gretchen's sense of adventure got the better of her and she reached for the next letter, excited to find out more. She skimmed Ben's bolder, slightly crabbed handwriting until she came to the answer.

It's the brick to the right of the mantel, my love. If you look closely, you can see my initials carved into the caulk.

Okay, this she had to see for herself. Putting the letter aside, Gretchen got up and scanned the library for a fireplace. There were two of them, one at each end of the long room. She headed to the closest one and scanned the bricks, running her fingers along the grout, looking for imperfections. Nothing. She moved to the other fireplace, but it was nothing but smooth marble.

Huh. Gretchen paused, thinking. This was a large house and it was bound to have multiple libraries. Perhaps this was the wrong one? With the letter in hand, she gave Igor a quick pat on the head and headed out. She had no idea where another library was, but Hunter would know. Brightening, she headed for his office, smiling to herself. Now was she excited at the prospect of the fireplace door and having an excuse to interrupt Hunter. Did it even matter? She loved interrupting Hunter. This was just a delicious opportunity that had presented itself.

Gretchen headed to his office and knocked lightly on his door.

"Enter."

She peeked inside and smiled at the sight of him. Even though no one was in the house but her and Hunter and Eldon, and Hunter worked alone, he was still dressed in one of his suits. Today's was a dark brown jacket and a lighter brown tie to match. His hair was slightly tousled, as if he'd been running a hand through it. His brows were furrowed but his expression eased when she entered.

"Finished working?" Hunter stood to greet her. "It's early."

"Just momentarily distracted," Gretchen told him, sauntering over to give him a kiss in greeting. She lightly brushed her lips across his and smoothed a stray cowlick of his hair. "Am I bothering you?"

"Yes," he said bluntly. His hand moved to her waist, pulling her against him. "But I don't mind it."

She grinned, wrapping her arms around his neck and sighing with pleasure when his hands caressed her ass. "You're going to make me forget my mission."

"Mission?"

"Mmmhmm." She lightly traced a finger along his jaw, admiring the strong lines of his face that were marred by scars. "I'm looking for a secret passage."

"Is that so?"

"It's mentioned in the letters," she told him, dragging her fingers along his shoulder even as she slipped out of his arms. She seemed to recall seeing a second library off his bedroom wing. "Where are the other libraries in the house?"

Hunter seemed to stiffen. "There's no secret passage."

"There is," she insisted, pulling the letter out and pointing at it. "I swear I'm not lying. They go on and on about it in the letters. I thought it would be terrific to see. We could take pictures of it and add some excitement and reality to the book."

His mouth thinned. "There's no secret passage."

"Of course there is. Just look at this."

He wouldn't look at the letter. Puzzled, Gretchen pushed it in front of his face. He pushed it aside again and gave her an annoyed look.

"Wow, what's crawled into your panties?"

"Nothing." He rubbed his face. "I'm just tired."

"Then will you quit acting like I'm bothering you?" She held the letter out to him again, her expression daring him to take it. "I don't know what the big deal is."

His expression was immediately contrite. He pulled her into his arms, rubbing his hands on her back. "You never bother me," he said huskily. "My day is better every time I see your face."

She leaned in and gave him a light kiss, brushing her fingers over his scarred cheek. "Then help me find this secret passage."

He took the letter from her and scanned it. "The house underwent many renovations over the last fifty years. The main library was destroyed. If there was a secret room, it's there no longer." He folded the letter carefully and held it back out to her, his face impassive. "I'm sorry. I know it's disappointing."

"Oh." Gretchen couldn't quite hide her regret. "That's a shame. I was hoping to see it. I'm sorry to have bothered you, then."

As she turned away, he grasped her arm, forcing her to turn back around. "Gretchen, you are never a bother. I'm just distracted."

"By what?"

"Work . . . and you."

She gave a mock-hurt sniff. "Well, if I'm bothering you, I'll just go."

He snagged her around the waist as she turned to leave. "No you don't. Now that you have my attention, you're not going anywhere."

"Is that so?"

"It is." His hands went to her shirt and began to tug it upward. "I can't help myself. You look ravishing."

She snorted. "I'm wearing a T-shirt and yoga pants."

"You always do."

"Now is that some slight upon my wardrobe choices?"

"No, that's me telling you that I find you impossible to resist every time I see you." There was the slightest hint of color to his face, and each word was said precisely, as if flirting came hard won to him.

But he was doing it for her.

She found that enchanting. Her heart melted into a little puddle of goo and she smiled at him, her hand going to his tie. She put the letter down on a nearby table and moved into his arms. "So there's no more secret passage?"

"Nope."

"Then it seems like I came in here for nothing," she said lightly.

"Not for nothing," he murmured. "I think I have something to show you."

"Oh?"

"In my room. Perhaps you'd like to search it for secret passages."

"What are the odds of me finding one in there?"

"Slim," he said, and one side of his mouth tilted into a smile. "But there's always that chance."

"Sounds like my kind of party." She turned and tugged on his tie, dragging him toward the door.

———

Later, when Gretchen was curled in his bed, sleeping and sated, Hunter got up and went back to his office, shrugging on a robe over his naked body.

He picked up the letter she'd discarded and studied it. A secret room. *Damn it.* When he'd had Eldon purchase the trunk of letters, he'd had them tested for authenticity. They'd been carbon dated and he'd been assured the dates were real and that the letters not a hoax. He'd never imagined that he was purchasing Victorian porn. Even worse, he'd never considered that they'd point to architectural oddities that would mark the location.

If Gretchen pushed about the secret room or if she found more compelling evidence about the house in the letters, she'd piece together that the letters weren't about Buchanan Manor at all. They were a fraud.

Just like he was. He'd orchestrated all of this to bring her to him, never imagining such happiness. He'd simply wanted to experience being around her bright personality for a time.

Except he'd fallen for her. Hard. And he wasn't going to lose her to a stupid mention of a secret room in a few letters.

He resisted the urge to crumple the letter into a ball and instead set it down carefully and rang for Eldon.

Eldon arrived a few minutes later, in his own pajamas and robe. His hair was slightly mussed as if he'd just come from sleep, but the look on his face was carefully neutral. "You called for me, Mr. Buchanan?"

Hunter gestured at the letter on the table. "You didn't read these before purchasing them, did you."

Eldon's face remained impassive. "I did not. I procured them as you wished, but my instructions never included reading the letters myself."

"They mention a secret room." Hunter tossed the letter toward Eldon, his temper getting the better of him. "Gretchen came here looking for it."

Eldon neatly plucked the fluttering letter out of midair and began to read. His mouth thinned with displeasure as he did. "This letter is quite vulgar."

Hunter snorted, clasping his hands behind his back as he paced. "They're all quite vulgar, or didn't you know that?" At Eldon's silence, he shook his head. "This is supposed to be a very innocent batch of letters, Eldon. From Buchanan Manor. Not some other nameless house with secret doors and libraries. If she finds out this is a fraud, she'll leave." Sudden panic seized him and he clenched his teeth. "I don't want her leaving here. Leaving me."

"She's not a dog," Eldon said in a dry voice. "She's allowed to leave your property on her own wishes."

He gave Eldon a cold look. "You know what I mean. I want her here for as long as possible."

Eldon's long face studied him. He sighed, his expression softening just a touch. "You do realize she's almost done with the project, Mr. Buchanan?"

Hunter's pacing increased. "I thought she was here for a full month. How long has it been?"

"A little over three weeks. And she's nearly done with the trunk. She'll be leaving very soon."

His hand raked through his hair rapidly, his thoughts furious. *No. Not when everything was going so well. Not yet.* "I . . ." Words failed him. He turned to Eldon. "Fix this."

Eldon held up the letter, unperturbed by Hunter's bad mood. "Fix this? Or fix the part about her leaving?"

"Yes. To both."

"Very well. Shall I shackle her left leg or right?"

Hunter glared at him. "That's not funny."

"What do you suggest I do to prevent her from leaving?"

Hunter's mouth settled into a grim line. "I don't know. Just think of something. She needs to stay longer. I'm not ready for her to leave my side. Not yet."

"I see." Eldon ran a finger down the crease of the letter. "I shall see what I can do."

"Thank you," Hunter said quietly. "Do this for me and I'll see that you're well compensated."

"You always do," Eldon said, and turned to leave. He paused and turned around again, his gaze searching Hunter's face. "You seem troubled, Mr. Buchanan. Would you like to . . . talk?" The question fell flat at the end.

Hunter's mouth twisted into the grimace that passed for his smile. "I'm fine."

"You don't seem fine, if you don't mind me saying so."

"I'm not, actually." He gestured at the letter in Eldon's hands. "But I will be once you fix that." He was struck by the sudden overwhelming urge to hold Gretchen in his arms. "I'm heading back to bed, Eldon. Get some sleep."

"Of course," Eldon said drily.

The two men parted, and Hunter slipped back into his dark bedroom, then moved into the bed next to Gretchen. She gave a small sigh and shifted in the bed, automatically moving a bit closer to him. His arms went around her and he pulled her tight against his chest, but he was unable to sleep.

Gretchen . . . leaving soon? Leaving him? Even though he'd declared love for her and they made passionate love every chance they had? Even though they enjoyed the endless hours spent together, and she made every day worth living, every hour of work sweeter because he knew she was waiting for him?

Not if he could stop it. She would be at his side for as long as he could make it happen. He didn't care how or why.

He just knew he needed her.

TEN

~~~~~~

Gretchen crawled over Hunter, yawning, and tugged a T-shirt over her body. She searched his room for her panties, which were flung off hours ago. They hung on a lampshade, making her chuckle as she snatched them and put them back on again.

He reached for her, his eyes closed. "Come back to bed. It's too early."

"Can't," she said, moving to his side of the bed and pressing a kiss to his forehead. He reached for her and she danced out of his grasp, laughing. "Nice try, but I've got a lot of work to do."

He reached for her again. "Come back."

She wiggled away. "Nope. Can't. You sleep, though. You were up too late last night working." She'd had to come into his office to drag him to bed. Of course, he'd been reluctant until she'd started to strip. Then he couldn't go to bed fast enough, she thought with a grin.

"I'll get up in a minute," he mumbled sleepily, then rolled over and went back to bed.

She watched him for a moment, resisting the urge to reach down and smooth his tousled hair. It was a mushy, silly moment, but she didn't care. Watching him sleep filled her with an odd, easy sort of pleasure. When his breath evened out, she turned and left the room.

Breakfast could wait. She wasn't all that hungry, and she'd dreamed about deadlines. Dreaming about work always left her in an anxious mood, and today was no different. She had to finish at least one project that was on her plate—if not the letters, then that last chapter of Astronaut Bill and Uranea that she kept promising to her publisher.

But the thought of writing more Astronaut Bill filled her with the usual loathing. She'd concentrate on finishing her cataloging of the letters, then. A week or two after she was already this late wouldn't make much of a difference. Plus, she was a fancy bestseller now. Her mouth twisted into a sour smile at the thought. *Yippee.*

She padded across the manor on bare feet. The house was silent and dark, the sun not quite up yet. Hopefully that meant Eldon wasn't up yet, either. A few minutes later, she opened the door to her library.

Igor stretched and meowed at her from the couch.

"Oh, no. Did I leave you in here all night?" She moved to pet his velvety head, making kissy noises at him. "I've been neglecting you shamefully, haven't I? I can't help it. I've got a new man in my life and he doesn't even need kitty litter."

The cat gave her a disgruntled look and then meowed again, flicking his tail at her and walking away.

Gretchen chuckled to herself, then headed to her desk.

And stopped, her heart dropping.

The vase of water that she normally kept her daily rose in was tipped over, the contents spilled all over the antique wood of the secretary . . . and her laptop.

"No, no, no!" She rushed forward, yanking her laptop out of the puddle. The case in her hands dripped, and when she turned it on one side to shake out the keyboard, droplets of water went everywhere. Frantic, she pushed the power button and held her breath, waiting.

Nothing.

Oh *no.*

Disbelieving, she hit the power button again, and then set the laptop down on one of the old-fashioned couches, racing back to her room. A hairdryer. That's what she needed. She returned with it a few minutes later, plugged it into the wall, and flipped over the soaked laptop, her pulse pounding with anxiety. Maybe if she dried it out, things would be fine.

Twenty minutes later, she still had no power. Gretchen bit her lip, hard, her thoughts frantic. It was okay. She always made a backup of her work. Always. She normally emailed a copy to Kat—well, except this time she'd been avoiding Kat—and she always copied the file to her flash drive.

Which she always kept beside her computer.

Her flash drive! Gretchen bolted to her feet and ran for the sopping desk. Sure enough, her small, hot pink flash drive was sitting in a puddle of flower petals and water. She picked it up anyhow and clenched it in her hand, as if willpower could somehow restore her work.

Igor must have been thirsty, she reasoned. He'd knocked over the vase to get some water and her laptop had been in the way. She'd been so busy curling up with Hunter that she'd neglected her cat, and now she was paying for it.

Her stomach twisted into a sick knot.

All that work, down the drain.

Three weeks of work, gone.

The entire file of transcribed letters, gone.

Her latest Astronaut Bill manuscript, completely gone.

Any chance of getting paid before her landlord changed the locks? Gone.

Gretchen sank down on the couch, feeling wrecked. She stared at her poor laptop, at the flash drive in her hands.

No problem. She could fix this. She'd just start over . . .

on both projects. In a few months, she'd be able to turn both in. And then she could get paid.

Gretchen burst into tears.

When Hunter awoke, he dressed and immediately headed for the opposite wing of the house. He'd had nightmares about being abandoned, and waking up without Gretchen's warm body next to him hadn't helped things.

His loneliness seemed to be slowly ebbing away, replaced with a new, different kind of agony—fear of abandonment. Hunter shook his head to clear it, trying to will away the bad dreams. He had Gretchen in his arms. She cared for him. She wasn't going anywhere. After a visit to his greenhouse, he selected a white rose and set off in search of her, determined to deliver the rose himself.

Hunter found Gretchen curled up on one of the library couches, clutching her laptop and sobbing as if her heart had broken.

His own heart clenched at the sight. "Gretchen?"

She looked up, startled, and wiped the backs of her hands against her cheeks. "Oh. Hi. Sorry. I was just, um . . . working." Her face crumpled and she began to cry again.

Something was wrong. He'd fucked this up somehow and he was going to lose her. That gut-clenching feeling wouldn't leave. "Tell me what's wrong," he managed hoarsely, moving to her side.

She sniffed and set the computer down, moving into his arms when he reached for her. At that, he relaxed a little. If she was angry at him, she surely wouldn't be going to his arms, would she?

"My book," she choked out between sniffles. "It's gone."

Recognition dawned, and a queasy feeling hit his gut. Was that . . . shame? "Gone?" he asked, feigning ignorance. "What happened?"

"Igor must have knocked over the vase," she said,

burying her face in his shirt. "The laptop is soaked. It's ruined."

Her sorrow was tearing him apart. Hunter stroked her back. "We'll fix it. I'll call someone to come take a look at it."

She shook her head against his chest, as if denying his words. "It's my fault. I left Igor in here all night. I'm so stupid."

"You are not," he said, his tone vehement enough to make her look up in surprise. He reached out and brushed the tears from her cheek. "You're not stupid, Gretchen. Not by far."

"I should have emailed my backups to Kat," she said mournfully. "I just . . ." She shrugged.

"You just what?"

She gave him a tiny smile. "The more I work, the less I seem to enjoy it. That's all. I guess I've been avoiding Kat. Talking with her just feels like too much pressure."

It was on the tip of his tongue to offer her money or work or whatever would take that miserable look off her face. But Gretchen wouldn't want a handout. She was strong and capable. He'd have to handle this carefully.

His fingers touched under her chin and he tilted her face toward him. "We'll fix this," he told her in a firm voice. "Give me your laptop. I'll send it off with Eldon."

"O-okay," she said in a wavery voice that made him ache with the need to comfort her.

He took it from her and then leaned into kiss her lightly. "I'm going to send this off with him and instruct the technicians to not come back until they've recovered your files. But for the rest of the day, we're going to relax and enjoy ourselves."

"I don't think I can."

"Oh, you can. And we're not going to think about work. We're just going to enjoy each other."

She gave him a miserable look. "What if I have to start over, Hunter?"

He quelled the part of him that rejoiced at the thought

of another month of her in his house. Her sadness was making his soul ache.

He'd asked Eldon to fix this, but he hadn't anticipated the destruction of her computer. It was brilliant—and a bit evil. But the worst of it was that Gretchen somehow seemed . . . defeated. His brilliant, vibrant Gretchen had been replaced by a sad woman weighed down by the world.

And that wasn't what he'd wanted at all.

Hunter caressed her cheek. "I'll be back."

"I'll be here," she told him with a wobbly smile, sniffing loudly.

He tucked the laptop under his arm, noting that it still dripped when he picked it up. It was definitely soaked. He didn't know if it could be fixed. He hoped—for Gretchen's sake—that it could. Either way, Eldon had bought him time with her, just as he'd asked.

Hunter headed back to his office and shut the door, then buzzed Eldon.

Eldon arrived a few minutes later, his eyebrows going up at the sight of the laptop dripping on Hunter's coat.

Hunter held it out to Eldon. "Your work, I assume?"

He said nothing, simply took the laptop and gave him a meaningful look.

"She's crying," Hunter said raggedly. He began to pace. "I didn't want her upset."

"You said to fix it," Eldon said, deadpan as ever. "You didn't say how. You needed her work to continue to keep her here." He gestured at the laptop. "I have ensured that, just as you asked."

Yes, but now Hunter felt like a heartless bastard. The thought of Gretchen's tearstained face still drove him wild with anger and self-loathing. He'd made her cry, and he couldn't even apologize.

"Take the laptop to a technician. See if they can fix it." He glanced at Eldon, and then hated himself for saying, "Not too soon, though."

"I shall escort it in myself," Eldon said in a toneless voice. "I am sure that no one will get to it for at least a week, no matter how much I ask."

"Good."

"And if the file can be recovered?"

He had to bite back the urge to tell Eldon to delete the file. His need for Gretchen warred with the sight of her tearstained face, her misery. "I . . . I'll cross that bridge when I get there."

"Very well," Eldon said as unflappable as ever.

"Cancel my meetings today. I'm going to spend the day with Gretchen."

"Very well," Eldon said. His face was neutral, but his tone was disapproving. It didn't matter what Eldon thought, though.

Only Gretchen. And he needed to somehow bring a smile back to her face.

When he returned to the library, Gretchen's weeping was under control. Her eyes were still red, but she was moving around, carefully laying out several of the letters on a nearby desk, the surface cleaned off. She glanced up at the sight of him and waved a hand over the piles of letters, Kleenex still clutched in her fingers. "I think I can come up with a system of some kind. Not all of the letters are important, so if I make a pile of the ones—"

"No," he said, and threaded a husky, enticing note in his voice. He moved to her side and took her hand before she could reach for another one of the letters. "Today, we're taking the day off."

"I can't." She gestured at the letters and then wiped her nose with the Kleenex in an oddly fragile-seeming gesture. "If I have to recreate the document, I need to get started right away. I can't afford to lose any time. I—"

He tugged on her hand, shaking his head when she

resisted. "Gretchen, you work every day. Even on week-ends. You can take a day off. When was the last time you had a day off from writing?"

She looked up at him, a dazed expression on her face. "I'm not sure."

"You're stressed and you're unhappy. I don't like seeing you like this." He pulled her closer, pressing a light kiss to her mouth. "Take a day off. I've cancelled all my meet-ings. We can just relax."

"But my projects—"

"Can wait one day." At her disbelieving look, he forced a smile to his lips. "You can call your agent in the morning and explain what happened and tell her you need a dead-line extension."

"She's not going to be happy." Gretchen's voice wavered.

He made a mental note to contact the editor he'd hired and have a delay in launch. Give Gretchen another month or two to work on the project—and at his side. That pinched, stressed look would be gone from her face and they could relax once more. Already he missed her cheer-ful smiles and flirty banter.

He felt like he'd crushed her, and his heart ached at the thought. This was his fault because he was a selfish ass-hole. Hunter grasped her by the back of her neck and pulled her close for a sudden, fierce kiss.

If he lost her, he . . . he didn't know what he'd do.

Gretchen looked startled at the vehemence of his kiss, but her mouth softened against his and her tongue stroked into his mouth once more. A soft moan rose in her throat when he lightly sucked on her tongue.

Her stomach growled, ruining the moment. They broke apart, and Gretchen giggled softly, her hand going to her stomach. "I think that was me. I guess I got so distracted that I didn't eat."

"Shall I have Eldon prepare something?"

She made a face. "I'm a much better cook than he is. You

haven't tried my three-cheese omelet yet, have you? It'll make you a believer." Her eyes sparkled with challenge.

"I'm willing to give it a try," he said slowly, pleased to see the light returning to her eyes. "But I'm not a big fan of eggs."

"I'll make you a fan," she proclaimed proudly, taking his hand. "Come on. I'll make you a treat."

He protested, digging his feet in for a moment. "Today's about your day of rest, Gretchen. I don't want you waiting on me."

She rolled her eyes, a semblance of her normal attitude returning. "Cooking's not a chore, silly. It's fun. Now, come on."

———

Gretchen was right—she could make a mean omelet, and even he, who normally didn't eat breakfast, cleaned his plate. She didn't stop with the omelet. Before he could even suggest otherwise, she was preparing a breakfast smoothie and then chopping potatoes for home fries.

This kitchen, she told him, was a shame to waste. So she talked and told him about recipes and things her mother had cooked for them when they were children. She seemed to glow with internal peace while she turned on the oven and picked an overripe banana off the counter, then began hunting for bowls. "I swear, Eldon lets most of this food go to waste. I'm going to make some muffins for the cleaning crew. It seems a shame not to use up these groceries." She paused for a moment, then tilted her head at him. "This is lame, isn't it?"

He was surprised by the sudden shyness in her voice. "What do you mean?"

She gestured at the ingredients spread on the marble countertops. "Me. Cooking. You think it's stupid and you're probably bored."

"Not at all." It was the truth, too. Gretchen in the kitchen seemed to be a whirling dervish of ideas. "I like watching you work. I don't mind."

She gave a wry, self-deprecating snort and began to peel the ripe bananas, dropping them into a bowl. "That's funny. You never want to watch me write."

"You don't look as happy when you write," he pointed out, reaching over to snag a chunk of banana and tossing it into his mouth. "You look happy now."

Gretchen gave him an almost shy smile, her gaze on the bowl in front of her. "Writing's my job. I don't do it because I love it. It just pays the bills." She picked up a small bit of banana clinging to the edge of the bowl and nudged it back with the rest. "I thought when I first started that writing would be an amazing job. Spend all day in your pajamas and no one to answer to but yourself, right?"

"I suppose." Years of business had taught him that there was always someone to answer to. He didn't correct her, though, because he liked hearing her thoughts and perspective on things.

"Yeah, well, I get to spend all day in my pajamas, but it seems like I have more bosses and deadlines than ever before. And I'm not crazy about the work. Like . . . not at all." She frowned to herself and grabbed the potato masher, then began to vigorously smash the bananas in the bowl. "I kind of hate it, actually. Fucking astronauts and their stupid bimbo girlfriends."

"What are you talking about?"

"You know. My ghostwriting work."

He had no idea what she ghostwrote. He'd been told, but it hadn't been important to him. Apparently Gretchen wrote about astronauts . . . or bimbos. What she wrote had never been important to him, though. Only Gretchen was. "So what would you do if you could do anything?"

Gretchen glanced over at him. "Be right here? With you?"

He smiled. God, he loved her.

For the entire morning, Gretchen cooked and baked in the kitchen. It seemed therapeutic and distracting for her to pull ingredients out of the well-stocked fridge and begin to make delicious treats. And while she baked, she chatted. She told him about how when she was a little girl, she was the eldest. The twins were Audrey and Daphne, and their mother worked two jobs to make ends meet. As the eldest child, Gretchen had been the one in charge of the food, and during the summers she'd watched cooking shows to learn how to prepare meals for her sisters. She'd enjoyed working in the kitchen and it had taken off from there. Now she baked for the coffee shop and loved to cook for friends.

By the time Gretchen looked fully relaxed, there was a fresh-baked set of banana nut muffins on the counter, something she referred to as a gingerbread soufflé, tiny, perfectly shaped white chocolate scones, and pudding-filled lemon cupcakes decorated with hints of lemon zest, freshly grated by Hunter. She seemed utterly content.

She was beautiful and incredibly sexy, and he found that he could watch her for hours and never get bored.

When the last pan was out of the oven and cooling, she began to whip up frosting. She glanced over at him and then dipped her finger in the frosting, offering it to him. "Want to taste?"

His cock jerked at the husky note in her voice and the soft look in her eyes. Ah, damn. Gretchen was thinking pleasant things, and it automatically made him hard to recognize that. Hunter leaned in and took her finger in his mouth, sucking on the fingertip.

A soft whimper of lust escaped her throat.

He licked her with languorous pleasure, his cock hard as a rock in his pants. When he released her finger, her gaze was still riveted to his mouth.

It seemed they were thinking along the same wavelength. "Is it too early in the day to throw you down on the floor and fuck you?"

Her entire body seemed to tremble with that. "God, no. Never too early."

"Then come here," he growled.

She moved toward him slowly, all cooking forgotten. Her hands reached for him automatically, moving to smooth along his jaw and the scars there. He didn't flinch away at her exploring touch. Gretchen's gaze was appreciative and hot with desire, not disgusted and flinching with revulsion.

She saw him beneath the scars.

Hunter's arm went around her waist, dragging her against him. Her eyes widened and she smiled, placing a hand on his already erect cock through his slacks. "It doesn't take much to get you going, does it?"

"Not when it comes to you," he told her, wrapping his other hand in her hair and tilting her neck back. He leaned in and pressed a kiss there, running his teeth over her skin.

She shivered against him, her hand automatically clenching around his cock. "Oh, Hunter, that feels amazing."

"I want to make you feel good," he told her, licking at the delicate cords of her neck. "Tell me what you want."

"Sex. Right here, right now." Her hand pumped over his cock, rubbing through his clothing as if she could give him a handjob through the layers.

He groaned in response, sliding the yoga pants down her hips. "Yes. God, yes."

She froze in his arms. "Wait. What about the staff? What if they see us? Maybe we should hide somewhere."

He groaned at the thought. He wanted to sink into Gretchen right then and now. But she was right. "We need condoms, too." Fuck. He needed to learn to keep one on him at all times. "Fine. We'll go to your room."

"So far away? It's an entire hall or two down," she teased. "I don't know if I can walk that far."

He grabbed her under her thighs and lifted her into the air. "Then I'll carry you."

She squeaked in surprise, her legs automatically wrapping around his waist, her arms going around his neck. "I was joking. I can walk."

Hunter thrust against the juncture of her sex, settling her against his erection. "But I like to carry you."

Gretchen sighed, and she automatically leaned in to kiss him, her thighs squeezing tight around him. "I'm out of objections."

He kissed her back, his tongue slicking against hers in a wild tangle. With her lifted into his arms, he began to walk slowly out of the kitchen, each step pushing her against his aching cock. He turned his back to push open the swinging kitchen door, then continued down the hall. All the while, she moaned and continued to kiss him, clinging to him.

The walk down the long hall of the east wing to her room seemed endless. Why was his damn house so big? And yet, him carrying her back to her room was exquisitely pleasurable. Every step pushed Gretchen's warmth against his cock, and her thighs squeezed against his hips. Her breasts pushed against his chest, and her mouth sweetly accepted every thrust of his tongue.

It was delicious torture.

She moaned loudly when they got to her door, and he had to pause to twist the doorknob and push the door open. "Don't stop moving," she told him, rolling her hips and working against his cock.

He groaned, his entire body stiffening with need. "Gretchen, don't."

"Don't do this?" She tightened her hands around his neck and ground her hips against him, her lips brushing against his scarred cheek. "I want you deep inside me."

Hunter staggered into the room, kicking the door shut behind him. He carried her to the bed and laid her down onto her back, immediately rolling on top of her.

"Mmm," she said, working her hips again. "I liked it when you held me. Felt so close to you."

He sat up, stripping off his shirt and jacket. "We don't have to stop. We can make love like that, with me holding you. I just need to get a condom on."

She gave him a surprised look, and ran a hand along his bare chest, tracing the muscles of his pectorals. "I'm not too heavy?"

"Not at all." He undid his belt, releasing his pants to the ground, quickly followed by his boxers. "Shall I show you?"

"Absolutely," she breathed, her voice excited. She began to strip her own clothing off with rapid hands, dragging her shirt over her head as he moved to the dresser and got out one of the condoms. He unwrapped it and rolled it down his aching length, resisting the urge to take himself in his hand and ease the ache a little. He'd be seated deep inside Gretchen soon enough, and that would be sweeter than any pleasure he could give himself.

When he turned around, she was laying on the bed, completely naked. She spread her legs wide at the sight of him, a beckoning gesture that he couldn't resist. But instead of going to her outstretched arms, he leaned in and nuzzled at her pussy, licking the delicate, slick folds and enjoying the choked gasp that she gave in response.

"You taste so sweet, Gretchen. Sweeter than anything I've tasted." He pushed his tongue through her wet petals, flicking it against her clitoris. "I can't get enough of you."

"Then don't stop." Her hands twisted in his hair, holding his head in place while he tongued her. "Oh, God, don't ever stop."

"But you'll come," he said raggedly, and sucked on the small button to make up for the fact that he'd paused.

She cried out, her back arching, and then whimpered a protest when he pulled away. "Why are you stopping?"

"Because I need to be inside you," he said, his voice rough with need. "Right now."

She made another wordless sound of protest, but he grasped her hips and pulled her to the edge of the bed.

"Put your arms around my neck," he commanded, even as he placed the head of his cock against her slick core.

Gretchen did, and he lifted her back into his arms again, tugging her against him.

The movement caused her weight to slide down, and then she was sheathed around him, her heat enveloping him like a glove. The feel of her was indescribable and he groaned at the sensation.

"Oh," Gretchen breathed. "You're so deep." Her muscles seemed to clench around him, sucking him deeper inside, holding him tighter. Her thighs clenched against him, her ass squeezing against his palms as he held her.

He thrust shallowly, rocking his hips even as he clenched her thighs, holding her in place. His mouth sought hers, but the motion only allowed him to graze his lips against her. "Feel good?"

She moved her hips a little, rocking down on him. The movement caused her erect nipples to brush against his chest, further driving him wild. "Oh, Hunter, don't drop me."

"Never." He was strong. He could bench press hundreds of pounds. Her weight was slight in his arms. "I won't let you go."

Gretchen's hips rolled against him, and he thrust at the same time, enjoying her gasp of reaction. "Harder, Hunter."

He began to rock his hips a little harder. It was a tricky position, though. He needed more leverage. Glancing around, he spotted a bare section of wall a few feet away and moved toward it.

"What . . ." she murmured in protest as he began to move.

Hunter thrust her up against the wall, anchoring her there. She wanted to be fucked hard? He'd give her hard. The leverage of the wall allowed him better support, and when he thrust the next time, her eyes widened, her pussy clenching around him.

"Oh! Just like that!"

She was bossy in bed, his Gretchen. He loved that. Harder and harder, he pounded into her, enjoying her little cries with every thrust. Her eyes were closed tight and she clung to him so hard that her nails dug into his shoulders. And she was making deep, quivering motions with every rough thrust he made.

And he loved it.

A painting fell off the nearby wall. He didn't give a shit. He thrust harder, each movement rocking her up the delicate floral wallpaper and bouncing her back down on his cock.

"Hunter," she cried.

"I'm here," he told her, his mouth swooping in to capture hers in a rough kiss. "I've got you." Her cries were loud and wild, and it drove him fucking mad with pleasure. He ground his hips into her, his cock buried inside that perfect warmth.

She screamed against his mouth, and he felt her go over the edge, felt that flutter of muscle deep inside her, and then she clenched all around him, milking him with her body.

He bit out a curse, so close to the edge himself, his thrusts becoming rougher. She continued to whimper his name, the body shivers continuing on and on. And then he was coming, too, his own orgasm unleashing with a wild groan. He thrust into her again and then stiffened, remaining there as he went over the edge with her.

Gradually, awareness returned and he realized he still had her pinned against the wall, her legs around his hips, her heavy panting in his ear. Hunter shifted, pulling out of her and letting her slide to the ground.

She clung to him, her knees wobbly. He thought she would say something clever, something bold. Something uniquely Gretchen.

But she only wrapped her arms around his neck and buried her face against his skin, as if she needed to be held.

And he was all too happy to comply.

They spent the rest of the day in bed, leisurely exploring each other's bodies. They chatted for hours about the house, her projects, and about his work. She'd been under the impression that he didn't leave the house to work but it turned out that he did, just not often. He had several real estate companies where he owned and leased enormous amounts of land and buildings. He might not oversee every sale, but he was involved in multiple projects at once.

Her own confessions about her job had surprised him. He'd had no idea that she'd had such an intense dislike for writing. He thought she did it because she loved it. But whenever Gretchen mentioned writing, there was a cagey, unhappy look in her eyes, as if she felt . . . trapped.

And here he'd thought he'd make her happy by making her a bestseller. But she hadn't even brought it up. Perhaps it meant nothing to her. He'd have to think of another way to make her melt.

It seemed he existed solely for Gretchen's teasing smiles.

A few days later

"We could have had this catered," Hunter said, reaching to steal a piece of bruschetta from the hors d'oeuvres table.

She smacked his hand and arranged the remaining appetizers to hide the fact that he'd stolen one. "How many times do I have to tell you? I like cooking. Besides, this is only ten additional people. I can handle that."

Tonight was the night of the small dinner party that she'd wheedled out of Hunter. It was a mixer of close friends and her editor and agent. At first, she'd wanted to do it to show the house off a little and get her editor excited about the project.

Now she was hoping that with a few bottles of wine in her editor, she'd be able to get an extension.

She'd made a feast for their guests—delicate pastries, savory appetizers, and a light salad. For the main course, she'd gone with an easy favorite—pasta—and had made a few different things for dessert to show off her skills. The entire day had been spent in kitchen-bliss, as she'd worked on one dish after another.

Why she couldn't transfer some of that happy peace to her writing, she didn't know. She hadn't worked on her manuscript notes ever since she'd lost her file. Part of her kept hoping that she'd hear that they were able to recover the data.

Part of her was just really, really mentally done with the entire thing.

So she'd taken a few days off. She'd baked delicious treats for the cleaning staff, who were delighted at her efforts. She'd reorganized the kitchen and tested out new recipes. She'd made scrumptious dinners for Hunter and even baked cookies for Eldon. She didn't write a lick. When she wasn't puttering in the kitchen, she spent her time with Hunter, watching movies in his personal screening room, working out together, or learning the basics of how to cultivate roses.

This week, she was happier than she'd been in a long time. She should have been miserable, but being around Hunter soothed that part of her. He made it okay.

And he didn't mind that she might have to spend a few more weeks at his house.

It didn't fix the issue with her apartment, of course. Audrey had called her and had forwarded the rent money to her account so her check would clear, but next month's rent was coming up fast and she still had no plans. Nor had the check for the new project arrived.

She was fucked. And she didn't care. Which was weird.

Tonight's party would either make things worse or better she thought as she surveyed the dining room. Buchanan

Manor had a formal dining room with dual crystal chandeliers, wood paneling, and pastoral paintings that she was pretty sure cost a small fortune. It boasted a long, narrow table that could seat twenty and looked like something out of an old-fashioned movie. Soft classical music was piped in through the house's speaker system. Fresh roses from Hunter's greenhouse adorned the table.

Her guests would be impressed.

Hunter seemed on edge. He was dressed in a crisp designer suit with a pinstriped navy tie and navy shirt. He looked like a dark god, right down to his hair that fell rakishly over his forehead.

Gretchen set out the appetizers and eyed the wine selection. "What time did we ask everyone to get here?"

Hunter shrugged. "It shouldn't matter. It's just a gathering of friends." The words sounded curiously flat.

"Poor baby. Are you nervous?" Gretchen moved to his side and pretended to straighten his tie, all to give herself an excuse to put her hands on him. "You shouldn't be. You look amazing."

His gaze smoldered as he glanced at her. "You're the one no one will be able to take their eyes off of."

"Flatterer." She grinned and adjusted one of the tight sleeves of her black cocktail dress. She'd ordered it online at Hunter's insistence and had it overnighted. The dress was a cute, low-cut number designed to show off her curves. The body of the dress was form fitting, the skirt tightening at her knees. She'd worn a white rose in her hair just to set it off and to please Hunter. "With that glib tongue, I think you'll do just fine at this party tonight."

He gave her a quelling look. "Not so sure about that. You know I don't entertain."

"Not even your friends?"

He looked uncomfortable again. "I've never invited them here."

Really? That was surprising. She knew he kept himself

remote from others; she just had no idea *how* remote. "Well, I'm here tonight. You let me handle everything." And she leaned in and gave him a grazing kiss on the mouth.

He grasped her and turned the kiss into something deeper, darker, and far more passionate. She moaned in response, making soft noises of pleasure when his tongue thrust into her mouth with searing ownership.

Someone clapped mockingly behind them. "Dinner and a show. You really know how to treat your guests, Hunter."

Gretchen gasped and turned around, whirling out of Hunter's arms. A man stood behind them in the doorway, dressed in a casual sports jacket, his collar open. He was handsome in a rakish, too-slick sort of way that she'd always despised. And he was assessing her with a speculative gaze that made her cheeks flush with embarrassment.

At her side, Hunter had gone stiff, and she glanced over at him, expecting to see a sharp scowl. But there was none. He just looked . . . resigned.

His hand went to her waist. "Come. Let me introduce you to Reese."

They crossed the dining room, and Gretchen kept a hostess smile pinned on her face even as she extended her hand to him. "You're our first guest," she said cheerfully. "You must be one of Hunter's friends."

"I am. You must be Hunter's new ladylove." He gave her an approving smile and then lifted her hand to his mouth. "I applaud his taste."

"Thanks."

"I do hope Hunter doesn't monopolize you the entire evening," Reese said, giving her his best seductive look.

She pulled her hand out of his with a little grimace. "Cool your jets, lover boy. I'm not into dual penetration."

He looked startled, then laughed, glancing at Hunter. "I see why you like her."

Hunter simply gave his friend a tight smile, looking more uncomfortable by the minute. She moved back to his side, giving him a light squeeze on the ass to distract him before drifting away to straighten up the table again. Though she was a safe distance away, she pretended to look busy, all the while watching Hunter furtively.

Reese was still chuckling as she drifted past and began to whisper something to Hunter. He nodded, the uneasy look leaving his face. He began to whisper back to Reese, and the other man burst out laughing. One of Hunter's rare smiles touched his mouth, and she relaxed a bit.

Maybe this wouldn't be as painful as she expected. Hunter really seemed on edge about having people in his house. Still, she hoped the presence of his friends would calm him.

One by one, the guests began to arrive. She was introduced to a charming, aristocratic businessman named Griffin, and another gentleman named Jonathan, who owned an auto business. To her surprise and pleasure, Cade Archer showed up a short time later.

He arrived with a smile on his face, flowers in his hand, and gave her a big hug. "I'm so pleased that you're here, Gretchen."

She laughed, hugging him back. "A bad Petty always turns up."

He groaned at her pun, then set her down on the floor. "Look at you. Gorgeous. Not an ounce of bad in you."

She glanced over at Hunter, smiling. "I didn't know you were friends with Cade."

"We go back to college," Cade said, flashing a white grin.

"Not nearly as far back as we do," she said. She then turned to grin at Hunter, who had moved to her side.

"I see I don't need to give introductions," Hunter said in a guarded voice.

"You can, if it'll stop Cade from giving me a noogie," Gretchen teased.

Cade looked a bit embarrassed by her words. "I haven't given a girl a noogie ever since I discovered they don't have cooties, Gretchen. I think we've missed out on a few years in between."

She smiled at Hunter to answer his enquiring look. "Cade grew up on the same street as I did. The twins, Cade, and I were the only children in the neighborhood, so we tended to play together quite a bit," she told Hunter. Gretchen glanced over at Cade. "You know Audrey's going to be here tonight, too."

He nodded. "I'm not surprised. She's Logan's assistant, correct? Sometimes she shows up at these sorts of functions."

Gretchen gave a little frown. So he knew Audrey was in the city and working for Logan? Why did no one tell her these things? "That's right. I'm sure she'd love to catch up." Another pair showed up at the door and Gretchen excused herself, heading over to greet her agent and her date.

Soon enough, everyone had arrived to the party, including Hunter's friend Logan and his fiancée, Brontë. Brontë was good friends with Gretchen, so she immediately began to help with the food and drink. Her editor had arrived as well, along with his assistant and the publicist, and Gretchen spent a few minutes showing them around the dining room and talking about the house and the letters with great enthusiasm.

Gretchen introduced them to Hunter as well, but his normally reticent manner had gone stiff and cold. She couldn't help but notice that Kat stared at his scars a bit too long and then whispered to her date. She felt a flare of irritation at her agent's callousness. No wonder Hunter hated gatherings like this. People acted like he was a sideshow instead of just another person.

The only guest missing in their small party was Audrey. When Eldon showed up at the door of the dining room to announce another guest, Gretchen headed to his side, anticipating her sister's arrival. To her surprise, Eldon moved into the room alone and headed to Gretchen's side, leaning in to whisper.

"Your sister is here, Ms. Petty. And she has brought a . . . problem. Could you please follow me?"

Gretchen's eyes widened. "Of course." She glanced across the room where Hunter stood in silence near Jonathan and Reese, and she gestured to him that she would be back. She quickly followed Eldon down the hall and asked, "What's the problem?"

"Follow me, Ms. Petty," Eldon said in a disapproving voice. "You'll soon see."

She hurried behind him, anxiety ratcheting up a notch. Had something happened to Audrey? Her sister was always so self-contained and capable. If there was something wrong, it usually didn't have anything to do with Audrey. Audrey strove to be perfect.

When they arrived in the massive main foyer, everything was made clear. Audrey was in the doorway, dressed in one of her coordinated suits and low-heeled pumps. Her pale red hair was drawn back into its usual tight bun. She also looked miserable.

Draped over Audrey's shoulder was the heavily braceleted, too-skinny arm of Audrey's twin and Gretchen's sister, Daphne. Audrey's polar opposite, Daphne's hair was a dyed mess of black and pink streaks, and dark makeup pooled under her eyes. Her clothes were torn and dirty.

And she gave a goofy smile at the sight of Gretchen. "Oh, hey sis," she slurred. "Heard you were having a party and thought I'd crash it."

ELEVEN

I'm so sorry, Gretchen," Audrey said in a tight voice, shifting her weight even as Daphne slid against her. "She showed up earlier today and I couldn't leave her alone."

"It's okay," Gretchen said, moving forward to take Daphne's arm. "Hey, Daph. How's it going?"

"Greaaat," Daphne said cheerfully, and her breath reeked of booze. She transferred her weight from Audrey to Gretchen, and Gretchen noticed how slight her troubled sister was. Audrey—sensible, sturdy Audrey—was rounded thanks to her desk job. Daphne was skin and bones, and she seemed unnaturally twitchy. She put a finger to her lips and then grinned. "I'm avoiding my manager. He's trying to take my money again."

"You mean put you on an allowance?" Gretchen said mildly, turning to look back at Eldon. "Can we add another seat to the party?"

"Are you sure you want to do that?" Eldon gave Gretchen an unhappy look.

She wasn't sure at all, but she didn't have much of a choice.

"'Course she does," Daphne said, and blinked rapidly. Gretchen noticed her pupils were huge and dilated. "I'm the entertainment. Don't you know who I am?"

"He doesn't care who you are, and you're *not* the entertainment," Gretchen told her.

"I'm really sorry," Audrey said, hurrying behind her. "I didn't know what else to do. Should we leave her in a room somewhere to let her sleep it off?"

"Can we trust her not to steal the silver?"

"Um, no."

"Then no, we can't. This is Hunter's house." Gretchen sighed. "Come on. Let's introduce my junkie sister to my boyfriend and my new editor. This'll be fun."

They returned to the dining room and the soft, casual voices of conversation died at the sight of Daphne's skinny, listing form.

"Hi, everyone. This is my sister Audrey and her twin, Daphne." Gretchen winced, waiting for the explosions. The gasps. The whispers. Something always happened when Daphne entered a room.

It didn't take long. Kat was the first to arrive at her side. "Oh, my God. Is that . . ." Her gaze went to Gretchen. "You're Daphne Petty's sister? *The* Daphne Petty?"

"Daphne! I am such a big fan." The editorial assistant arrived at Daphne's side, gushing with clear excitement. "I loved your first album. I even saw you on tour in 2010 with the Lipstick Project."

"Yeah, that was me," Daphne said, brightening to the subject. She put an arm around the editorial assistant's shoulders and leaned in way too close. "They sucked, didn't they? That fucking tour was a nightmare. Hated every moment of it. Couldn't wait to get backstage and get loaded every night, just to get through the goddamn day. The drugs were the only thing that made it worth it. Shit, they had some fine ass drugs." She peered at her new friend's face. "You don't have any drugs on you, do you?"

"Um." The editorial assistant's eyes widened and she looked to Gretchen for help.

"Daph," Gretchen said in a warning voice.

"Oooh, wine," Daphne said, heading for the table.

"No wine!" Audrey said, hurrying after her sister.

"I can't believe you didn't tell me that Daphne Petty is your sister," Kat hissed at her. "She is a gold mine of Hollywood gossip. Do you think she'd let us do an autobiography? We could sell it. We're talking millions."

"No, Kat," Gretchen said, turning her agent away from Daphne and Audrey. "She's not interested and neither am I. Her life is private."

"Not that private," Kat pointed out. "She's in the tabloids every week. Is it true that her manager has her on a strict allowance? Is it true that she slept with Thomas Steele and aborted his baby? That her label assigns her handlers?"

Gretchen gave Kat a stern look. "I'm serious. Drop it. Daphne's off the table."

Kat raised a hand, indicating that she was backing off. "I'm just saying. You know where to go if she ever needs an influx of cash. Which, according to *Star Trax* magazine, is any day now."

Ugh. Gretchen rubbed her forehead, stress returning. Count on Daphne to mess things up tonight. She'd been hoping to have a low-key dinner to excite the publishing house, not try and put her sister up for auction to a group of vultures.

Brontë stepped in, smiling apologetically. "I hate to break in to the conversation, ladies, but dinner's going to be served in a few minutes. Gretchen, where do you want to seat Daphne?"

Gretchen hesitated. Daphne's high-pitched giggle cut through the air, grating on Gretchen's nerves. "Put her on the far end of the table. Let's make sure nothing but water gets close to Daphne."

Brontë nodded and moved to Daphne's side. As a

former waitress, Brontë had experience in dealing with loud, obnoxious patrons, so Gretchen was assured that Brontë could handle her.

"Is everything all right?" Hunter was at Gretchen's side in the next moment, his arm moving protectively around her shoulders. "You look unhappy."

"Just surprised," she told him softly. "Though I shouldn't be. Daphne just brings trouble wherever she goes."

"Do you want me to have her escorted off the premises?"

"No." Gretchen shook her head. "Let's just try and ignore her through dinner. I think Brontë has her handled."

Indeed, Brontë was chatting cheerfully with Daphne and escorting her to the far end of the table, away from the wine and her new editor. Reese and Jonathan were watching Daphne with an amused expression, but the look on Cade's face was sad. She knew how he felt—she wanted to cry every time she saw Daphne. She was a shadow of her former self.

"Wait," Daphne slurred. "Where's my sister?" She scanned the room, and then her gaze moved to Gretchen.

And then stopped on Hunter, still protectively looming over Gretchen's side.

"Oh, my God," Daphne said. She leaned over to Brontë and whispered loudly, "That dude is fucking hideous."

The room grew immediately silent.

Ah, hell. Gretchen put her arm around Hunter's waist and smiled, even though she wanted to punch her sister in the mouth. She knew Hunter had to be humiliated. "Daphne, this is my . . . boyfriend, Hunter." Were they boyfriend and girlfriend? He'd confessed love, so she felt comfortable saying that. She hoped he didn't mind.

Daphne just stared, blinking her stoned eyes. "He's like a bad acid trip."

"Daph! Stop it! You're embarrassing me."

Daphne giggled. "Me? What about Quasimodo at your side there?"

"That's enough," Gretchen said through gritted teeth. She strode forward, pushing Brontë aside and grabbing Daphne by the arm. "I don't care if you're my sister. If you can't be polite, you're out of here. I'm going to call your manager and rat you out."

"Daphne, please just be quiet," Audrey said in a low, unhappy voice. "Please."

Daphne ignored her twin, wrenching her arm out of Gretchen's grip. "Why are your panties in such a wad, Gretchen? So you're dating an ugly dude. So what." Her eyes widened. "Oh, I get it. He's rich, isn't he?"

Horror burned Gretchen's cheeks. Oh, God. That wasn't it at all, but everyone at this party was going to think that of her, weren't they? "You are leaving, Daphne. Right now." She grabbed her sister's thin, veiny arm. Audrey grabbed the other side. "Tell everyone you're sorry and I won't call your manager."

"Gee, I'm sorry everyone," Daphne slurred as they dragged her out of the room. "Sorry my sister is being such a lame piece of shit. Gretchen was always the fun, slutty one. Guess Audrey made her boring."

Gretchen inwardly groaned at the shocked chuckles in the room. *Great. Just fucking great.* Now she was a slut *and* a gold digger in their eyes.

Eldon escorted them down the hall, moving valuable objects out of Daphne's writhing grasp. It took the two sisters a few minutes to drag their protesting sister to the front door, but when she was finally there, Daphne seemed to calm down. "All right, all right. I'm going." She looked at Gretchen with a pitying smile. "If you needed money, sis, all you had to do was ask. No need to whore yourself out to fugly guys."

"Get. Out."

"Can I be of assistance?" Cade arrived, glancing at Audrey before moving toward Daphne.

Daphne's drunken expression softened. "Cade. You

remembered me." She held out her arms for a hug, and he moved into them.

"It's going to be okay, Daphne," Cade said in a soothing voice, stroking the thick tangle of Daphne's hair. "I'll take care of you." He nodded at Gretchen and headed out the door, Daphne huddled against him.

Audrey followed them, a stricken look on her face.

Gretchen waited until she was sure they were gone, then turned from the door, feeling as if she wanted to vomit. God, Daphne was ruining everything.

In the hallway, Eldon stood there, staring at her. A look of hatred was on his face. "I never liked you much, Ms. Petty, but I never thought you were deliberately cruel. I see I was wrong."

"You're still wrong," Gretchen told him, but it was clear her words weren't getting through. "I'm not dating Hunter because he's rich."

Eldon ignored her, clearly choosing to believe otherwise. "I am returning to the party to serve dinner," he told her a moment later, then left without bothering to see if she followed.

This was going to be a long, long evening.

———————

Gretchen paced the halls of Buchanan Manor, trying to compose herself. What a mess. She'd have to go in and apologize to everyone. She'd wanted a nice, quiet party among friends, perhaps impress her editor a little. She'd gotten a nightmare instead, and the urge to run away and not return was overwhelming. Hunter had to be miserable.

It was the thought of his misery that prompted her to return to the party. Gretchen headed back to the dining room.

Before she could open the door, though, Kat stepped out. She looked relieved at the sight of Gretchen. "Hey, kiddo. Can we talk?"

"Right now?" Gretchen bit her lip and gestured down

the hall. "Let's go to the kitchen, then. I need to make sure the desserts are ready to serve."

They walked down the halls in silence. Once they pushed into the kitchen, Kat whistled, gazing at the enormous room. "This is impressive."

"There's three of them in the manor, actually." Pride for Hunter made her offer the tidbit. "The entire house is lovely, isn't it?"

"I imagine." Kat gave her a knowing look and picked one of the slivered almonds off a delicately frosted cupcake and popped it into her mouth. "So is that why?"

Gretchen sighed at her friend. If Kat was going to pick at her creations, she'd have to fix them: She turned and headed for the large walk-in pantry. "Why what?"

"Why you're with you know who. Scarface."

She jerked open the door to the pantry and stepped inside, shoving aside cans, searching for the bag of slivered almonds. Irritation flared through Gretchen. Did everyone have to call Hunter names? She didn't even notice his scars anymore. They gave him character, nothing more. Why was everyone fixated on them tonight? And where the hell were the damn slivered almonds?

She pushed aside a bag of chocolate chips with force. "I don't know where you're going with this, Kat."

"I just wonder if you and him is about money more than lust. I mean, I get it. I like money, too, but jeez. He's a lot to take in."

"You know me," Gretchen said sarcastically, "I'll do anything for a paycheck." If her agent believed that about her, they clearly weren't as good friends as she thought. Still, Kat did seem to see the world in terms of money. She couldn't grasp the concept of dating a man simply because she was fascinated by him. Annoyed, she continued to search the pantry. "I can't believe you even had to ask me that."

"I just have concerns for you. Do you need money that bad?"

Where were the damn slivered almonds? She shoved aside a tin of baking powder and spotted the bag. Finally. Gretchen grabbed it. "Honey, I always need money. But—"

She turned.

Hunter stood in the doorway of the kitchen and had listened to every word they'd said. His face was mottled red, the scars a livid white against his angry flush.

Kat was still seated, picking at a cupcake. As Gretchen's voice died, she turned around and sucked in a breath.

"People are asking about you," Hunter said, his voice cold enough to freeze the Arctic. "I thought I'd come and check on things."

"We're coming back," Gretchen said brightly. "We were just making sure dessert was ready." She bustled to the doorway and moved to give Hunter a quick kiss.

He sidestepped her embrace, avoiding her.

Hurt spiraled through Gretchen, but she ignored it, keeping a smile on her face. "Shall we get back to our dinner guests?"

"If we must," Hunter said, his voice still ice-cold.

With a sick feeling, Gretchen suspected he'd heard far more than he cared to. She needed a chance to explain.

She wondered if she'd even get that chance.

———

Dinner was an excruciating affair. Her food was praised, but Hunter was silent to all parties, and everyone seemed incredibly awkward and uncomfortable. Kat drank glass of wine after glass of wine, and Brontë kept casting Gretchen concerned looks from the far end of the table. Determined to make the best, Gretchen was a little bit loud, a little bit brash, and kept the conversation going even when it died an awkward death time after time.

Soon enough, dessert was served and demolished, and guests began to slowly trickle out. Brontë and Logan were two of the first to go, and Brontë promised to call her in the morning, no doubt to offer support or simply to get details out of her. Hunter's other friends quickly followed, until there was no one left but her new editor, Preston Stewart.

As Gretchen walked him to the door, she chatted on and on about the letters and the history of Buchanan Manor.

"It sounds like a fascinating project," he said. "I can't wait to see the finished manuscript. When do you think you'll be done?"

Gretchen kept her too-fake smile pinned to her face. "I wanted to ask you about that. I've had a bit of a setback and need a few more weeks to hit my deadline. Is that going to be a problem?"

He frowned slightly, then shrugged. "I'll run it past our boss and see what he says."

Gretchen paused, surprised. He wasn't making sense. "Our? What do you mean?"

The editor grinned. "I'm sure you can wrangle an extension out of him." He gave her a lewd wink. "Just do what you do best."

She took a step backward, appalled. "What are you talking about?"

"Hunter? It's obvious you're sleeping with him."

"What does that have to do with anything?"

For the first time, her editor looked puzzled. "Hunter's the owner of Bellefleur Publishing. It was his idea for this project, and he insisted you work on it."

Her jaw dropped. "I . . ." She paused, flabbergasted. She didn't know what to say to that.

This new publisher that had requested her specifically . . . was set up by Hunter? Bellefleur? The floral name should have tipped her off, since he loved roses so much. The contract offered specifically to her with no logic behind it.

But why? It didn't make sense.

She needed to talk to Hunter right away. Giving the editor a tight smile, she excused herself, wished him a good night, and then hurried back to the formal dining room, where she'd last seen Hunter.

He wasn't there.

Heavy with dread, Gretchen calmly walked to the north wing and headed for Hunter's rooms. She headed for his office and turned the doorknob.

It was locked.

He didn't want her in there. Well, damn it, she wanted to talk to him. Gretchen knocked, hating how embarrassingly awkward it felt to wait for him to deign to let her in. All the while, she kept thinking about what the editor had said.

I'm sure you can wrangle an extension out of him.

She felt dirty at the thought. She knocked on the door, ignoring the twist in her gut.

A long, interminable moment passed before the door opened. Hunter glanced at her, his face rigid, and then turned away, walking back to the large desk in the center of his office. He hadn't spoken a word to her.

Gretchen followed him in, unsure of how to begin the conversation. Apologize for Daphne's behavior? Explain the sarcastic conversation he'd overheard between her and Kat that made her look bad?

But she kept coming back to something else, instead. "Why does my editor think that if I ask you for an extension, I'll get one?"

Hunter looked up from his computer screen, then flicked his gaze away again as if she were unimportant. He began to type once more. "He has a big mouth. It seems to be a trend with our dinner guests."

"Daphne's not herself." Gretchen moved toward his desk, wishing that he'd stop typing for just a minute and look at her, really look at her. "She's under a conservatorship because she can't seem to stay out of drugs and alcohol. Audrey's spent half her life cleaning up Daphne's messes."

"I don't give a shit about your sister," Hunter said coldly. "Is that what you came in here to talk about? I'm busy."

She flinched. "You overheard me talking to Kat, didn't you? You can't possibly think all that is true."

"What part's not true? You weren't exactly refuting her claims."

"I would never sleep with you just to get to your wallet. I'm a little hurt that you think I would."

"What am I supposed to think, Gretchen? Your sister proclaims to our dinner party that you enjoy the company of men. Quite a few men, it seems."

"So I was a little loose in my teenage years. So what?"

"And that you're sleeping with an ugly man for money. And you don't deny it." He stopped typing and gave her an icy look. "And I find you having the exact same conversation with your agent, and again, you don't deny it. Exactly what am I supposed to think?"

"Well, for starters, you can trust me," Gretchen snapped.

His jaw flexed, as if he were trying hard to keep his temper in check. He said nothing.

"You really think I'm sleeping with you because you're rich?" She was incredulous.

"I'm trying to think of another reason why you would," Hunter said, his voice crisp. "After all, it is acknowledged that I'm quite ugly. And looking back, you came on to me. So yes, it's looking rather suspicious in my mind."

"Your feelings are hurt," she said, shaking her head. "And you're taking it out on me."

He shook his head. "You're not the person I thought you were. That much is clear."

"And who did you think I was? I've never lied about my family or my finances. You never asked. Why do you think I work all the time at a job that makes me miserable?" She snorted. "It's not my stunning work ethic."

He said nothing.

"And for the record, I came on to you because I wanted you. Because I was drawn to you. You seemed lonely and ached to have someone touch you. And I guess I'm stupid, because I wanted to touch you and rock your world. I guess that was a bad call on my part."

"I guess it was."

She bit her lip, thinking. This conversation was going nowhere. Worse, it was making her confused. She'd come in here to apologize to him for her sister's behavior, and now she was having to apologize for her own? For the grave crime of falling for a man who didn't trust her? It was laughable.

No, it was heartbreaking.

Gretchen crossed her arms over her chest. "I'm sorry if my friends hurt your feelings—"

"They didn't hurt my feelings. They simply showed me the truth of who you are. I should have known you were too good to be true. All those words you said, just words."

She flinched again. "What words?"

"Your talk of not caring what a man looked like as long as he made you happy. It turns out that you don't care what a man looks like as long as he has a full wallet."

"That's a lie and you know it. And what are you talking about? When did I ever say anything about men and their looks?" Where on earth was this coming from? She couldn't recall having a conversation with him where they discussed what she looked for in a man. Strange.

"Ask Brontë. Remember? You told her that rich men thought they were the heroes of the fairy tale but they were truly the villains."

Huh? She stared at him, trying to piece together the whirlwind of accusations. The last long conversation she'd had with Brontë was when they were picking up books on Audrey's request. They'd talked about men then, but they'd been alone in the empty house. Unless . . .

"You were spying on me," she said slowly. "That day at the house."

He gave her a cutting look and turned away, but not before she saw the hint of red rising in his cheeks.

"It's true, isn't it? You saw me that day. How? And what does that have to do with anything?"

He was silent.

Her mind raced. She vaguely recalled her conversation with Brontë in the empty house, but only because she'd tried to give her friend relationship advice. Not that she was a great expert on relationships herself. "I don't understand what that has to do with anything. We didn't know each other then. I didn't meet you until I moved into this house."

This house.

Something clicked. Her publishing contract specified that she had to live in the house that Hunter Buchanan owned. Hunter, who'd been spying on her before she knew he existed. She gasped. "And you own a new publisher that contacted my agent out of the blue and offered a big paycheck as long as I lived on location. At your house. You set this all up, didn't you?"

He stared at her, silent, his jaw clenched. But he wasn't denying it.

Suddenly, things clicked into place. The weird contract. The editor's odd comments. The fact that Hunter didn't seem to know a thing about what kind of books she wrote. Eldon's dismissive dislike of her. Her mysterious bestsellerdom.

She gasped again. "I didn't become a bestseller, did I? Not really? Did you buy all those books?"

"I wanted to do something nice for you. It seems I am a fool."

Horror crashed through her. "You set this all up to bring me here. There's no new publisher. The letters . . . are those fakes?" When he continued to be silent, her stomach churned. She felt sick. "No wonder the details never matched the house. It's not this house, is it? None of it's real. You basically paid me to come and live at your house for a month so I'd be around you and fall in love with you?"

His mouth twisted, the scar at the corner of his lip livid. "Don't try and throw love into this now, Gretchen. We're both not fools enough to believe you're really in love with me."

Revulsion hit her. She *did* love him, and he was a monster. "I can't believe you did this," she said brokenly. "I can't believe you went to such levels just to try and get me to sleep with you."

"It's not like that," he snarled.

"Isn't it? Isn't that what you did?" Gretchen waved an arm, furiously gesturing at her surroundings. She was angry, but more than that, she was hurt. Betrayed to her core. "Isn't all this and me being here because you wanted to fuck me? Don't you care that you're ruining my life? You can't just play with people's livelihoods because you're bored and lonely, Hunter Buchanan. Reality doesn't work that way."

"Doesn't it? You certainly came running the moment you heard the dollar amount."

She reeled as if struck. "You really do think that of me. After all we've been through."

"What am I supposed to believe, Gretchen? That you saw my face and thought you needed to have a man like me? You'll forgive me if I don't quite fall for that again."

She wanted to vomit. She had been excited about the money and the adventure. Now she wanted nothing to do with it. She just wanted to get away from here. Away from him and his awful, cold accusations. "Well, thank you for making me feel like a whore," she told him in a light voice, though it trembled with control. "It's good to know where I really stand with you. I thought I cared for you and that you cared for me, but I guess I was mistaken in that, wasn't I?" She laughed bitterly. "I guess we're both in love with a person who didn't exist."

He said nothing. After a long, pregnant pause, he began to type again.

The conversation was done. She shook her head sadly

and left the room, closing the door behind her. As soon as the door closed, the tears began to flow. Hot and painful, Gretchen swiped at them but they seemed to keep coming no matter what she did.

You certainly came running the moment you heard the dollar amount.

The walk back to her lonely room seemed endless. The halls were silent and dark, Buchanan Manor as austere and forbidding and unfriendly as ever. When she opened the door, Igor looked up from his position on the foot of the bed and mewed a greeting.

She closed the door behind her and leaned against it, her limbs feeling heavy and lethargic. "We're going home tomorrow, Igor," she said softly. "We're done here."

The cat simply flicked an ear at her, and then lowered his head again.

It seemed no one was impressed with her lately. Figured. She headed to the bed and moved to stroke his ears. "I wonder if it was even you that knocked over that glass of water, Igor. I'm starting to think Hunter tramples on anyone just to get what he wants. No wonder he's alone."

But even as she said the words, she ached inside. Why was it that the man was slowly and methodically destroying her life and she wanted to comfort him? She must be crazy.

What was even sadder? Her accidental declaration of love hadn't been a lie—she did love him.

She loved him, but she couldn't be in a relationship with a man who claimed to love her but didn't respect her and treated her like a pawn.

With a heavy sigh, Gretchen picked up her suitcase from under the bed and laid it flat. Time to pack.

TWELVE

She'd lied to him the entire time.

The agony of it tore through Hunter all night. Over and over, he heard the conversation in his mind.

You know me. I'll do anything for a paycheck.

He'd thought she was different. He'd dared to hope that someone as vibrant as Gretchen would care for him. No—he hadn't even hoped for that. He'd simply wanted to be around her, to bask in her presence like an adulating teen boy. It was her who had made the first move, her who had seduced him and made him hope for more.

And that made it worse, so much worse.

Because now he knew what he was missing out on. He craved her body and wanted her curled up against him. Wanted to sink deep inside her and forget the outside world. Wanted to hear those soft cries she made when he pleased her. He wanted to talk to her, hear her laughter, see her eyes shining with joy.

He didn't want her to go. Even after all that had been

said and done, a heartless woman at his side that pretended to love him was torture, but it was better than being alone.

He simply needed to swallow his pride and offer her a new kind of deal—no pretenses to their relationship. No lies. No pretending. Gretchen clearly had a price tag and he could pay it.

And over time, perhaps the ache of it would go away. Perhaps he'd learn to not care that when she cried out under him, she was repulsed by his face and the scars that lined his body. Perhaps he wouldn't mind that when she smiled, she was simply biding her time.

He'd simply have to become better at hiding his own emotions.

———————

After a fitful night of sleep, Hunter awoke and dressed in one of his more somber suits. He'd confront Gretchen and offer her a new business deal this morning. But when he arrived at her suite, he found the room straightened and her heading for the door with her suitcase under one arm, cat carrier in the other.

"Where are you going?"

She looked surprised to see him, but then the hurt look returned to her face. She wasn't good at masking her emotions. Maybe she never had to, not like him. Because right now she looked miserable and wounded. "I'm leaving. I just need to call a cab."

He pretended to straighten his sleeves, adjusting his jacket. "You haven't finished the project you were hired for."

"It was delayed," she said in a cutting voice. "Though I'm guessing the delay was just as manufactured as the project, wasn't it?"

He didn't deny it.

She sighed, as if defeated. "Good-bye, Hunter."

"Wait." He stopped her when she tried to move past him. "You need to hear what I'm going to say."

A wary hope shone in her eyes and she paused, setting down her suitcase. "What is it?"

Hunter studied her upturned face, which was so lovely. So hopeful. So deceitful. "I've decided that I don't care that you only want me for my money. I have more than enough of it. If you stay with me, I'll continue to pay your bills as long as you continue to provide companionship . . . at all levels."

The hope in her eyes withered and died. Now she simply looked angry. "You said you loved me just a few days ago."

"What I feel for you has no bearing on a business arrangement. I want your body. I want what we had before. Name your price."

Gretchen shook her head at him, incredulous. "You're killing me, Hunter."

"One million."

Her breath caught. "Fuck you. You can't buy me like that."

"No?" His mouth twisted into a bitter smile. "You don't approve of the direct route? Very well, then. I'll speak with Preston Stewart and see about contracting another on-site project for you. I'm sure we can arrange something."

Her eyes brimmed with tears. "I ache for you, Hunter," she said in a quiet voice. "That you think such awful things of me, and that you're so lonely that you're still willing to have someone at your side despite thinking they loathe you. That they're turned off by your face. You deserve to have someone who loves you." A tear slipped down Gretchen's cheek. "I wish you nothing but the best. I really do."

She moved to go past him and he stepped in front again.

"Two million."

She shook her head. "Someday you're going to learn that money can't buy everything, Hunter. You can't manipulate people just because you have a bigger wallet. It's going to make you very, very lonely."

"Three million," he said quietly.

"Good-bye, Hunter."

She left the room, leaving him a little surprised and feeling a bit more alone than ever. He'd thought she'd wanted his money. But he'd offered three million dollars for her to give him exactly what they'd already had. Did she want more money? Was this another game just to fleece him out of his wealth?

Or could it be that she truly didn't want his money? Just him?

He touched the scars on his face.

Scarface. Quasimodo.

Impossible.

———————

The office phone rang.

Without letting it go to a second ring—the assistant in her couldn't stand to leave someone waiting—Audrey picked up the phone and gave her cheeriest, most efficient greeting. "Logan Hawkings's office, Audrey speaking."

"Hey, it's me." The soft, sweet voice of Brontë Dawson, Logan's fiancée, was impossible to mistake. "I need to talk to Logan, but I'm glad I got you first."

"Oh?"

"I wanted to see how things were going with your sister," Brontë asked. "How is she doing?"

Her sister. Audrey's mind immediately filled with mental flashes of sickly, wasted Daphne, sprawled facedown on her floor. Daphne, who was on the cover of the latest tabloid, staggering out of a club at four a.m. with coke-ringed nostrils. Daphne, who kept promising her twin over and over again that she was going to change. That this time, she meant it.

"She's a mess," Audrey said in a flat voice. "Nothing new about that."

"Oh, no. Poor Gretchen. She must be taking this breakup so hard."

For a moment, Audrey didn't follow Brontë's comment. "Gretchen?"

"Yes. Your sister?"

"Oh." A hot flush crept up her face. That was right. She had two sisters. It was just that she normally didn't have to worry about Gretchen nearly as much as she did Daphne. Gretchen was impulsive and headstrong, but she knew how to take care of herself. Daphne was a mess. "Gretchen's having a tough time," Audrey said. "She lost her apartment so she's staying with me."

"Does she need money?"

"Money's not a problem. Daph has money. Gretchen could ask me for money. She wouldn't take it, though. And money seems to be the least of her problems." Audrey sighed, trying to hide her annoyance. "She just sits on my couch and cries all day long."

"Cries? Gretchen? Really? She seems so . . . strong."

"Well, not when she's dumped," Audrey said briskly, pulling out the stack of mail on her desk and beginning to quickly sort it. "She hasn't moved from my sofa in two days. She just keeps watching bad movies and reading my books and weeping. I came home yesterday to find her sobbing her brains out at *Phantom of the Opera*. She kept going on and on about how Christine was a bitch because the Phantom needed her love and support."

"Oh, jeez. That's awkward."

"You're telling me."

"You know, I never thought Hunter would hook up with Gretchen. He just seems so . . . remote." Brontë sounded distressed. "I wish I could help her."

"I can send her to your place for a few days."

Brontë laughed. "Somehow I don't think Logan wants to watch *Phantom*."

Yeah, well, neither did Audrey. She had enough trouble on her hands with Daphne. Gretchen's misery just compounded things and made her feel even more helpless. If there was one thing Audrey didn't like, it was feeling helpless. Give her a problem she could tackle any day of the week. Emotional stuff? She was not good with that. "I'm not quite sure what to do with her."

"Well, it's obvious! We have to get the two of them back together. Hunter's so lonely and Gretchen's so bold and clever. I think she's good for him. Logan said that he'd never seen Hunter happier than when they were together."

Audrey tried to picture the grim-faced billionaire as happy. She couldn't. Still, it was obvious that their breakup had devastated her normally easy-going sister. "I'm not good with match-making, Brontë. Fair warning."

"Me either. But we'll ask Logan to intercede. Hunter will listen to him."

"What's this 'we' stuff?" Audrey said drily. "You're his fiancée. I'm merely the hired help."

Brontë laughed again. "Okay then, I'll handle it. Put me through to him."

"Just get her off my couch," Audrey said with a smile, and then patched the call through.

Having one troubled sister was plenty for Audrey. The last thing she needed were two miserable sisters living with her. If Brontë and Logan could fix the situation with Gretchen, so much the better. Audrey loved her sister, but she was helpless when it came to relationships.

Her twin was proof of that.

THIRTEEN

～

Even a week later, Hunter still craved her.

He'd fucked up somehow; he'd offended her with his offer and instead of going back to his bed and resuming their stable relationship full of lies, she'd left him.

He felt more alone than ever before.

There was Eldon, of course, but Eldon was hired to assist him with tasks, not to offer companionship. He'd preferred that for so long, and yet now? Now the house seemed too quiet, too lonely.

Hunter hadn't realized how quickly Gretchen had changed his life. How much he'd had to look forward to now that she was in it. When he reached across the bed, it was empty. There was no warm, cheerful smile to wake him in the morning, no one to bring him coffee before turning to her own work. No one to walk through the gardens with. No one to appreciate his efforts in the greenhouse. No one to talk over his day with. No one to caress and hold and love. No one to say bold, exciting things to shock him out of his shell.

He needed Gretchen back.

Rubbing his face to clear his mind, Hunter scanned the ever-growing list of unopened emails in his inbox. For some reason, he hadn't had much of an appetite for work this week, and things were piling up. He scanned them with disinterest, pausing at Preston Stewart's name. He clicked on it.

Buchanan,

It seems we're in need of a new ghostwriter for our launch book. Any suggestions? Let me know who you have in mind.

Preston

Hunter immediately dialed the man's phone number, his heart pounding.

"Preston Stewart speaking."

"Why do we need a new ghostwriter?"

"Ah. Mr. Buchanan. Very nice to talk to you again. I wanted to tell you how much I enjoyed the party the—"

"Explain to me," Hunter said, cutting in through the editor's niceties, "why we need a new ghostwriter."

"Well," Preston said. "I got a call from Ms. Petty's agent earlier today. She's off the project. Since we haven't signed anything, there's no money to collect as of yet. Kat and I were still working on negotiations—"

"What do you mean, she's off the project?"

"I mean she quit. She doesn't want to do it."

"Did you offer her more money?" *Gretchen needed that money, didn't she?*

The editor laughed. "Mr. Buchanan, that's not how publishing works. I—"

Hunter hung up. He stared at the phone, thinking. Gretchen had quit. To teach him another lesson? But her agent had said she needed money. He didn't understand.

Damn it, he didn't understand women. He didn't

understand any of this. Frowning, he thought to himself for a moment, then stared at his monitor. He wanted to call Gretchen's agent, see what was going on. He didn't remember her name, though. Kat something. That wouldn't get him very far. There were a million agents in New York City. He drummed his fingers, thinking.

Then he jolted to his feet. Of course. Logan's assistant was Gretchen's sister. She'd know where Gretchen went off to . . . and she'd know why Gretchen declined the contract. He wanted answers.

Hunter hit the speaker button on his phone. "Eldon?"

"Yes, Mr. Buchanan?" The assistant's voice was as cool and monotone as ever.

"Bring the car around. I need to go out."

He waited for Eldon to ask where. To protest. To tell him he was busy and couldn't drop everything at a moment's notice. To crack a joke.

Something.

But all Eldon said was "Of course."

Hunter was on edge the entire drive. Traffic was bad this time of day, and he had to bite back his impatience. It wouldn't do any good to lose his temper at Eldon since he wouldn't even raise an eyebrow.

Eventually they pulled up in front of Hawkings Conglomorate's primary office building. "Wait here," Hunter said in a clipped voice. He got out of the back of the sedan before Eldon could get out to open his door. "I'll be back shortly." He slammed the door to the sedan and crossed the sidewalk, dodging pedestrians. Normally he'd tense up, his nerves on edge, waiting for people to stare at his face and flinch. To stagger backward and move out of his way.

Today, he didn't have time for any of that bullshit.

He headed into the building, ignored the lobby full of people, and headed for the elevator. The receptionist didn't stop him because he was a recognizable face and had been here several times before. Jamming the button on the elevator, he impatiently waited for it to rise to the top floor. When it did, he stalked down the hall to Logan Hawkings's office.

Audrey would be there. And she would know where Gretchen was and why she'd refused the contract that he'd more or less put together specifically for her.

But when he burst into Logan's office, the secretary's desk was empty.

Hunter gritted his teeth in frustration. Was fate working against him? He raked a hand through his hair and then pushed open the door to Logan's office.

Logan had his feet kicked up on the corner of his desk, a headset on. He was obviously on a conference call. He frowned at Hunter's burst into his office and toggled a button on his headset, speaking into the microphone. "I've had something come up. Someone send me the meeting notes when you're done." He disconnected the call and swung his feet down from the desk, casting an irritated look at Hunter. "Don't you knock?"

"Where's Audrey?" A sharp burst of fear hit him. What if Gretchen left town just like Brontë had? Logan had had hunted her down, only to find out that she was right under his nose. He didn't want Gretchen leaving. He wanted her back, damn it.

"Probably getting my lunch from the cafe downstairs. Calm the fuck down. What's wrong with you?" Logan's brows furrowed.

"I need to find Gretchen." Hunter moved in front of Logan's desk, ignoring the chair offered to him. Instead, he clasped his hands behind his back and began to pace.

"So you admit that you fucked up?"

He gave Logan a scathing look. "What are you talking about? What do you know?"

Logan shrugged, putting his hands behind his head and leaning back in his chair, his pose far too leisurely to suit Hunter. "I know that Brontë's been talking to Gretchen."

"And?"

"And," Logan stressed, "she says she's really upset. Cries a lot. You fucked it up, didn't you?"

He'd thought Gretchen was angry at him. She was crying? Hunter's heart felt like it was being ripped out of his chest. "What did she say?"

"First you tell me what you did."

Hunter collapsed in the chair, frustrated with the situation. With everything. "She found out the project was a sham."

"And that made her cry? Damn, she's a sensitive type, isn't she? I wouldn't have pictured her as the type—"

"Then I accused her of sleeping with me for money."

"Ah."

"And then when she was packing, I told her that I didn't care if she loved me or not. I'd pay her to use her body regardless of how she felt." Now that he was recounting it, it sounded awful even to his own ears. "She turned it down."

Logan grimaced. "Yeah. I'd say you fucked it up."

"Shit." Hunter suddenly felt weary. "I thought for sure that she was using me for my money. Her agent said—"

"Her agent thinks everything's about money," a tart female voice interrupted. "Or didn't Gretchen tell you that?" Audrey strolled forward and came into sight, no-nonsense in a stern bun and oatmeal-colored tweed, her round face scowling. "Or were you too busy calling her a whore and a money grubber?"

"Audrey, this is not the place—" Logan began.

"The door was open," Audrey replied in a cool voice. "I'm sorry. I overheard. I'll leave."

"No! Stay." Hunter studied Gretchen's sister. "What makes you so sure she wasn't with me for my money?"

Audrey's mouth drew into a thin line. "Because," she bit out. "If she wanted to freeload off someone, she'd freeload off Daphne, who has millions. Or Cooper, who's so in love with her that he'd buy her whatever she wants. Why would she need to sleep with someone for that?"

Hunter's hands clenched into fists. Cooper. The friend

who was in love with her. That bastard had better stay away from his woman.

"I suppose the better question is, what made you think Gretchen wanted you for your money?" Audrey asked. "Did she ever give you reason to think that?"

"Every time she looked at me," he snarled. "I'm supposed to believe that she wants to be with this?" He gestured abruptly at his face, at the scars that were impossible to miss, that distorted the side of his face.

Audrey's cold expression softened. "Why is that so hard to believe?"

"Because I'm a monster."

"My sister's a romantic," Audrey told him. "Maybe she likes monsters."

He didn't care. He just wanted Gretchen back in his bed. In his life. Laughing and smiling and bringing brightness and joy to every corner of his life. "Why'd she turn down the writing project? She needs the money."

"She doesn't need the money that bad," Audrey said, sidling towards Logan's desk and setting down a paper-wrapped sub, along with a soda. "She'd rather be broke than work on that project a moment longer."

Because he'd fucked it up. He'd had a woman—a smart, funny, beautiful woman who loved him for him and didn't give a shit about his hideous face—and he'd somehow driven her away.

He'd been so utterly convinced that he was unlovable that he'd pushed away the only person who had given him kindness and affection. He'd been so broken that he automatically assumed the worst.

But he needed Gretchen. And he'd do anything to have her return to his side. "How do I get her back?"

"Groveling," Logan pointed out. "Take it from me. Lots of groveling."

Audrey's lips quirked in a hint of a smile. "That's a start."

FOURTEEN

⌒

Gretchen turned the page in her paperback and reached for another Kleenex, weeping.

"You okay?" To her side, Cooper was scooping out coffee beans to put into the grinder. He gave her a concerned look.

"Yeah." She sniffed and waved the paperback. "It's just my book."

"Sad ending?"

"Something like that," she mumbled, dog-earing the page and tucking the book under the counter. Actually, it was a romance. Audrey read the darn things like crazy, and her house had been full of them. Gretchen had picked one up on a whim and then been unable to stop reading them. The stories were so perfect. Even though bad things happened to the hero and heroine, everything would turn out okay in the end. They always did. She'd teared up when the hero had admitted love for the heroine, and then the heroine had joyfully exclaimed that she'd loved him back as they'd galloped on horseback to the hero's castle. The epilogue was full of sweet cuddling and hints of future babies. It was saccharine and ridiculous.

And she could not stop crying over it.

Her own relationship? Hadn't exactly been that clean cut, that fairy-tale wonderful. She'd gotten the admission of love, but she'd chickened out. Of course, then her Prince Charming had accused her of wanting him for his money, and more or less called her a gold-digging slut.

Strange how being called a whore by the man you loved tended to hurt so much, she thought wryly.

Gretchen opened up the back of the glass pastry counter and began to add some of the fresh-baked cookies she'd made to the decorative plates in the front. Some things just didn't work out like the stories, she supposed. Some people were too damaged.

Even as she thought it, she scowled. There was no reason for her to be thinking like that. The only thing damaged on Hunter was his damn pride.

Gretchen picked off a wedge of broken cookie and tossed it in the garbage. Hunter needed to get over that hang-up about his face and come to terms with the fact that not everyone was out to get him. He needed to learn how to trust people.

"You sure you're okay?" Cooper said, coming to her side. He patted her shoulder awkwardly, then dropped his hand. "I hate seeing you so unhappy."

"I'm fine, really," she told him, but couldn't force a cheerful smile to her mouth. Things were still awkward with Cooper. She'd come back to work because she needed money—though not badly enough to beg druggie Daphne—and because she was driving Audrey crazy after a week of lounging on her couch in her pajamas. Even Igor seemed to be giving her cranky looks.

But Cooper was still hovering in a way that made Gretchen edgy. Any minute now, she expected to turn around and see him ready to confess his love again. They were nothing but friends, but—

"Gretchen," Cooper began, his voice soft.

She squeezed her eyes shut. "Oh, Cooper, please don't—"

"I know," he said quickly. "I know. It's weird between us right now, isn't it? I should have never said anything."

He sounded so unhappy with himself that she winced. "It's not that, Cooper. I just . . . wish we could go back to the way things were before, you know?"

"Before I gave you my heart and you stomped it to pieces?"

Gretchen turned, her eyes wide in shock. "I—"

"I'm kidding," he said with a sheepish grin. "I'll be honest, I wish things could be different between you and me. But even what we had before was better than what we have now. I know you don't care for me the way I care for you. And that's fine, Gretchen. But it hurts me that we can't even be friends anymore. I'd rather we acknowledge the problem, move past it, and get back to being just Gretchen and Cooper."

Her eyes began to water again, and she sniffed, reaching for the wads of Kleenex she had stuffed in her apron. "I'm so sorry, Coop."

"Hey," he said softly. "Don't apologize." He reached out and pulled her into a friendly, warm hug. "I'm sorry I got all weird on you when you needed a friend the most."

She wrapped her arms around him, sniffing hard. "You're such a good friend. I'm not normally this emotional."

"I know," he said dryly, rubbing a hand up and down her back.

She clung to him for a moment, enjoying the hug and the simple comfort of a friend. "I'm glad that we're going to go back to just being Gretchen and Coop," she mumbled against his shoulder. "And I'm sorry I didn't fall in love with you. If I could have picked to fall in love with someone, it would have been you."

He chuckled, and for once, there was no pain or sadness in it. "It's okay, Gretch. I know you're in love with Buchanan.

It was obvious as soon as I saw him with you. You lit up around him in a way I've never seen. I've had a few weeks to get over you now."

She smiled over his shoulder, opening her eyes and gazing out into the coffee shop.

Behind them, a scarred man in a long tailored jacket stood in the doorway of the coffee shop, a dozen roses in his hand. He wore sunglasses despite the cloudy weather, as if it might obscure the scars on his face—and he was watching her hug it out with Cooper. Then, he took the glasses off, and she felt sick with dread.

Hunter's heart was in his eyes, and it was being broken all over again.

The man had shit timing.

"Hunter," Gretchen gasped, pulling away from Cooper.

Hunter's mouth tightened. He said nothing, simply turned and walked back out of the coffee shop. As she watched him disappear into the crowd, he tossed the roses into the nearest waste bin.

She felt as thrown away as those roses in that moment. Everything was all messed up again.

Even as she asked herself why she cared, Gretchen pulled out of Cooper's embrace and dashed out from behind the counter, crossing the coffee shop quickly and bursting through the door.

The streets were busy, but not so busy that she couldn't pick Hunter's bulkier form out of the group. That, and his stiff, angry stance and the way people paused when they glanced at his face.

She raced after him. "Hunter!"

He ignored her, his shoulders set.

"Hunter Buchanan." Gretchen planted her feet, fists clenched. "Turn around, damn it, or I'm going to run straight into all this traffic."

He slowly turned around, a good twenty feet from her on the bustling sidewalk. He didn't move forward and his hands were stuffed into his coat pockets. "What do you want?"

She paused at the icy tone of his voice. "You were bringing me flowers?"

"I was not."

"Really? I suppose you just throw flowers into every garbage can outside of a coffee shop, then?"

When he flushed, she had to hide her grin of delight. Why was it that she loved teasing Hunter so very, very much? She'd fallen back into her comfortable sense of joy with him, forgetting all about that he'd broken her heart.

"I threw them away," he bit out after a moment.

"I noticed. You shouldn't have."

"Why not? It's clear you've moved on. Anything I say will fall on deaf ears." His jaw clenched furiously.

She folded her arms over her chest. "Were you coming to apologize?"

He gave her a mutinous look.

"Then why does it matter if I've moved on? You made it clear you just wanted my body. You think I'm for sale."

"I was wrong. I should have trusted you." He looked so tortured that she softened for a moment. Just a moment.

"You should have. You should have believed that you can't buy my affection."

"What other choice does a man like me have?"

For a moment, she was dumbfounded. What did he mean, a man like him? Then, she realized he meant his face. Did he truly think he was so very hideous that he'd have to purchase affection? Sure, he was scarred, and the scars weren't pretty. They distorted the one side of his face, but they couldn't hide the fact that Hunter had a delicious body and a generous, sensitive soul. She remembered his long fingers caressing the petals of a flower and the way he'd smiled as if it were something new and joyous to him to be happy.

Her heart ached. "You're not ugly, Hunter. Not to me."

"You'll have to forgive me if I don't believe that," he

said in a cold voice. "I've had a lifetime of being reassured that I'm only wanted for my fortune."

"Well, if you don't believe that, then I guess you don't have much faith in me," Gretchen said, her voice light. "And that hurts me that you think I'm that shallow and mercenary."

For a moment, he looked stricken. "I didn't mean—"

"Didn't you? You're saying I'm an awful person who will only fuck a man if he's got a fat wallet." People on the street were starting to stare at them, but she ignored them. If Hunter could stand out here in the middle of New York City having a frank conversation with her, then she certainly could, too. "How do you think that makes me feel?"

He scowled. "Not bad enough, it seems. I see you've already moved on to your friend."

Fury pushed through her and she stomped her way toward him. "Ugh! Will you just listen to yourself for a moment? You're so convinced that you're some sort of hideous beast that you think that someone can't possibly see the true you inside. Yeah, well I saw the true you, buddy."

Hunter said nothing, but he didn't pull away. He simply watched her.

She was close enough to touch him now, and she stabbed a finger at his chest. "I saw a man who isolates himself because he's worried about making other people uncomfortable. I saw a man who doesn't leave his house very often, but makes sure that the staff is well paid. I saw a man who works all day tirelessly and tends to roses because he enjoys their beauty. I saw a man who expects perfection in himself but is okay with others treating him like dirt. I see a man who shuts out the world because he's so afraid of getting hurt again. And you tell me I'm the one with the problem? How about you look in the mirror?"

Astonishment crossed his face and his mouth slackened.

"How about you take a long, hard look at that asshole butler of yours? How about you hire someone who you actually enjoy being around? You're a wonderful person, Hunter.

You're shy but you're incredibly giving and thoughtful, and you have a poetic soul under all that muscle. If you're lonely, it's because you've isolated yourself. You have friends!" she exclaimed. "Your buddies thought you were happy at the dinner party and I saw their faces. They were happy for you. Why can't *you* be happy for you?"

And she jabbed him in the chest with her finger again.

Hunter caught her hand. She was momentarily astonished at how warm he was against her cold skin, and longing flared through her. But when he lifted her hand to try and kiss the palm, she wriggled free.

"No, Hunter," Gretchen said quietly. "I care about you, I really do. But I'm still mad at you."

"I want you with me, Gretchen. If you can forgive me for what I said, I want you at my side. I just have a hard time believing that someone as perfect as you would want to be with someone like me." He looked pained at her rejection, his scars stark on his face.

She wanted to kiss him and make him feel better. She wanted to grab him by his tailored lapels and shake some sense into him. So she just shook her head.

"Am I too late?" Hunter asked in a low, intense voice, full of pain. "Is that it? You've moved on? To him?"

Gretchen gave him an exasperated look. "I was sad and Cooper was comforting me. We're just friends. That's all we'll ever be."

"You were sad?" His attention focused on her words. "Why?"

"Why do you think?"

For some reason, his face broke into one of his rare smiles.

And she found herself smiling back at him. "I'm still mad at you."

"But you'll forgive me."

"Not today."

"Tomorrow, then." His eyes gleamed with anticipation.

"Maybe not tomorrow. I'm still deciding," Gretchen told him playfully, and began to walk back to the coffee shop. "You need to make some changes first, though."

"I will," he said.

"Good!" she called over her shoulder. "And next time, don't throw away my roses!"

She didn't look back as she went inside the coffee shop, but she could have sworn she'd heard him chuckle before she closed the door. A hint of a smile touched her face.

They were good. Sort of. They weren't great. Hunter needed to come out of his shell. But they were starting in the right direction.

And she smiled.

———

The next day, as Gretchen walked into the coffee shop, she was met by a surprising scene.

Every table was covered in enormous vases full of roses. The interior of the cafe looked more like a florist, and customers were milling around, sniffing the flowers and exclaiming in wonder as they held their lattes.

Every rose was exactly the same color—that icy pale blue-purple that she'd come to associate with Blue Girl. It was the rose she'd told Hunter that she liked the best.

Gretchen unwound her scarf from her neck, feeling warmth throughout her bones. She headed to the counter, unable to stop grinning. She knew who those were from and what they meant.

And while she couldn't be bought, well, it was a start.

Cooper gave her a relieved look as she arrived. "Thank God you're here. Did you see this mess?"

"Mess?" she inquired innocently. "I think they're beautiful."

"The first delivery showed up a few hours ago, and they've been coming in all morning. I think someone bought every purple rose in the entire city."

"Blue," she corrected him absently, pulling a long-stemmed rose from one of the vases and smelling it. "They're blue."

"Well, there's no name for the recipient. No sender. Just flowers coming in from every single florist in all of Manhattan. It's crazy." He looked frazzled.

Gretchen dragged her fingertips across the bud of the rose, feeling the soft petals and smiling. "I think it's sweet."

"I don't know what to do with all of them."

"Give them out to customers," she said, taking scissors and snipping the stem from the rose in her hand and tucking it safely into the pocket of her apron. She'd take this one home tonight.

————————

The next day, dozens of yellow roses showed up. The day after that, white roses with pink edges and a delicious scent that was so thick it made her nearly dizzy with delight. The roses never came with a card, but that was okay. Gretchen knew who they were for. Each day, she'd carefully take one of the flowers, wrap it in tissue and tuck it into her apron, and then take it home and press it between the pages of a book, carefully preserving it.

She didn't work for the next two days, but she still passed by the coffee shop, unable to stop her curiosity.

No roses. For some reason, that made her smile even more broadly. Hunter knew when she was working and made sure the flowers were delivered just for her. That was sweet.

She spent her days off with Audrey, baking, cleaning Audrey's apartment as payment for letting her live there, and shopping. Her normally capable sister seemed a bit morose and stressed, and Gretchen wondered if Audrey was worried about Daphne. The rest of the family had written off Daphne long ago, but Audrey refused to give up on her twin. Every time Daphne sauntered back into their lives, Audrey was the one who paid the price.

Gretchen had invited Kat to lunch, but Kat had called off, citing work. Gretchen suspected her agent was still mad at her since canceling contracts had meant that it cost Kat money, too. And her agent was probably not very pleased with the mess she'd scraped together for the last Astronaut Bill book, but she didn't care.

She wasn't writing a single thing and, for once, she felt wonderfully, gloriously free. She hadn't realized how unhappy writing had made her until she no longer let it rule her life.

Maybe, like Hunter, she was still figuring out parts of herself.

———

The roses continued for a week and a half, until one day Gretchen walked into the cafe and saw only one bouquet sitting on the counter. The roses were the deepest, darkest velvety red, and she immediately recognized them—Papa Meilland.

"Well," Cooper said as she came around to the back of the counter, tying on her apron. "We finally got a note with the roses."

"We did?" Gretchen perked up, her hands suddenly twitching with want. "Where is it?"

Cooper's brow furrowed. "How'd you know it was for you?"

"Just a hunch. Now, where's my letter? Gimme." She made a grabbing motion at him.

He dropped a cream envelope into her hand. It simply had a large *G* printed on the front, and the back was sealed. Hastily, she tore the envelope open and was surprised at the sight of the paper inside.

It was soft, yellow with age, and wrinkled. Gretchen sucked in a breath as she carefully removed the folded paper with reverent hands.

"What is that?" Cooper asked, peering over her shoulder. "Looks old."

"It's a letter," Gretchen said in a soft voice. "And it's very old." She touched it with reverent fingers, remembering the contents of the letters at Buchanan Manor. "I need a moment in private."

"Sure," Cooper told her, giving her a puzzled look.

She raced to the back room and then shut herself into Cooper's office, sitting at his messy desk. With trembling fingers, she unfolded the letter and began to read.

My lovely Lulabelle,

I never thought a day could seem longer than twenty-four hours. Once, I cursed that the days were so short, for they seemed to rush past. I have found a way, though, to make the day seem interminably long, for the hours to slow to molasses and minutes to crawl past as if unmoving.

I simply need to be parted from you.

I miss you, my darling. I miss you so very much that my heart aches in my breast. I long for you, for your body next to mine. I long to wake up and feel your hair against my cheek, to taste your sweet breath against mine, to hear your warm and happy laughter. I miss your body, of course, but it is your mind and your spirit I miss most of all. It is you who brings the light and warmth into my life. I am cast into darkness without you at my side.

And so I sit, watching the minutes descend into hours, and count the days until you return to my arms. I live for the day that I can see your brilliant smile again, touch your lips to mine, and know that we will never be parted again. I know that day will come soon, and my aching heart is eased at this.

All my love,
Benedict

Tears pooling in her eyes, Gretchen clutched the letter to her chest. No raunchy words of love this time. No longing for sex. Just a simple, aching loneliness that spoke to her soul. She hadn't seen this letter before. Had it been at the back of the box that she'd been unable to get to? Had Hunter read through them, thinking of her? Looking for just the right letter to soften her heart?

It had worked. It had worked wonderfully.

She looked over the letter again, touching it with amazed, trembling fingers. She'd ripped open the envelope in her haste and now she regretted that move. She wanted to keep it and press it into her scrapbook like she had with the roses. Gretchen carefully folded the letter and placed it back into the envelope.

There was an address printed in the top left-hand corner. A return address.

Curious, she read it. Then she read it again.

And then she bolted from her seat. Rushing back into the main room of the cafe, she shrugged her jacket back on, winding her scarf around her neck once more. "I have to run out, Cooper."

He gave her a concerned look, a frown wrinkling his brow. "You coming back?"

"I am. I just need to see something," she told him, and rushed out the door before he could question her further.

Gretchen raced down the streets of New York City, her heart pounding as she wove through the crowds. SoHo was always busy this time of day, but she didn't pay attention to anyone. Instead, she was lost in thought, running her thumb over the green embossed return address on the envelope.

She took the subway toward Madison Avenue. Envelope in hand, it took her a few minutes to locate the building, and then she entered, eyes wide, as she read the placard at the front of the office building.

Buchanan Real Estate—4th floor.

He had an office here in the city? She thought he only

worked out of his house. In the entire month she'd stayed with him, he hadn't left it. Mystified, she entered the elevator.

The fourth floor was a bit of a surprise. Not because it wasn't the Buchanan offices at all—it was—but that the walls seemed to be made entirely of glass. For a man who prized his privacy, this struck her as either bizarre . . . or deliberate. Glass panels displayed the waiting room of the office, with six chairs neatly lined up next to end tables that were covered in real estate magazines. Fresh roses decorated each table, and at the far end was a reception desk. If she headed further down the main hall, the glass walls continued, and she could see straight into Hunter's office. She touched her fingertips to the glass, staring at the office. It was set up exactly the same as his office at home, right down to the mirrors on the wall, the enormous TV, and the vase of roses at his side.

His desk was empty.

When had he gotten an office here? Had he always had it and she wasn't aware of it? More questions that she had no answers to. Gretchen paced the hall, not willing to go inside, not quite yet.

A woman appeared out of one of the back rooms and paused at the sight of Gretchen, and then waved enthusiastically, beckoning her in.

With a deep breath, Gretchen pushed open the glass door and smiled.

"Well, hi there, ma'am," the receptionist said in a thick twang that told Gretchen that she wasn't from New York or anywhere north of the Mason-Dixon Line. She wore a cheap suit that was a little too ugly to be anything but homemade, and she had freckles going across a snub nose and rounded cheeks. She also had the palest, most wild corkscrew blonde hair that Gretchen had ever seen. She waved Gretchen in again. "Don't just stand in the hall like you done lost your britches. We don't bite in here!"

Gretchen blinked. My God, this girl was . . . country. What was she doing working for Hunter? "Um, hi."

Gretchen gestured at the hallway that she'd been stalking. "I was just, uh, looking for someone."

"Well, I'm someone," the girl beamed. "Can I help you find something?"

She held up her envelope. "Is this the Buchanan office?"

"It surely is," the girl drawled. "My name's Maylee— that's all one word, not two. It's after my Nana and Pepaw," she said casually, as if these were things you normally tossed out into conversation. "I'm Mr. Buchanan's secretary. It's nice to meet you."

"Nice to meet you, too. I'm sorry, I'm just . . . is Mr. Buchanan here?"

"Naw. He went to lunch with some fancy-looking guys." She pulled a Post-it note off her desk and sat down, whirling in her chair. "Gimme your name again and I'll tell him you stopped by."

"It's Gretchen. I—"

"Oh, my lordamercy!" Maylee clapped her hands together in excitement. "Mr. Hunter's your beau, ain't he? Oh, my gosh. You are so pretty! Of course you are."

Gretchen was having a hard time reconciling stiff, proper Hunter with this secretary who seemed straight off the turnip truck. Had he paid for a new assistant who could take care of *all* of his needs? Maylee was pretty in a disheveled sort of way. Jealousy gnawed at Gretchen. Was she thinking he'd turned over a new leaf when he'd just decided to buy a cheaper model?

"Mr. Hunter's gonna be so dang sad he missed you," Maylee continued, scribbling on the Post-it. She stuck it to her monitor, where dozens of other Post-its fluttered. "He makes me call all the flower shops in the city lookin' for your flowers, you know. Man's lost his cotton-pickin' mind over you, if you don't mind saying so. It's really cute."

And just like that, Gretchen blushed. Maybe Maylee wasn't a replacement after all. She shouldn't have doubted him. "Do you know what time he'll be back?"

"No ma'am," Maylee drawled. "But if you'll give me your number, I'll give you a holler when he gets back."

"That's okay," Gretchen said, her lips twitching to contain her smile. "I'll swing by tomorrow."

"I'll be sure and tell Mr. Hunter," Maylee beamed. As Gretchen turned to leave, she called out, "Y'all have a nice day, now."

She barely stifled her giggles until she got to the elevator. Well, she *had* told him to get himself a nicer assistant, but Maylee wasn't exactly what she had in mind.

———

The next day, before she stopped into the coffee shop, she headed straight for Hunter's office. It was just after lunch and she hoped she'd catch him before he left again. She'd chosen her clothing carefully today, too—casual but still sensual. She wore leggings and knee-high leather boots that showed off her long legs, and a draped tunic sweater that clung to her body. She wore a fringed scarf that she'd borrowed from Audrey—who was always perfectly accessorized—and had worn her hair in a soft ponytail, deliberately leaving her bangs and a few tendrils loose. She'd even worn makeup for the man.

Of course, the look was slightly ruined by the peacoat she'd had to toss over the ensemble thanks to the cold weather, but that was okay. She'd strip it off as soon as she got to his office and show him what he'd been missing out on.

As soon as she emerged from the fourth-floor elevator, her breath caught. Hunter was in his office, typing on the computer. He was intent on his screen, and he hadn't noticed her in the hallway yet.

His scarred side was facing the hallway, exposed for all to see. Was it deliberate? She hadn't realized his desk was set up so anyone coming up the elevator would see it.

As she stood there studying him, Hunter glanced up.

His gaze caught hers, and he slowly colored red even as he got up from his chair.

Her heart began to pound, and she smiled at him, slowly, sweetly, and then opened the door to the main lobby.

"Well, hi there, Ms. Gretchen," Maylee called cheerfully. This time she was dressed in a lavender plaid suit, her baby-blonde corkscrew hair pulled up into a messy, frizzy knot. "You caught Mr. Hunter in the office today. Ain't that somethin'?"

"It sure is," Gretchen said, smiling. She gestured at the door to his office. "Mind if I go on in?"

"'Course not. Lemme just ring Mr. Hunter." Maylee picked up the phone.

"He saw me come in," Gretchen said.

"I know, but I'm s'posed to ring everyone, Ms. Gretchen. Mr. Hunter says it's the rules." She held the phone to her ear, beaming. "Mr. Hunter? Ms. Gretchen's here to see you." After a moment, she nodded. "You can go in now."

"Thank you," said Gretchen, her lips twitching again. This time she was able to contain her laughter until she shut the door behind her in Hunter's office.

His expression was unreadable and wary. He stood behind his desk but made no move to approach her. "Hello, Gretchen."

She shook her head, still chuckling. "Where exactly did you find that secretary of yours?"

He grimaced. "It's a long story." His gaze moved over her, devouring her. "You look gorgeous."

Oh, right. She was supposed to shrug off her bulky coat and show him what he'd been missing. Gretchen fumbled with the buttons of her coat, then struggled to pull her arms out of the sleeves. Not smooth. By the time she got her coat off, her sweater—and her ponytail—were sticking to her body thanks to static. *Lovely.* "I thought I'd come by and say hi."

Her lack of grace didn't matter, though. She was pleased to see that his fascinated gaze was riveted on her.

He gestured at the seat across from his desk. "Please sit."

She did, deliberately crossing her legs in a slow motion, enjoying when his eyes followed her. Now this was a heady, feminine power. "I wanted to come by and say thank you for the roses."

Hunter inclined his head, studying her.

She suddenly felt awkward and unsure. What did she want to come out of this meeting? For him to beg for her to return to him? Keep teasing him for another week or two and make him suffer?

Actually, she kind of just wanted to bask in his presence for a bit.

Gretchen glanced around. "Nice office. I didn't know you had one here."

"I didn't until last week."

She looked at him, startled. "What made you decide that you needed one?"

"You were right," he said bluntly. "I've been hiding away from the world for a long time. I told you about my accident. Things weren't easy for me after that. It became easier to hide from the world than to go out into it. When I . . . returned to my father's house after the hospital, he hired private tutors for me and I hid from the world. He'd insisted I go to college, though. I tried to get out of it, but he refused. It was like living in a waking nightmare. Being amongst all those strangers . . ." His voice trailed off, and then he cleared his throat. "College wasn't easy for me. If it weren't for the friendship of . . ." His words died and he looked frustrated for a moment, then said, "Logan and the others, I would have never made it through. I was picked on and women flinched at the sight of me. When I inherited my father's business, I set up in my house and it was just easier not to leave unless necessary." He shrugged. "It became easier to avoid the world than to live in it . . . until I met you. You're why I bought this place."

Gretchen's cheeks warmed. "So I made you buy real estate? That's a pretty good super-power, I have to admit."

His mouth tugged up on one side. "I already owned this office. I just decided to keep it for myself." He glanced out the window onto the main section of the floor. "It reminds me to be out there in life, instead of hiding away."

"I'm very proud of you," she said softly. "And I hope that you someday realize that you're not this monster you've painted yourself to be. You're just a man."

The man who I love.

But the words clung to her throat.

"I took your advice about Eldon, too." Hunter folded his hands on his desk. She noticed his knuckles were white, as if he were gripping his hands tightly despite his casual pose.

Oh, no. Did he fire his assistant-slash-butler? Now she felt bad. "He's very loyal—"

"He's a cranky old bastard," Hunter admitted. "But yes, he's very loyal. He's also elderly and has family in the west. I gave him a very large retirement bonus as thanks for his tireless work, and I suggested he visit his daughters for a time. And I hired some additional staff at Buchanan Manor. It's rather . . . quiet lately."

She inclined her head back to the main room. "Maylee's not exactly what I had in mind when I suggested you hire a new assistant."

To her vast amusement, he grimaced. "Maylee is a . . . problem."

"She seems like a sweet girl."

"That is the problem." Hunter sighed and rubbed a hand over his mouth. "When I had Eldon call the agency, I told them to find me someone pleasant. She's very pleasant," he said in a sour voice. "But I feel I should have been more specific. She's not good with computers. Or phones. Or the copier."

A giggle escaped her throat.

He gave her a vexed look, seemingly aggrieved. "Yesterday, she set up a meeting for a client and then didn't tell me about it because she couldn't find her sticky note. I was extremely . . . annoyed."

"Oh, no. What did you do?"

"I suggested she use the computer to keep my schedule instead of Post-it notes."

Gretchen thought back to the sea of yellow sticky notes on Maylee's desk. "And what did she say?"

"Nothing," he said in a pained voice. "She cried."

"What did you do?"

"What else could I do? I gave her a raise."

Gretchen burst into laughter. "Really?"

He looked aggrieved. "This is her first job since leaving Arkansas and no one else will hire her because she is a hick, as she likes to tell me. I can't fire the poor girl simply because she's unorganized."

"You big softy," Gretchen teased, her heart swelling with warmth. "Maybe you should hire an assistant for your assistant."

"Maybe so." His gaze moved over her with obvious pleasure. "You look beautiful."

She shivered at the husky tone of his voice. He looked so delicious that she wanted to crawl across the desk, start kissing him, and never stop. She forced herself to look at the gigantic windows instead.

"Forgive me," Hunter said in a tight voice. "I'm not trying to make you uncomfortable. Did you see my invitation?"

She glanced at him in surprise. "I haven't been by work yet. You sent me an invitation?"

His nod was short. "Today's flowers came with an invitation to a charity fundraiser scheduled for this weekend. A ball. It's at Buchanan Manor."

Her eyes widened and she sat on the edge of her chair. "You're hosting a charity ball? Are you serious? Who are you and what have you done with Hunter?"

Hunter gave her a patient look. "I was approached because the venue that the charity ball had originally been scheduled for cancelled on them. They were desperate. It seemed like the polite thing to do."

Polite had never bothered him before, though. "What should I wear?"

His eyes warmed at her question. "Something formal. I'm told there will be dancing."

"Do you plan on dancing with me?"

"If you'll be my date."

"Oh, you just want me to be your date because I put out," she said in a teasing voice.

His face flushed an angry red and he jerked to his feet. "I'm sorry you think that of me."

And just like that, their easy banter ended. Gretchen felt a moment of sadness. She'd messed it up this time, and it was clear from Hunter's stiff posture that the moment had vanished.

"The invitation is yours if you want it," he told her in a cold voice. "Feel free to decline with no obligations. It was meant as a friendly gesture."

And she'd killed it. Clearly if she was going to bring them back together she'd have to be the one to do it.

"I'll think about it," she lied.

FIFTEEN

When Gretchen's taxi pulled up to Buchanan Manor several days later, she did a double take. She knew that having the charity event at the house was a big move for him, but it took seeing the throngs of people and the endless line of limos curving up the driveway to impress into her mind just how much of an effort he was making.

She smoothed her little black dress nervously. He'd made an effort. Had she done enough? She pulled out a compact and checked her hair. Her upsweep—so different from her normal messy ponytail—still looked perfect thanks to Audrey's help, and she had a yellow rose tucked behind one ear. It was the only accessory she wore, and she hoped it was enough. Her dress was plain since she didn't have the money in her bank account to buy something. But she'd had a dress in the back of her closet that was simple, but elegant. It was a black dress with tight, elbow-length sleeves, shirred sides, and a boatneck collar. It made her red hair stand out, and she knew Hunter liked her hair.

Staff in white shirts with black ties opened the doors

to the house to let her in. Had he hired more staff only for the party? Or was this a new change? She thought she recognized a few of the women wandering the room with trays as the housecleaners, but she didn't approach them for fear of making them uncomfortable. Instead, she mingled with the crowd and scanned the room. Buchanan Manor looked as gorgeous as ever, but it was unnerving seeing it full of guests. She was used to seeing the rooms empty and silent.

Oddly enough, the house no longer felt lonely.

As she pushed through the throngs of people, a woman whirled past her with a tray and then turned. "Would you like a hors d'oeuvres—oh, Gretchen! Hello!" She broke into a smile.

"Brandy, how are you?" Gretchen smiled back at her. She recognized the maid from her excursions into the cleaning wings. Brandy was fond of Gretchen's banana nut bread and always talked about how much her children enjoyed Gretchen's cooking.

"Busy," she said, offering Gretchen a fig-covered confection from her tray. "But happy. There's been lots of changes in this house in the last two weeks."

"Oh? What kind of changes?" She pretended to be casual, though anticipation strummed through her body at the thought. Had Hunter made changes because he wanted to impress her? Why did that make her positively giddy?

"Well, first of all, he got rid of that nasty assistant of his."

Gretchen grinned. "So I heard."

"Yup. From what I hear, he's got three assistants now. Two localized here in the house and one at the office."

"Three. That seems like a big change."

"It is. And that's not all. That man of yours hired more staff and gave the rest of us a raise." She patted her pocket. "I got a Christmas bonus, too."

"That's wonderful," Gretchen said with a smile. "But I don't know that he's my man. I—"

But Brandy was already on her way to the next group, a cheery smile on her face. "Hi there. Hors d'oeuvres?"

Her man. Gretchen popped the appetizer into her mouth and tasted the words. *Her man.* She liked that. Did he miss her like she missed him? God, she hoped so or this was going to get awkward, fast. She turned around and sucked in a breath.

There he was, at the center of the room, in the thick of the party. He looked pained and uncomfortable . . . and utterly gorgeous. A black tuxedo fit him to the nines, and his hair had been cut recently, his new hairstyle keeping his hair off his forehead and giving him a slightly rakish air. He stood with a group of people, a flute of champagne in his hand. A stiff-looking silver-haired couple were talking to him animatedly, and he kept a polite smile on his face even though he looked a bit trapped.

She giggled at that, even as her fingers curled with the need to touch him. Instead, she just watched him from a distance, enjoying his every move, noting the way his cheek pulled when his mouth curved into a lopsided smile. How could anyone think of that raw, masculine, delicious man as anything but beautiful? She couldn't take her eyes off him.

Then he turned, and his attention seemed to head unerringly for her. His gaze lit up.

Gretchen's feet felt glued to the floor. She should go over and say hello to him. Interrupt the conversation he was having. Something. Anything. Instead, she stood there like a dummy, her brain unable to work.

Hunter was having a party and entertaining people. Her Hunter. He was breaking out of his self-imposed exile. Was this all for her?

How could she possibly be mad at a man who was going to such lengths to prove to her that he could be the man she needed him to be? He'd manipulated her—and others—with his influence, that was true, but now she understood why. He'd never thought that she'd be interested in him, never thought she would give him the time of day, so he'd done the only thing he could do to bring her close. And while it was low-down, dirty, and craven . . . she understood it and even felt a twinge of sympathy for him that he'd felt the need to go so very far for something as simple and basic as human need for another person.

He extricated himself from the conversation, handed his glass to a passing waiter, and strolled toward her, adjusting the front of his tuxedo jacket as if to make sure he looked his best. She found that utterly charming. Here was Hunter Buchanan, the most sexy, glorious, powerful man in the room, and he was making sure he looked good enough for her.

It was a heady feeling.

He walked up to her, reached out, and then dropped his hand. A hint of unease flashed across his face but he couldn't seem to stop looking at her. "Gretchen. You look . . . lovely."

She smiled at him, shifting when someone passed too close to them. "Hi, Hunter." She didn't know what to say. This hadn't been a problem she'd had often. Normally words just ran right out of her mouth whether she wanted them to or not. A tall, slinky woman strolled past, her tight bandage gown glittering with sequins. "I seem to be underdressed."

"On the contrary," Hunter said. "You're the most gorgeous thing in this room. You don't need flash to improve your beauty. Just your smile."

She couldn't resist smiling at that. "You flirt."

He flushed a little.

"Nice party," she told him, stepping aside as another couple moved past them. The room was positively packed. "You did well."

"I did it for you," he told her in a voice so low she almost didn't catch it.

She swallowed hard. "You did, huh?"

"All for you. Everything. I want to prove to you that . . . I can be who you need me to be."

She shook her head. "Hunter, all I've ever needed was—" She paused as someone in the crowd called his name. "Maybe this is a bad time."

"Not a bad time," he told her with a growl, and then he was at her side, cupping her elbow and steering her through the crowd. "Come with me."

They wound silently through the throng and escaped down a back hallway—the north wing. Hunter's wing. At the sight of the familiar paintings hanging on the wall, she felt a sharp stab of longing. If they continued down a second hallway, they'd get to his room. Was his bed lonely without her? Was this thing they had too broken to be fixed? Had she been too hard on him when she should have been understanding as to what drove him?

Hunter stopped in front of the large windows at the far end of the hall, where the corridor split and branched toward Hunter's suite of rooms. From here, the wintry gardens were visible and the evergreen bushes were peeking out from under a blanket of snow. His hand lifted as if he wanted to reach for her and he just as quickly drew back.

"You're well?" he asked in a clipped voice, clasping his hands behind his back and glancing out the window.

"Actually, no," she told him. When he turned to her with a stricken look, she said, "There's this guy who kind of broke my heart. He lied to me and sabotaged my work just so I could stay around him a bit longer."

The look on his face was tense, his expression intent as he focused on her. "And would you have gone out with me? Not knowing me? Not knowing who I was except for this?" He gestured at the deep gouges scarring his face. "How am I supposed to believe that? People turn away at the sight of me."

His sadness and pain broke her heart. "Oh, Hunter. Just because most people are shallow assholes doesn't mean that I am."

"But how would I know this?"

"It doesn't matter, does it?" she said briskly. "We'll never know that, because you manipulated the situation and lied to me. You messed with my career. You can't just make up jobs to bring people into your life."

"You can still have the money, you know," he told her quietly. "I never meant to force you to choose between your happiness and me."

She threw her hands up in the air. "It's not about the money, Hunter. When will you get that? It's about you and me and trust. How can I trust that you're not pulling strings behind the scenes again anytime something goes my way?"

"How can I trust that you truly want me for who I am and not what I am?" There was a wealth of pain in his voice.

"Oh, Hunter. You have to have faith in me." She moved forward and gently cupped his cheek, feeling the grooves of the scars.

He closed his eyes as if in ecstasy, his hand moving to hold hers there. "I love you so much, Gretchen. Please don't leave me again."

"Then trust me."

His eyes opened. "It's hard for me to trust."

An amused smile curved her mouth. "I get that you're damaged, but how do you think I feel knowing you've been manipulating things since day one?"

He flinched, and she could feel it against her palm. "I never meant to hurt you."

"I know. And that's why I've come back." Her thumb lightly stroked over the jagged scar that twisted at the corner of his mouth. "It was the only way you knew how to reach out to me. I forgive you for that."

He leaned in and kissed the heel of her hand.

"I still haven't forgiven you for the sabotage of my laptop, though," she said lightly. "That was kind of low."

"I didn't realize Eldon was going to do that," he told her. "I just wanted him to delay you."

"Oh, he delayed me all right. Killed my contract dead in the water."

Hunter winced, but his fingers stroked the back of her hand. He still held her palm to his cheek, as if fearful that if he released her, she'd slip out of his grasp again. "The files were recovered, by the way. I can send you the information."

She shrugged. "I'm a lot happier without writing, honestly. It's not a profession I'm very good at. The constant deadlines drive me crazy, and if I have to write one more astronaut story I just might jump off your balcony. Without the contracts, I'm pretty broke but I'm also a lot happier—and less stressed—than I've been in a long time."

"Preston will be sorry to hear that. He contacted me the other day and suggested that if you didn't want to do the epistolary novel that perhaps you'd be interested in doing a cookbook. He loved your cooking at the dinner party."

"A cookbook, huh?" She gave him a skeptical look. "Your idea?"

He grinned and released her hand. "It was all him, I'm afraid. For once, I had nothing to do with it."

"I'll think about it," she told him softly, though in her mind she was already racing through her favorite recipes. Well, she'd let Hunter stew on it for a bit before deciding. Gretchen reached forward and slid a finger along Hunter's lapel. "So what about the letters?"

He leaned into her touch, stepping forward. His hands went to her shoulders. "They were simply a means to an end."

"Were they real? All those dirty, naughty things they wrote to each other?"

"They were real," he told her. "Just not in this house."

"I'm glad. I like to think that those two were crazy in love for so long and that they eventually get together. They do, don't they? Get together and have a happy ever after?"

He shrugged. "I didn't read far enough."

She snuggled into his embrace, sighing. "I like to think that they did. I feel like their story is ours, just a little. Two lovers separated and reunited."

"Their story's not ours," he told her in a husky voice, his fingers brushing at a lock of her hair. "I want us to make our story, not follow someone else's."

Her heart melted a little at that, and she curled her fingers into his jacket, tugging him close enough to kiss her. "You hurt me bad, you know."

"I'm changing. For you, I'll change everything I am." His intense gaze swept over her face. "I meant it, Gretchen. I love you. It doesn't matter to me if you love me or not. Just stay."

"Well, it's a good thing for you that I love you, too."

His eyes warmed. He brushed a finger along her jawline. "Do you mean it?"

She thwacked him on the shoulder. "We're going to have to get past this trust thing. Of course I mean it. Why would I lie to you after all this?"

A wide grin crossed his face. "I just never thought I would be so lucky." His fingers moved over her lips and he pressed a kiss to her mouth.

It was a soft, gentle kiss, and it was over far too soon. All it did was stoke a fire in her belly that was impossible to put out. She moaned when he pulled away. "You want to see how lucky you can be?" she murmured to him.

"Always."

She took his hand and led him toward the greenhouse.

As soon as they shut the door behind them, he wrapped an arm around her waist. She closed her eyes and leaned into his embrace, taking in the lush scents of the rows upon rows of roses and the smell of damp earth.

"Tell me I am not dreaming," Hunter whispered against

her neck, pressing kisses there. "That you're truly in my arms and I'm forgiven."

"I'll just pinch you instead," she told him playfully, sliding out of his arms and turning to face him. "Got a preference as to where?"

"Don't care." He grasped her hips and pulled her against him so she could feel the hard length of his desire against her. "I want you, Gretchen. So badly."

She smiled and sauntered away, passing by the black table that he did the more delicate gardening on. While most of the roses grew in large, deep pots, he had seedlings and a scatter of tools on the table at all times. Currently there were rows and rows of carefully planted seedlings marching across the table and taking up almost all of the space.

Gretchen ran a finger along the edge of the table. "Kind of a shame that this is occupied. I can think of some naughty uses for such a nice, flat surface."

Hunter moved past her and, before she could protest, he lowered his arm and raked everything off the table in a loud crash. Plants tumbled to her feet, splashing dirt on her serviceable black sandals. A long smear of dirt marred his expensive tuxedo.

Then he stood there, watching her with intense eyes, breathing deep.

She kicked off her shoes, her panties growing wet at his impulsive move. A man who would destroy hours of careful work simply because he wanted to fuck her on the table? *Hot.* She tsked at him. "You're ruining your jacket. I think it needs to come off."

Hunter's eyes narrowed, and he shrugged the jacket off his shoulders, dropping it to the ground. His gaze never left her.

Mmmm. His intensity was doing delicious things to her. Her pulse throbbed low, her sex growing slick. She moved forward, edging between him and the table. "My, you're quite responsive today, aren't you?"

He captured her hand when she reached for his bowtie. His other hand slid under her dress and pressed up against her now-wet panties. "You're ruining these," he whispered huskily, turning her words against her. "I think they need to come off."

Gretchen moaned at the feel of his hand there. "How quickly the tables turn," she breathed. Excitement was rushing through her and she wriggled against his hand, unable to resist pressing her mound against his fingers. "If I take them off, are you going to fuck me on this table?"

"Yes." His eyes gleamed. "And it won't be polite."

Her hands trembled as she reached for the hem of her dress. "No?"

"It's going to be hard and rough," he murmured, sliding his fingers up her mound to drag down the fabric of her panties in a possessive gesture. "You'll probably scream my name a few times."

"Oh, wow," she said, dazed at his words. Her thighs clenched in excitement. "When you take control, you really take control, don't you?"

"Is that a problem?"

"God, no."

"Good. I want you, and I don't want to wait another minute," he murmured, dragging her panties down her thighs. She obediently spread her legs so he could tug them downward, and then she let them slide to the greenhouse floor and kicked them aside.

As soon as she did, his hands were on her hips and he lifted her to the table surface. She perched on the edge, her breathing rushed and excited. Lordy, this was hot.

He pushed her backward a little, and then he hiked up her dress, exposing her pussy. She sucked in a breath when he placed his mouth on her. "Oh, Hunter." Her fingers curled in his hair. "You are way too good at that."

He didn't respond, but simply tongued her clit harder,

his fingers spreading the lips of her sex to expose her fully to his mouth.

She whimpered at the barrage of sensations, her hips flexing involuntarily. Her hands scrambled for something to hold on to, to brace herself on, but there was nothing but Hunter. She moaned when his tongue circled her clit with fierce little circles, her fingers tangling in his hair again. "Need you so bad, baby," she breathed.

He jerked up, and his face looked furious for a moment. "Damn it."

Fear suddenly flooded through her. "What is it?"

"Condoms. Don't have one."

Relief swam through her. "Is that all? Fuck it." Her legs dragged around his shoulders, hooking him in place. "I'll get on the Pill."

"But today—"

"Today," she murmured, "just pull out. Come on my belly."

His groan of need was loud and brutal. "You sure?" he asked even as he continued to drag her dress up her body, exposing her all the way to her bra.

"God, yes. I need you inside me." She squeezed her hips again. "Right now."

That was all the incentive he needed. Hunter stood and she heard his zipper before he pulled her hips down to the edge of the table. She felt his cock against her entrance, and then he hammered into her with a single move.

Her groan of pleasure matched his.

"I love you, Gretchen," he gritted out, even as he began to thrust into her with rough strokes. "You're the best thing that's ever happened to me."

He sounded wild, out of control, and it excited her even more. Each pounding stroke slammed her into the table and sent a wave of intense pleasure through her. She whimpered again, digging her fingernails into his shoulders as he continued to ram into her, his thrusts hard just like he promised.

And when she began to come, she did, in fact, scream his name.

He bit out a curse when she began to clench around him, and he pulled out of her. A moment later, hot seed splashed on her stomach as he stroked his cock, groaning.

She lay still beneath him as he finished, and when he was done, he inhaled deeply, opened his eyes, and fixed his intense gaze on her. His cheeks flooded with color. "I think I ruined your dress."

"Or gave me a great excuse not to go back to the party," she told him languidly. Man, she felt amazing now. She didn't even mind that she had dirt in her hair. "But I suppose you have to go back, right?"

"Hell no," he growled, tearing off his bowtie and then unbuttoning his shirt. When he pulled it off, he began to towel his cum off her stomach. "They can all leave as far as I'm concerned. I'm not letting you get away from me ever again."

She smiled up at him. "You say the sweetest things, you sexy beast."

"I mean every word of it," he told her, his eyes serious. "I love you. You have no idea how much."

Emotion clogged her throat as she sat up on the table. She carefully put her hands on each side of his face and gently kissed him. "I might love you more."

He grinned, a boyish smile of delight crossing his face that made her heart clench with emotion. "Using this table might have been a regrettable action."

"I'm not so sure about that," she said in a low, purring voice. "I feel pretty good."

"I destroyed all of the roses I was working on for you, though. The crossbreeds."

She shrugged and wrapped her arms around his bare

shoulders. "Guess I'll have to stick around for the next batch."

"It might take months before they're ready again."

"I'm in no rush," she said softly. "I plan on being at your side for quite a while."

He smiled.

Turn the page for a sneak peek at
Jessica Clare's next Billionaire Boys Club novel

THE WRONG
BILLIONAIRE'S BED

Available now from InterMix

The three teens sat on the end of the rickety wooden dock at the pond.

"Today's my thirteenth birthday," Daphne Petty told the boy at her side, giving him a coy look and winding a bright red lock of hair around her finger. "You know what that means, right?"

"That it's Audrey's birthday, too?" Cade glanced around Daphne's shoulder to smile at the quieter twin.

Audrey gave him a shy smile, flustered that he'd remembered her. She sat on the opposite side of her vivacious, flirty twin, saying nothing. That was usually how it went. Daphne commanded attention and Audrey just sort of stood by her side. Not that she minded much. Daphne was also the bad twin, and Audrey liked being the good twin. You got into trouble a lot less when you were the good twin, and if there was one thing Audrey hated, it was being in trouble.

"That's not it," Daphne said with a pout. She nudged his shoulder. "Pay attention to me."

Instantly, Cade's amused gaze went back to Daphne. "I am paying attention to you."

"No, you're paying attention to Audrey. Don't you like me, Cade?" She continued to twist that lock of hair around her finger, imitating a move they'd seen their older sister Gretchen pull, to great effect. Gretchen always had interest from boys, and Daphne wanted to learn everything she knew.

"I like both of you," Cade said in a cheerful voice, then ruffled Daphne's hair like she was a child. "You two are my friends."

"Best friends," Audrey said shyly, swinging her legs.

Daphne rolled her eyes at her twin. "We can't be best friends with a guy. Guys can only be boyfriends."

Cade choked on a laugh. "You two are too young for me. I'm fifteen now. You just turned thirteen."

"Well, it's my—" she turned to look at her twin "—our birthday and you need to give us a present."

Cade tugged on the frayed collar of his shirt. It was faded and worn, much like everything he owned. No one talked about it, but the Archers were the poorest family on a rather low-end block of the neighborhood, poorer even than Audrey and Daphne's parents, who worked long hours for little pay. "I don't have money, Daphne. I can't get a job until next year, remember?"

"It's okay," Audrey said. "You can give us something that doesn't cost anything."

"Like?"

A kiss, Audrey thought dreamily, staring at Cade's handsome blue eyes and blond hair.

"You could teach us how to make out with a boy," Daphne said slyly, that wicked tone in her voice. "I need to practice so I'm ready for my first boyfriend."

Cade sputtered. "Make out? I don't think so. You two are like my little sisters."

That was not the first time he'd referred to them as his little sisters. It crushed Audrey's heart a bit, but she could tell her twin was undeterred. Daphne usually didn't take no for an answer.

"Maybe just a hug, then?" Daphne asked sweetly.

"Of course," Cade told her, leaning in and reaching an arm around Daphne.

Daphne immediately wrapped her arms around Cade and thrust her mouth against his, trapping him into a surprise kiss. Audrey's jaw dropped in shock as her twin kissed—no, *mauled*—the boy she knew that Audrey had a crush on. Their friend.

Cade made a noise of surprise and tried to pull away, but Daphne clung to him like a leech.

"Daph, stop it," Audrey hissed. Anger began to bubble inside her. How dare Daphne make a scene with Cade. It was bad enough that she monopolized him constantly. "Just stop it!"

But Daphne didn't stop. She made a loud *mmmmm* in the back of her throat, just to goad Audrey.

So Audrey shoved her twin into the pond.

Daphne fell with a splash and a yell, and Cade barely managed to scramble backward onto the dock. He stared at Audrey in surprise.

That was okay, because Audrey was pretty surprised at her actions, too.

Dang it. There went her impulsive temper. Audrey tried to keep it under control, she really did, but sometimes it got the better of her.

Like right now.

Daphne surfaced in the pond's scummy water, screeching as she flailed. "Audrey, you suck!" she yelled. "Cade, help me out!"

"That was not cool, Audrey," Cade told her, leaning over the side of the dock and extending a hand to Daphne. When she continued to flounder in the water, he sighed and looked over at Audrey, who stood on the dock, frozen in horror.

She tried so hard to be the good twin, she really did.

"Here, hold this," Cade told her, and pulled off his T-shirt. Then he jumped into the water and grabbed Daphne, who went into his arms, sobbing, and began to pull her to the nearby shore.

A moment later, both of them were dripping on the bank of the shore. Audrey still stood on the dock, clutching Cade's shirt and mortified by what she'd done. She'd pushed her twin in, all because Daphne'd been kissing the boy Audrey wanted.

But it wasn't just any boy. It was Cade. Audrey had adored him for what seemed like forever, and Daphne only wanted him because Audrey did. That was how it always went.

"You came for me," Daphne sobbed, clinging to Cade.

"Of course," he soothed. "I'll always come for you, Daph. You know I will."

It was true. Though two years separated them in age, the three of them had roamed their neighborhood for years, fishing for crawdads, playing in the pond, and riding bikes. It never failed that Daphne would get into some sort of scrape—like the time she'd pulled up a manhole and climbed down—and Cade would have to come after her.

Daphne caused trouble, and Cade rescued her. And Audrey stood by, because she was the good twin.

Until today, of course, when Audrey's temper got the better of her, and she'd suddenly become the bad twin in a blink.

Daphne wiped streaming hair off her brow and scowled at Audrey. "I'm going to the house and telling Mom. You'll be sorry, Audrey." She turned and stomped off, heading back to the neighborhood.

Audrey sucked in a breath. She was totally going to be grounded.

"Looks like the birthday celebration's going to end early," Cade told her, heading down the dock and reaching for his shirt. He pulled it over his head and then ran his fingers through his wet hair.

"It's okay," Audrey said. "She'll forgive me. We're twins. We can't stay mad at each other."

Cade smiled, reaching out and ruffling Audrey's hair. "Well, since you're twins, I can't give one a present and not the other, can I?"

And he leaned in and kissed her on her freckled cheek.

Audrey flushed bright red, her mouth gaping.

Cade pulled back, tousled her hair again, and grinned. "Happy birthday, Audrey." When she continued to stand there, he added, "You should probably go home and check on Daph."

Audrey nodded, then raced after Daphne. Her cheek throbbed in the perfect, perfect spot where he'd kissed her.

Sure enough, Audrey was grounded that day. Daphne had sobbed her story to their parents, who were appropriately horrified. Audrey was sent to bed early, without TV or computer while they let Daphne stay up late, feasting on birthday cake. Daphne was upset, and that was almost as bad as getting in trouble on its own.

As of that day, Audrey learned two things.

One, that she was never going to slip up and be the bad twin again.

And two, that she was absolutely, without a doubt, in love with Cade Archer.

Twelve years later

Audrey glanced in the bathroom mirror, smoothed a stray lock of hair into her tight bun, and then straightened her jacket for the eighth time that morning.

Time to approach the boss.

She left the bathroom, her nerves tingling with a mixture of dread and wariness. Not that her outward expression showed it. She was very good about remaining calm and in control in a stressful situation, and this was definitely a situation. Her low heels clicking on the marble floors of Hawkings Conglomerate's headquarters, she swept the mail out of the delivery basket and returned to her desk. Once she'd sorted all the envelopes for Logan's personal attention, she rubber-banded the rest and set them into her mailbox to attend to later.

Her hand paused over the tabloid on her desk. After a moment's indecision, she folded the magazine in half lengthwise and tucked it under her arm. Then, with mail in hand, she headed to Logan Hawkings's closed door and rapped twice.

"Enter," he called.

She did, her stomach churning just a bit.

He didn't look up as she approached, continuing to type on his laptop. As was their usual routine, Audrey moved to his outbox and picked up any outgoing memos or faxes that he needed her to handle. She slipped his personal mail into his inbox, picked up his faxes, and glanced over at him. But she couldn't make her mouth form the request.

So she stalled. "Coffee, Mr. Hawkings?"

"Thank you."

She moved to the Keurig machine in her adjoining office and brewed him a cup, waiting impatiently for the machine to finish. Once it was done, she sweetened it, added creamer, and stirred, all the while mentally cursing herself for not broaching the conversation yet. She returned to his office with the cup in hand and set it on his desk.

Again, he didn't look up.

"Dry cleaning today, Mr. Hawkings?"

"No." He picked up the mug and gave her a suspicious look. "Something wrong?"

And here she thought she'd hidden it so well. Audrey clutched the folded tabloid in her hand, hesitating in front of his desk. "I . . . need some time off work."

Over his coffee mug, Logan frowned. "Time off?"

Just as she'd thought, it hadn't gone over well. In the three and a half years since she'd been working for Logan Hawkings, she'd never missed a day of work. She was here before he was, left after he did, and took her vacation time concurrent with his so as not to disrupt his schedule.

She was the model employee. She kept things quiet and running as smoothly as possible for Mr. Hawkings. When he needed something handled, she took care of it.

And she never, never asked for time off until today.

Audrey swallowed. "I'm afraid so."

"How much time off?"

"I . . . don't know. It's a personal matter." And very quietly, she unfolded the tabloid and offered it to him.

Logan tossed it down on his desk, eyeing the picture on the cover. The headline was a bold yellow that screamed out of the grainy photo. POP PRINCESS CAUGHT IN A COKE-FUELED ORGY! PICTURES ON PAGE 17! And there was the unmistakable face of her twin, blade-thin, her hair matted and dyed a hideous shade of black, a dopey smile on her face as she snorted lines in a club bathroom and leaned on an equally dopey-looking pair of men. Audrey didn't know who they were. She never knew who Daphne ran with any-more. Daphne's manager handled all that . . . theoretically. She suspected Daphne's manager took care of his own needs first, and Daphne's second.

Logan glanced at the magazine, then back up at her. "Your sister?"

She nodded succinctly. "I understand that this is an inconvenience, but I've taken extra precautions to ensure that your schedule is not interrupted. I talked with Cathy in personnel, and she's agreed to send a temp for me to train on daily duties."

"It's fine."

"I'll make sure she's prepared before I leave. I'll have my phone with me so you can contact me—or she can—if you need something. And I've made sure that your address book and calendar are up to date. The meeting next week—"

"It's fine, Audrey. Take the time you need." He folded the magazine and offered it back to her. "I take it you're getting her some help?"

She took it from him, her fingers trembling with a rush of relief. "She refuses to go to rehab, but she's agreed to go away for a time if I go with her. No parties, no drugs. I'm basically going to chaperone and try to get her to sober up." She hesitated. "It might be a few weeks. It might be longer. If that's a problem—"

"It's fine."

"If you need personal errands run—"

"I said it's fine, Audrey." Now he was getting annoyed with her. She could tell by the set of his eyebrows. "If I have personal errands, I'll ask Brontë to step in and help. It's not a big deal. Take the time that you need. Your family comes first."

Words that she'd never thought she'd hear billionaire Logan Hawkings say. His fiancée must have mellowed him quite a bit. She nodded. "Thank you, Mr. Hawkings. I'll make the arrangements with Cathy."

"Close the door when you leave." He turned back to his computer and began to type again.

She quietly exited his office, then shut the door behind her. Only when it was shut did she allow herself to lean against it, the breath whistling out of her in relief.

That had gone much better than she'd anticipated. Mellowed out, indeed. Two years ago—heck, six months ago—Logan would have given a few thinly veiled hints that if she'd valued her job, she'd find a way to make things happen. He paid her very well, after all, and if she couldn't find a way to perform her job to his satisfaction, he'd find someone who could.

Of course, that was BH—Before Hurricane. And before

Brontë. Still, Audrey hadn't relished asking him for the favor. Logan knew she was twins with Daphne; he'd met her at a rather unfortunate dinner party once. Most people didn't know she had a twin, and Audrey didn't volunteer the information. She'd learned the hard way that the conversation usually went in one of three directions:

Scenario one: Oh, my God. You're related to Daphne Petty? *The* Daphne Petty? The singer? Can you get me her autograph? Free tickets? A visit to my kid's birthday party?

Scenario two: Daphne Petty? Really? You don't look anything like her. She's so thin and glamorous. You're . . . not.

Or Scenario three: Daphne Petty? You poor thing. Is she really like that?

Scenario one was simply annoying, but she'd learned to deflect it a long time ago. No, she couldn't get free swag/tickets/CDs of Daphne's latest. No, she couldn't have Daphne show up at someone's birthday party. She kept business cards of the manager of Daphne's fan club and handed them out when pressed.

Scenario two was irritating, but again, she'd learned to deal with it a long time ago. Stage Daphne dressed in wild, colorful outfits and thick makeup. She never left her car without six-inch heels, a thick fringe of fake eyelashes, and her hair dyed some trendy shade. She'd gone Hollywood thin years ago at her label's suggestion (though secretly Audrey suspected drugs more than a healthy diet) and it was just another way that Audrey no longer looked like her twin.

Audrey's hair was straight, smooth, and a pale orange-red that hadn't faded when childhood did. Her skin was still lightly freckled, which was only obvious when she didn't wear makeup. She never wore much either because it would have looked out of place with her conservative business suits. And she was several sizes larger than Daphne. Where her twin had been a svelte size two, Audrey was soft, curvy, and just this side of plump. She didn't wear false eyelashes or six-inch heels. She looked like Daphne, but only if one squinted hard and compared photos.

She was used to being insulted about her looks and being asked for favors. But worst of all was scenario three: the pity. The look she'd come to recognize all too closely in the last two years. The look on someone's face as they recalled one of the more recent tabloids with Daphne's escapades splashed across them, her stints of jail time, her public fiascos, the rumors of drugs, alcohol, men, and excess. The train wreck that bright, wild Daphne Petty had become.

And Audrey hadn't been able to do a thing about it. She'd stood by, helpless, as her headstrong twin pushed her away and embraced all that her fast-paced lifestyle had to offer.

It was killing her. And that was why Audrey hated the pity more than anything else. Because she desperately wanted to do something about it, and now she had the chance. Daphne had called her last night at three in the morning, crying, from the back of a squad car. She'd called Audrey instead of her handlers, and though she'd been in LA instead of someplace that Audrey could have actually helped out with, her sister's misery had broken her heart.

Daphne was reaching out to her. She wanted help. Not rehab, she said, because that would be all over the tabloids and she'd already been to rehab twice, without success. Just a chance to get away and reconnect with her old life, with Audrey's assistance. This time, Daphne swore, it was going to be different. This time she'd leave behind the drugs and alcohol, if Audrey would just help her. She didn't trust anyone else.

And so Audrey had promised to help. She'd go away with her twin. Put her life on hold and come to Daphne's aid once again. She'd soothed her weeping twin on the phone, and then quietly contacted Daphne's management about the most recent visit to the police station. Like most of Daphne's incidents, they were able to make things disappear and Daphne was released from custody and flying to New York in the morning.

And then Audrey would start the slow process of finding Daphne again. Hopefully.

———

Audrey nibbled on a pretzel stick, flipping the pages of the latest romance novel she'd picked up at the supermarket. She checked the clock, then sighed and dug back into the pretzel bag. It was late and she was in her pajamas. Daphne's plane was supposed to have landed hours ago, and she had promised—*promised*—to come straight to Audrey's apartment from the airport. Audrey had volunteered to meet her twin, but Daphne had demurred, laughing it off and claiming she knew her way around New York just fine.

Except that the later it got into the night, the more positive Audrey was that her twin had made a few pit stops along the way. And it made her furious.

Some time after one a.m., she heard a knock at her door, and then a giggle. Stifling her irritation, she headed to the door and checked the peephole. Sure enough, there was Daphne, along with a stranger. Audrey unchained the door, flipped the lock, and flung the door open to glare balefully at Daphne and her companion.

Daphne leaned heavily on a tall, skinny man wearing black clothes and enormous plugs in his ears. He had several brow rings, neck tattoos, and a bright green fauxhawk. Daphne was, as usual, a disaster. Her jeans and T-shirt were stained, her hair was in a messy braid that hung over one shoulder, and the small suitcase at her side had shed clothes all down the hall. They both listed to the side and couldn't stop giggling despite Audrey's clear displeasure.

They were drunk. Sloppy drunk.

"You were supposed to be here hours ago, Daphne,"

Audrey told her. "Where have you been? I've been worried sick."

Daphne shrugged, pushing her way into Audrey's apartment. "The flight sucked and made me all tense, so Stan and I went out for a nightcap."

Audrey eyed Stan as Daphne staggered past her. When her date tried to follow, Audrey put a hand on his chest, stopping him. She gave him a polite smile. "Thanks for bringing her home."

He grinned, showing a gold tooth. "Don't I get to come in, too?"

"No, you don't."

He looked as if he'd argue, but then began to head back to the elevator, too wasted to even realize he'd just abandoned his famous hookup. Audrey quickly shut the door and re-bolted it, then turned to glare at Daphne.

Her sister was passed out, face down, on Audrey's couch.

"I don't believe you, Daph," Audrey said. "Drinking? Weren't you coming out here to clean up?"

"Tomorrow," Daphne mumbled from the couch cushions, not bothering to get up. "I'm starting tomorrow. Quit yelling."

"I'm not yelling!" Audrey bellowed, then winced when the neighbor pounded on the wall in response. Frustrated, Audrey grabbed Daphne's suitcase and hauled it to the bedroom. *Fine then.* Daphne wanted to be like that? Audrey wouldn't give her a choice in the matter. She'd simply have to take control—again—and save Daphne from herself.

Tossing the suitcase on her bed, she returned to the living room to grab Daphne's purse. On the couch, her sister snored, oblivious to Audrey's movements. Audrey snagged the purse, returned to the bed, and dumped the contents out.

The usual clutter fell onto the bedspread—half a protein bar, three lipsticks, a few pens, hair clips, and credit cards.

Several prescription bottles fell out as well, and Audrey bit her lip, frowning as she read the names. Two of them weren't even Daphne's prescriptions.

She flushed those, along with the small baggy of white powder she found. Daphne would be pissed when she woke up, but Audrey didn't care. Next, she searched the luggage and found several more pill bottles under different names, more drugs, and a thick packet tucked into the liner of her suitcase. It all went into the garbage, and with every item tossed, Audrey grew more and more determined.

Daphne wanted Audrey's help in getting clean? She was willing to help, all right, but she was pretty sure Daphne wasn't going to appreciate it. And that was too damn bad for her twin, because Audrey was in this for the long haul.

She returned to the living room and watched Daphne, snoring, on her couch. Makeup was smeared across Daphne's delicate features, and her mouth hung open, slack, as she slept.

Audrey *would* get her twin back. No ifs, ands, or buts. Daphne would be furious and threaten her, but it didn't matter.

Audrey had to do this once and for all, because it felt as if she'd already lost Daphne.

Jessica Clare also writes as Jill Myles and Jessica Sims. As Jessica Clare, she writes sexy contemporary romance. You can contact her at jillmyles.com, or at twitter.com/jillmyles, facebook.com/jillmyles, or pinterest.com/jillmyles.

FROM *NEW YORK TIMES* BESTSELLING AUTHOR
Jessica Clare

STRANDED
with a
BILLIONAIRE

A BILLIONAIRE BOYS CLUB NOVEL

With a visit to a private island resort in the Bahamas, billionaire Logan Hawkings has a chance to mend his broken heart. Then a hurricane, a misplaced passport, and a stalled elevator lead to an encounter with a most unusual woman.

Brontë Dawson is down-to-earth, incredibly sensual, and even quotes Plato. She also thinks Logan is simply the hotel's domineering yet sexy manager. And after several steamy island nights in his arms, Brontë's ready to give her heart to the man in charge. There's just more to Logan than he's told her—a billion times over.

jessica-clare.com
facebook.com/AuthorJessicaClare
facebook.com/LoveAlwaysBooks
penguin.com

M1478T0414

FROM *NEW YORK TIMES* BESTSELLING AUTHOR
Jessica Clare

THE VIRGIN'S GUIDE
TO *Misbehaving*

A BLUEBONNET NOVEL

After being the quiet, shy girl her whole life, Elise Markham is tired of doing what's right. She's ready to throw caution to the wind—and let sexy, tattooed wilderness instructor Rome show her just how exciting being bad can be...

PRAISE FOR JESSICA CLARE AND HER NOVELS

"Sexy and funny."
—*USA Today*

"A fast, sexy read that transports you."
—*Fiction Vixen*

jessica-clare.com
facebook.com/AuthorJessicaClare
facebook.com/LoveAlwaysBooks
penguin.com

M1479T0414